For Love or Liberty

Other Books by Jennifer Hudson Taylor

Highland Blessings
Highland Sanctuary

Quilts of Love Series
Path of Freedom

The MacGregor Legacy Series
For Love or Loyalty
For Love or Country
For Love or Liberty

For Love or Liberty

Book 3

The MacGregor Legacy Series

Jennifer Hudson Taylor

Nashville

For Love or Liberty

ISBN-13: 978-1-4267-3386-4

Published by Abingdon Press, P.O. Box 801, Nashville, TN 37202

www.abingdonpress.com

Macro editor: Teri Wilhelms

Published in association with Hartline Literary Agency

Library of Congress Cataloging-in-Publication Data

CIP data has been requested.

Printed in the United States of America

1 2 3 4 5 6 7 8 9 10 / 19 18 17 16 15 14

To Dwayne & Celina

Your love and sacrifices made it possible for me to write this series.

Thank you!

Acknowledgments

Thank you to the Abingdon Press staff and my agent, Terry Burns, for your hard work in making this series a reality.

A Letter to My Readers

Thank you for reading The MacGregor Legacy series. I have enjoyed researching and writing these stories for you. As with the first two books, I want to mention a few authentic historical details used in *For Love or Liberty*.

During the War of 1812, President James Madison was in office. It is true that his wife, Dolley, wore turbans around her head, and many women began wearing them as a fashion statement, especially in Washington D.C.

The British blockade along the eastern coast was real and a great challenge not only for our military, but for our merchants who needed to trade for goods. It is also true that the British navy would impress our young men into service against their will.

Commander Perry was a real naval officer in the War of 1812, and I included some of his extensive accomplishments in the story. The USS *Niagara* and USS *Lawrence* were real American ships that fought against the British in the Battle of Lake Erie in 1813. The USS *Larkspur* was a fictional ship that I created for Captain Conrad Deaton. The Battle of Lake Erie happened in real life as I portrayed it in the story at Put-in-Bay. The Captain of the USS *Niagara* really held back and did not help Commander Perry. After the USS *Lawrence* was surrendered, Perry ordered his surviving sailors to row him to the USS *Niagara* where he took command and continued the battle and won. The incident caused a severe rift between Perry and Captain Elliot for the rest of their lives. Perry was only thirty-four when he contracted yellow fever in Venezuela and died in 1819.

Military titles were not as official back then as they are now. Perry has been referred to as Commander, Commodore, and Admiral. Commodore was used for senior captains in the absence of an Admiral. After the Battle of Lake Erie, Perry was more often referred to as Admiral.

Cleveland, Ohio, was named for General Moses Cleaveland in 1796. It was not incorporated as a village until 1814. Cleveland was not incorporated as a city with the new spelling until 1836. Therefore, I have elected to use the spelling of "Cleaveland," so please know it was not a mistake or a typo.

I hope you enjoy *For Love or Liberty* and The MacGregor Legacy series.

All my best,
Jennifer Hudson Taylor
April 2014

1

Wilmington, North Carolina, 1813

Charlotte stood in the sand as waves washed over her bare feet, burying her heels and toes like an anchor holding her captive in time. The cool seawater receded from her skin leaving a mist of white foam layered with broken shells along the shore—much like the residue of the broken pieces of her life.

Her grieving heart threatened to succumb to the pain engulfing her, but the glistening colors of the scattered shells across the wet sand painted a brilliant scene of hope. If she could still see something beautiful through the dark clouds residing in her heart, it was a tiny reminder that the Lord had not forsaken her. Even though Emma was gone, her twin sister had left behind two precious children for Charlotte to love and help raise. She clung to that thought with resolve, especially since it was Emma's last request of her.

Charlotte covered her aching chest with a trembling hand and released the aching sob she had held throughout the funeral. Here . . . alone . . . with the wide ocean as comfort, she could finally let out the pain. She wept until her empty stomach rolled and tears choked her. Charlotte's eyes and nose swelled and breathing grew difficult as the inside of her head swirled like a monsoon attacking her brain.

Charlotte lost track of time and dropped to her knees. Oncoming waves swept her black gown into a floating parasol around her legs. The sound of the rolling ocean slowly consoled her as she lifted her face to the warm sun. From her earliest memories, the sea had always comforted her in times of distress.

An aggressive wave tumbled over Charlotte, knocking her off balance and onto her side. Her head plunged under and her eyes burned from the saltwater. Once the wave passed, Charlotte sputtered and gasped for air, rubbing at her eyes.

"Charlotte! What are you doing?" A man's voice carried through the breeze and over the splashing waves.

She groaned at the idea of Conrad Deaton finding her in such a predicament. Why did he have the habit of always catching her at her worst? Ignoring the broken shells beneath her feet, Charlotte scrambled to regain her balance before he reached her. She winced as a sharp edge sliced through the bottom of one heel. She grabbed her foot as another wave slammed her under a second time. Charlotte splashed her arms and legs, determined to land on her feet before the next wave hit.

Strong hands grabbed her around the waist and pulled her out of the water. Charlotte gasped as cold air hit her wet skin and she could breathe again. Propelled against the warmth of a solid chest with her feet in the air, she clutched at his shirt.

"What are you trying to do? Drown yourself?" Conrad's voice sounded like a commanding officer.

Well, she wasn't one of his sailors to be commanded. Charlotte pushed against him and kicked in an attempt to be free. A lock of sandy brown hair fell across his forehead as he gripped her tight and grinned. His mustache moved with his mouth, revealing a row of healthy teeth in spite of his time commanding the *Victorious* at sea. His hazel eyes lit in challenge and a hint of boyish freckles peeked across his nose in the bright sun. Something in her chest skipped with light-hearted joy at seeing him in a different light, but she swallowed back the temptation to let down her guard. This was Conrad, the man who tried to sabotage his brother's courtship of her sister and would have succeeded if not for her wise intervention in distracting him.

He had shed his navy coat and wore a white buttoned shirt with blooming sleeves, navy pants, and black boots that sloshed in the water and crunched seashells beneath his heels. Conrad smelled of leather and musk from a fresh shave and bath, having at least made an attempt to look his best for her sister's funeral that morning. Charlotte closed her eyes and breathed in the scent of him. It had an unexpected calming effect on her. She rested her aching head against him, knowing her struggles would be futile against his strength.

"I realize you are grieving for your sister, but I am *not* about to sit back and watch you drown yourself." Conrad clenched his jaw as he tightened his hold on her and concentrated on a targeted spot in the sand. "Do you not think the family has been through enough these last few days?"

"Let go of me! I am deeply grieved over the loss of my sister, but contrary to your belief, I was not about to drown myself." Charlotte sighed in exasperation and shook her head. "I only needed a moment alone, to grieve freely without anyone watching and waiting for me to fall apart. Besides, I would never think of relieving you of my presence so easily. Whether you like it or not, I made a promise to help raise our niece and nephew and I aim to do it."

Conrad blew out a deep breath as he set her down on a mound of dry sand near his discarded coat. The rank of captain displayed in bold yellow threads on the shoulders. He settled beside her, propping his knees up and linking his hands between them. Conrad gave her a sideways glance, a look of determination crossing his expression. "Likewise, my dear, I am afraid you will have to put up with me as well. I have no intention of neglecting my brother in his time of need. I, too, intend to be part of my niece and nephew's life."

"We shall see." She shrugged and looked away, wiping wet strands of hair from her eyes. "I doubt you could stay in one place long enough to be much of an influence on anyone." Charlotte lifted her hand and gestured to the ocean. "The sea will call you back before little Davie turns six and Ashlynn is a year old."

Everyone saw him as a sea-loving adventurer who lived for the thrill of exciting heroism, but she knew him for what he was. Captain Conrad Deaton, a man bent on destroying true love because he could never give up his beloved freedom and adventures at sea. To him, marriage imprisoned men with responsibilities and trials. He had begged his brother to avoid it. Charlotte feared while the rest of them grieved, he secretly viewed her sister's death as a way out for his younger brother, David.

"Actually, the navy has already tried to lure me away. I received word yesterday I am being transferred to the war on the Great Lakes. They need a captain to command one of their new ships on Lake Erie. I shall be stationed in Cleaveland." He leaned closer, brushing her hair down the side of her face and behind her ear. "I suppose you shall get your wish. You shall be rid of me within the fortnight."

"What happened to not abandoning your brother in his time of need?" Charlotte jerked away from his touch, glaring at him with contempt.

"Which is why I requested David be transferred under my command, so I can look out for him. Do not be so quick to judge me." He reached for her again, but she slapped his hand away and scooted out of reach. Charlotte dug her palms into the thick sand for leverage and pushed her wet body to her feet.

"You would have him abandon his children only a few days after losing their mother?" Her voice rose as the waves crashed behind her. She shoved her fists on her hips and stared down at him in disbelief. "You are insufferable!"

"There you go again, assuming the worst about me." He pointed at her as he stood. Conrad frowned and turned to wipe the sand from his backside. "We are taking the children with us. Your father has agreed to help us find a nursemaid for Ashlynn. I am not as insensitive and uncaring you like to think."

"Indeed you are." She stepped closer, ignoring the ache in her neck from staring up at him. "My sister knew what she was doing in asking me to help raise her children. She knew David would be too weak to deal with the likes of you and your meddling." She poked his chest. "You will not take those children across the country in this war."

"No, their father is and there is naught you can do about it." He crossed his arms.

"We shall see about that." She turned on her heel and stomped through the sand.

Conrad groaned as Charlotte rushed from him. He bent to retrieve his coat and realized a trail of red stains followed her footprints in the sand. Was it blood? Concerned, he ran after her.

"Charlotte, wait!" He caught up to her, grabbing her arm. "Your foot is bleeding."

"Let go!" She jerked away and stumbled. Wincing, she reached for her heel. "I shall be fine."

"Not if you get sand in the wound and end up with an infection." Conrad reached for her again, but she avoided him. Tired of arguing with her, he strode after Charlotte and gathered her around the waist. He ignored her surprised gasp and lifted her up, tossing her over his shoulder. "I will not have the family blaming me for allowing you to be so foolish."

"Oh, so I am another one of your heroic deeds, am I?" She beat upon his back. "Put me down. You have no right."

Conrad pivoted around and carried her back to the sea. Charlotte continued to hurl insults at him, but he paid her no heed. He waded into the water to a foot deep and bent to one knee. Maneuvering Charlotte from his shoulder and settling her on his bent knee, Conrad dipped her injured foot to wash off the gritty wound.

She stopped her complaints long enough to bite her bottom lip, in obvious discomfort. It was all the confirmation he needed to know he had done the right thing. The blood washed away, and he could see a half circle cut, but it wasn't too deep. If she would stay off it a couple of days, stitches wouldn't be necessary, nor would she risk an infection.

"At least this nasty gash is on your heel and not the tender part of your foot." Unable to resist, Conrad lightly trailed a fingertip along the inside of her foot, tickling her. She kicked in reaction and jerked back with enough force to send him on his backside. With a chuckle, Conrad managed to keep her in his grasp and took the full brunt of the fall. His breeches were thick enough to protect his flesh from the shells, but not enough to keep from bruising his hide.

"That is completely inappropriate," she said, her green eyes blazing like fire. Charlotte's pink lips twisted into a frown and her wet blond hair tangled around her face and shoulders. Even now she looked beautiful in spite of her disheveled state. The fact she glared at him as if she wished she had a pitchfork in her hand did not discourage him in the least.

Another wave rushed at them. Conrad gathered her tight in his arms and stood to his feet in time to avoid it. Breathing a sigh of relief, he glanced down at her. "We had better get you back, but I must say, I have quite enjoyed the fun." A grin tugged at his mouth. He could never resist teasing her. She made the temptation too enjoyable.

"Fun . . . indeed." She turned and motioned to objects lying in the sand. "Do not forget my slippers."

"Would never think of it." Conrad carried her over to them. "Step down on your good foot and I shall retrieve them for you."

For once, she obeyed, leaning on his arm for support as he bent to grab her brown slippers. He dumped the sand out of them. She couldn't put them back on and risk getting sand in the wound. He held them out and met her gaze. She grinned. "You could rinse the sand out of them and then I could wear them again."

"And I could just carry you."

"All the way back to the house?" She lifted a golden eyebrow; her expression suggested he had gone daft.

"No, back to my horse." He bent and swept her up before she could protest. "Your mother asked me to find you. She was worried since you disappeared right after we arrived home from your sister's funeral. The longer it takes me to get you back, the longer she will continue to worry."

At the mention of the funeral, Charlotte's expression fell into a pensive frown. "I have been thinking, it would have been harder if Emma had not already married your brother and moved from home." Charlotte surprised him by laying her head against his shoulder. "Now I am used to having my own chamber and being alone. Still, the aching pain lingers and deepens."

"I know we have had our differences, but I am sorry you are going through this." Conrad wanted to comfort her, but he wasn't sure if she would allow it. Instead, he kept silent as he carried her to where he had left his horse tethered to a nearby tree. Once he settled her in the saddle, he took the reins and mounted up behind her. Now away from the water, the humid heat made his lungs feel like they were suffocating and the discomfort of his wet clothes and soggy boots scratched at his skin.

Conrad smelled the salty sea in her wet hair brushing against his chin. His arms pressed against hers as he guided the reins. Rather than increasing his discomfort, having her near brought a measure of satisfaction he had not anticipated. He wondered if she felt the same. Was it a bond between them or attraction? Charlotte had a way of confusing him like no other, but she also infuriated him quicker than anyone. He used to think his brother had that distinctive honor, and then he had met Charlotte.

They arrived at the two-story brick home half an hour later. As he rode up to the front porch, Charlotte sighed. "Now we will have to explain why we look so disheveled."

"Do not worry. I am sure they are used to it by now. Since the day my brother and I met you and your sister six years ago, you have been headstrong and in constant trouble." He didn't say it, but he had always thought Emma had been the voice of reason, keeping Charlotte from straying too far. With the passing of her twin, he feared Charlotte's behavior would stretch beyond the limits of what was considered proper. Her grief alone could launch her in any direction. The way the family watched her, and the comments they made, told him he wasn't alone in his concern.

The front door opened and her mother, Tyra, rushed out, wringing her hands, worry on her wrinkled forehead. Tall for a woman, Charlotte's mother remained thin and healthy for one nearing fifty. Her hair was swept up on her head in a mixture of red and gray locks. She wore a black gown, but had removed the black hat she had worn to the funeral.

Conrad helped Charlotte dismount as her father and brothers followed her mother out onto the porch with marked concern on their stern faces. A moment later her brothers' wives and children appeared as well, flanking around them and shielding their eyes from the sun.

"Charlotte, you have been worrying your mother—today of all days." Her father crossed his arms and shook his gray head in disappointment. He stroked his full beard in thought as if pondering how best to handle the situation. He wore a black suit and his gray eyes flickered as he assessed their rumpled attire and wayward hair. Unsure of how Captain Donahue Morgan would react, Conrad remained silent. Charlotte leaned into him, as if seeking his support to face them all. He swept her into his arms and carried her toward the house.

Tyra Morgan breathed deeply as tears filled her eyes, but she took an angry step forward and shoved her hands on her hips. "What have you gone and done now, Charlotte? Why can you not walk?"

"Where did you find her?" Charlotte's father's asked, stepping forward to take her.

"In the ocean." Conrad handed her over to her father, knowing the man was still in fine health and could handle her weight. "She has cut her foot on a shell, and we needed to clean sand out of it. I think she will be fine."

"Hugh, take her in and set her on the couch, so I can see if she needs stitching," Mrs. Morgan said.

"Thank you," Hugh said, his gray eyes meeting Conrad's. "Is there anything else we should know? Other injuries?"

"No, I am fine," Charlotte insisted. "You worry too much. I am sorry, I did not mean to concern everyone. I only needed to be alone. You all know how I find solace at the sea."

"Since we just buried Emma this morning, it would help if you would think of someone else besides yourself once in a while." Scott, her oldest brother, scolded her.

Someone cleared her throat and the whole family parted, creating an aisle for Charlotte's grandmother, Lauren MacGregor. She walked forward, leaning on a cane, as she approached Charlotte. Unlike the others, a smile lit her wrinkled face, but moisture gathered in her blue eyes as she reached over and cupped Charlotte's cheek.

"Lass, ye remind me so much of yer mother when she was yer age, strong-willed and stubborn. And Emma was more like me when I came from Scotland." She turned and stared up at her daughter and son-in-law. "This family has had enough sadness for one day. There is no place for anger in a grieving family. 'Tisn't unusual for Charlotte to go running off. She is back now. Let us take comfort in that and in each other. Right now, there is much to be decided for Emma's children."

Charlotte sat on the couch in the parlor and listened to her family's chastisement for disappearing after Emma's funeral. Painful memories flashed through her mind. Staring down at her twin's cold, empty body felt like she stared at herself in that coffin. As identical twins, she and Emma shared more than their looks, a bond that was beyond anything she could ever hope to explain. The moment she held her sister's hand and watched her breathe her last moments after Ashlynn's birth, something inside her snapped, and a deep loneliness engulfed her. She had forced herself to endure the funeral, including all the nods and condolences of their friends, but afterward, she could no longer cope and fled.

Little Davie came over and crawled onto her lap. Charlotte could only imagine what must be going through his five-year-old mind. While he seemed to understand his mother had died and would never come back, did he really comprehend death when Charlotte continued to struggle with it at a score and three years? Did he feel like his mother had abandoned him?

"Auntie, I thought you left like Mama." Davie swung his tiny arms around her neck and squeezed so tight he cut off her breath.

"No, I only went for a walk to the ocean." She hugged him back, resting her chin on his brown head. Not once had it occurred to her that he might think of her dying as well. The idea of hurting him was more than she could bear. The muscles in her chest closed in on her lungs, nearly suffocating her. She closed her eyes as she kissed the top of his head. Fresh tears squeezed past her eyelids and crawled down her face as the ache in her heart and chest deepened.

David couldn't take the children away. At less than a week old, Ashlynn wouldn't know any better, but Davie would. His reaction to her brief disappearance proved it. Besides, she had made a promise to her sister, and as she had told Conrad, she intended to keep it.

"While I am still living and breathing, I will never leave you. I promise." Charlotte stroked the back of Davie's head. His wide hazel eyes blinked up at her as a slow grin spread across his face.

"I love you, Auntie!" Satisfied and reassured, he gave her another big hug and scooted off her lap to go play.

Charlotte took a deep breath and used the back of her hand to wipe the tears from her face. She glanced over at Grandma Lauren rocking little Ashlynn to sleep in a wooden rocker her grandpa had made before his death two years ago. Grandma understood her grief. She once told Charlotte everything reminded her of Grandpa Malcolm. Now, everything would remind Charlotte of Emma. There was a childhood memory lurking in each room, lingering in every corner, all the places in town would haunt her, even her own face each time she looked in the mirror.

Resting her foot, Charlotte settled in as families dropped by throughout the afternoon to express their condolences, bringing dishes of food and baked desserts. While it was a strain on her family to keep up the fake smiles, the trivial conversations, and their true feelings at bay, it was expected. Their distant cousins from the Baker family were the last to leave.

Charlotte's father closed the front door in the foyer. A moment later, he walked back into the living room and paused to clear his throat. "David, it is my understanding from your brother that you are being transferred to the Great Lakes. I would like to know what you have decided to do about the children. Who will care for them during the long months you will be serving aboard a naval ship?"

Silence filled the room as the air thickened with anticipation. Like the rest of her family, Charlotte watched David's reaction, hoping he would be willing let the children stay where she could better care for them. They were familiar with their home here, their grandparents' home, and the city of Wilmington. Here, familiar faces surrounded them in love, comfort, and security.

Fear clutched her heart as she glanced around the somber room. The bottom half of the walls were made of dark paneling encased in carved squares and thick molding, while the upper half of the walls were painted beige. As the sun's light diminished through the windows, someone had lit candles around the room.

Charlotte's mother sat on the couch beside her, mopping at her damp face with the handkerchief her father had given her. Melanie, Charlotte's older sister at a score and five years, sat on her other side, no doubt charged with the responsibility of watching over her in case Charlotte decided to disappear again. She favored their mother with fiery red hair and green eyes. Her husband, Rob McCauley, was outside with their toddler son, making sure the older children behaved. He claimed to be out there to watch the kids, but Charlotte knew it was because he smoked his pipe.

Her oldest brother, Scott, and his wife, Caroline, sat on the settee by the window. He was named for their uncle, Scott MacGregor, who had fought and died in the War of Independence. At a score plus ten years, her brother now had four children, who all chased lightning bugs outside with their cousins. Like her and Emma, he had blond hair favoring their Grandma Lauren, but unlike them, he had the same deep blue eyes as their grandmother.

Her brother Duncan stood beside his wife, Elizabeth, seated in a wood chair by the pianoforte. Duncan was named for their great-grandfather from Argyll, Scotland. At a score and seven years, he was the second oldest with dark brown eyes and black hair like their father. During their seven-year marriage, they had a six-year-old son and a three-year-old daughter.

"David, we know you do not feel like discussing these decisions right now, but we have to find a permanent nursemaid for Ashlynn." Uncle Callum's deep voice carried across the room as he walked to stand beside Charlotte's father. After Grandpa Malcolm passed away, he now ran the MacGregor Quest estate and had taken over as the patriarch of the MacGregor family.

"Mrs. Brown has agreed to come over and feed her for the night, but only this one night. We need to hear your plans so we can help you, lad."

David stared at the wood floor where he sat in a chair in a dark corner. His eyes were red and swollen with the shadows beneath them testifying to his lack of sleep. He had not shaved so brown whiskers now graced his face and neck. Leaning forward, he placed his elbows on his knees and rubbed his chin with a weary sigh.

"I promised Emma I would be a good father, and I cannot do that if I abandon my children and leave them here. They have already lost their Mama. I cannot allow them to lose their father, too." His voice broke, and he looked away at the wall.

Charlotte closed her eyes as familiar pain sliced through her chest. Even though Conrad had already told her their plans, a small part of her still hoped David would change his mind. She glanced over at Conrad leaning against the wall near his brother. His warm, hazel eyes locked with hers as he remained silent. Doubt flickered in his eyes. Did he doubt his brother's decision but felt honor-bound to stand by him? Her unease grew.

"But David, have you considered how dangerous it would be to travel with a newborn infant?" Mama asked, disbelief thickening her tone.

"I have already spoken to the doctor, and we will wait a fortnight as he suggested before we leave." David brushed his hand through his hair, leaving a small gap on the side. "Once we arrive and get settled in Cleaveland, Ohio, I plan to hire a new nursemaid to stay with the children."

"A complete stranger?" Mama pressed the heel of her hand against her forehead. "I cannot believe this. Besides, you will need a nursemaid for the journey. You cannot wait until you arrive."

"I am sorry, Mrs. Morgan," David blinked back tears. "But I am their father, and war or no war, I will not abandon my children. My mind is made up. They are coming with me."

"It will be hard finding a nursemaid who is willing and able to travel with you." Charlotte's father crossed his arms, as a frown wrinkled his forehead. "However, I shall endeavor to do my best to find someone."

"Hugh! You cannot be serious?" Mama scooted to the edge of the couch, ready to battle all of them for the care and safety of her grandchildren. "The country is at war with England once again. And dare I suggest the worst? David will be fighting on a battleship. What if he cannot return to them? The children will be all alone in a strange place."

"I made a promise to my twin." Charlotte stood, ignoring the pain in her foot. Her chin trembled, and tears threatened to choke her, but she swallowed them back. "For as long as they need me, wherever they go, I will go. Unlike the rest of you, I have no husband, no children, and I am available."

2

Over the chaos of the next few days, Conrad's respect for Charlotte grew, but he wasn't about to let her know it. He feared this new responsible and sympathetic side of Charlotte would fade into obscurity. Her decisions were usually based on what Charlotte wanted, and it had always been her twin who considered others first.

This time, Conrad witnessed Charlotte make a difficult decision that pained her greatly. Deep down she didn't want to leave her home here in Wilmington. It was obvious in the lingering looks she gave her family, as if she didn't know if she would ever see them again. He could see it in how she hugged the treasured items she chose to leave behind. She took longer walks by herself and would return with red and swollen eyes. Conrad had to look away, unable to bear her grief.

Still, he cared about his niece and nephew and wanted the best for them. Right now, Charlotte *was* the best for them in the absence of their mother. Even though no one wanted to see her go, none of them argued against it. Conrad assumed they believed in her as much as he did. The family had rallied around her and the children to try and make the transition easier.

Conrad wrote his superior officers at the Great Lakes to inform them of the situation and explain why he and David would not be arriving as soon as planned. He paid a visit to the *Victorious* anchored at the Wilmington docks. His sailors greeted him with condolences and asked about David. Conrad ordered them to prepare for the arrival of David's family and made arrangements to have them stay in the comfort of his own cabin.

A frigate filled with lusty sailors was no place for a young lady in charge of two small children, but they had no choice. This way they could save time by sailing up the coast to Bridgeport, Connecticut, and limit slow travel over land further endangering them from marching troops, more battles, Indians, and wilderness filled with creatures of all types. As captain of the *Victorious*, Conrad could provide them safe passage—the only challenge would be avoiding the British blockades.

Late in the evening, Conrad bounced little Davie on his knee when the front door opened in the foyer. Charlotte walked in wearing a black gown, bringing out the purple circles under her eyes. His heart tightened as he set Davie down and rose to his feet. She untied the bonnet strings at her neck, while her father and David came in behind her. Conrad assumed Callum was still outside tending to the horses and putting up the carriage.

"Auntie!" Davie ran over to Charlotte. "Look what Uncle Conwad made me—a soldier." He held up the wooden toy for her inspection. "See? A blue coat. He is American!"

"Indeed." She bent to kiss the top of his brown head, and her eyes met Conrad's. He offered her a smile as he linked his hands behind his back. "Where is Mama?" Charlotte's gaze scanned the empty parlor as she pulled off her bonnet and crumpled it in her hands.

"I believe she is upstairs with Melanie, packing the children's trunks." Conrad gestured to the staircase in the hall. "Your sister brought over some clothes Ashlynn will grow into."

"They think of everything." Fresh tears filled her eyes. "However shall I manage without them?" Conrad stepped toward her, wanting to comfort and encourage her, but she turned away and walked into the foyer where she hung her wrinkled bonnet on the tall hat rack in the corner. The sound of her steady footsteps carried upstairs.

"Did you have any luck finding a nursemaid for Ashlynn?" Conrad asked, his gaze sliding from his brother's gaunt face to Mr. Morgan's tired gray eyes. The older man rubbed the back of his neck with a sigh and glanced over at David who sank into a nearby chair and stared at the floor.

"David, we shall be right back." Mr. Morgan tilted his head toward the front door and motioned for Conrad to follow. David didn't bother responding.

Outside, Mr. Morgan rubbed his bearded chin and strolled across the porch and down the front steps. Without a word, he kept walking, and Conrad followed, not knowing what else to do. They walked across a field with weeds up to their knees. When they came to a wooden fence, Mr. Morgan gripped it tight and leaned over, drawing in a deep breath. He held on swaying back and forth on his heels.

"Give me a moment, son." His deep voice cracked, and there was no mistaking the grief in his soul. After being at war with England for more than a year, Conrad had come to recognize the sound in a man's voice for his fallen comrades. Still, the agony in Mr. Morgan's tone was chilling, especially from a man he had always seen as the patriarch of the Morgan family—the strong one holding everyone together. "Seems like yesterday I held my newborn infant twins in each arm. I took it for granted they would be burying me." He gripped the fence so tight his knuckles turned white and the veins showed through the skin of his hands. "I pray you never have to feel what I am feeling right now."

"I am sorry, sir." Conrad placed his hand on the fence post. "Truly, I am."

"The reason I asked you to come out here with me is because I have something I want to say, and I cannot say it to your brother. In fact, I am worried about the lad." Mr. Morgan straightened and met Conrad's gaze. Moisture glistened in his eyes, but his stare was as deep and penetrating as ever. "I was about his age when I married Tyra. David and Emma had their whole lives planned, and it has been ripped out from underneath him. You have to find a way to pull him out of this depression he has gotten himself into. He has two small children to raise. He has to do this for them." He pointed at Conrad. "And you have to help him."

"I will." Conrad nodded. "It is why I wrote my superior officers and had him transferred under my command."

"I figured as much." Mr. Morgan leaned his elbows on the top rail. "As far as a nursemaid for Ashlynn, we thought it would be best to consult the town doctor. He knows all the women who have given birth in the last year. He was out, and we asked about him at the post office, the general store, talked to the pastor at church, and no one knew of any nursing woman who would be willing to travel away from home. They all have families here."

"It does not sound too promising." A small headache began to pump through Conrad's temples. "David has his heart set on bringing the kids. I hate to think how he might react if he has to be separated from them. I have always been his big brother, able to make things better for him, but this . . . this is too much. I cannot stand to see his pain."

"I know." Mr. Morgan propped his booted foot on the bottom rail. "It is how I feel about my whole family right now. All of them are hurting, and each of them is facing it in different ways, which brings me to another concern—Charlotte."

"Yes, sir?" Conrad lifted an eyebrow, wondering where this topic of conversation would lead. Even the mention of Charlotte's name made the hairs on his neck rise and his stomach twist into knots.

"Do not let her fool you. She is grieving over her twin more than she realizes—probably more than the rest of us. In fact, I fear her determination to go with you and David is an attempt to run away from her grief. Yesterday, she told Tyra everything here reminds her of Emma." Mr. Morgan shook his head. "Son, I hate to put more pressure on you, but you will need to be strong not only for David, but Charlotte as well."

"I will." Conrad thought about her attempt to escape at the ocean, her standing by Emma's grave in her black gown, looking lovely in spite of the dark circles beneath her eyes, and how she had cried the first time she gathered Ashlynn in her arms. A fierce protective nature welled up inside him, and he meant it. "Mr. Morgan, I will do my best to make sure no harm comes to your daughter or grandchildren."

"It is all I can ask." Mr. Morgan reached over and gave him a friendly pat on the shoulder. "Know you will be in our prayers."

Charlotte walked into her chamber to see tiny clothes spread across her quilted bed. Her mother bent over an open trunk and glanced up with a welcoming smile. Melanie gripped the bedpost and gestured to the bed.

"I thought it would be helpful if I brought some clothes of varying sizes for Ashlynn. Over the next year, she will grow quickly." A pensive expression crossed her face as she looked down at Ashlynn sleeping in her bassinet. "She will not even know us the next time we see her."

"Do not worry. I intend to make sure she and Davie do not forget any of you, especially Emma." A familiar ache pressed to her throat. Charlotte swallowed, needing to change the subject. "Thank you for the baby clothes. I daresay, Ashlynn will now be much better off than if she had to endure my sewing."

"Scott and Caroline will bring some things over for Davie later," Melanie said.

Charlotte nodded as she walked around to the side of her bed and sat on the edge. Silence followed as she linked her fingers on her lap and tried not to think of all the loved ones she would miss. She always imagined leaving home with her husband—only love could ever take her away from here. Actually, it was love, but not the romantic kind she had imagined. She would do anything for Davie and Ashlynn—even be their mama in Emma's place.

"Charlotte," Mama said, "I tried to finish packing your trunks, but I realized you had packed more of Emma's things than your own. You are going north and will need more warm clothes in the fall. Why did you pack Emma's wedding gown?"

"For Ashlynn. She may one day want to wear it for her own wedding." Charlotte shrugged with a broken sigh. "I do not know. I thought a few things would be appropriate for David and the children to remember her by."

"Indeed, but you must be sensible and take practical things on your long journey," Mama said. "Emma's wedding gown will be safe here. I promise. When Ashlynn has need of it, she may send for it." Mama blinked back tears, and her nose turned red. "Besides, I hope to see you all before then, even if I have to drag your father up North myself."

"Or we shall take you," Melanie offered. "I will want to see them, too."

"Must you take all of Emma's drawings?" Mama asked, lifting an eyebrow. "What if some were to get ruined or rained on? Or lost? You have no idea what kind of challenges you might face."

"You make a good point. Why not pick out a couple for each of you? I will frame the rest and hang them up around the new house for David and the children. I want to decorate the place as she would have done."

"Emma was too humble to do so, Charlotte." Melanie shook her head. "She would have framed and hung someone else's drawings before her own."

"Yes, but I would have insisted upon it, and she would have given in to appease me." Charlotte grinned, hoping she didn't look as wounded as she felt. How did one go about pretending to be happy when feeling so utterly wretched inside? She needed fresh air. It was bad enough dealing with her own grief, but she couldn't bear the sad faces of her mother and sister, knowing her decision had made things worse for them.

Charlotte tried to speak, but her throat clogged. She shook her head and tried again. "You both know me as well as I know myself. I trust your judgment. Right now I need some fresh air." She stood and walked to the door.

"But you have only returned," Mama said. "Charlotte, you may take all of Emma's drawings if you wish but do not leave. I want to spend as much time with you as possible before you go."

"It is not the drawings, Mama." Charlotte paused as she opened the door. "I cannot breathe. I feel as if I am suffocating and must get away." She closed the door behind her and hurried down the staircase and out the front door.

"Charlotte!" Conrad followed, his feet pounding down the porch steps after her.

She didn't stop but kept running until she reached her favorite oak tree covered in Spanish moss. It was as if the low-hanging strands welcomed her with open arms. Charlotte pressed her back against the wide trunk and took a deep breath, willing her heart to calm and the aching pain in her heart to disappear. She closed her eyes and embraced the gentle breeze blowing across her face and neck.

"Charlotte?" Conrad's soft footsteps approached slow and steady. A twig crunched beneath his boot.

"Go away, Conrad. I need to be alone right now."

He didn't respond. A moment of silence followed, with the exception of her struggle to breathe. She clutched her chest as she tried to make the suffocation go away. Out of curiosity, she peeked beneath her lids to see him sitting on the grass with his booted feet crossed at the ankles leaning back on his palms and staring up at her. He wasn't going away.

She waited in silence, hoping her breathing would soon ease and her heart slow to a steady pace. In spite of the heat, breathing was easier out here than inside. "My life will never be the same again." She opened her eyes and met his gaze. "I am suffocating. Is this what it feels like to have a heart attack?"

Two days later the family settled in the parlor after dinner. The children ran outside to play. Charlotte's older siblings, Scott, Duncan, and Melanie had gathered their families and taken them home the day before. David and Conrad were invited to dinner each night, which gave Conrad a chance to get to know the Morgan family better.

Melancholy settled over the whole house. With the exception of little Davie's childish chatter and Mr. Morgan's attempt at normal conversation, everyone around the dinner table remained quiet in spite of Conrad's fruitless efforts to liven things up a bit.

By the time they finished the main course and started eating apple pie for dessert, Conrad decided he needed to remove his brother and Charlotte from the premises. The sooner they were away from the downtrodden spirits around them, the sooner they could begin healing from their grief. He hated to see them all languishing in a pit of despair. When he attempted to cheer them with his typical jokes, a strange silence followed with questioning looks. Conrad feared he appeared insensitive, but he couldn't help himself. No wonder Charlotte felt as if she suffocated inside the house.

A knock sounded at the front door, and a male voice greeted the maid since they had no butler. A moment later, she appeared in the parlor with a brief curtsy in front of Mr. Morgan. "Dr. Hawthorne is here to see you, sir."

"Please show him in," Mr. Morgan said.

In walked a man of medium height wearing black breeches, a grey diamond-patterned vest, and a black jacket. He carried a hat under his arm and a dark bag in his hand. His bald head glowed in the candlelight framed by short gray hair on the sides. He surveyed the room, his brown eyes scanning each face until landing on Mr. Morgan who stood and held out his hand in greeting.

"Mr. Morgan, thank you for receiving me without prior notice." Dr. Hawthorne closed the distance between them, his boots a steady gait across the wooden floor. He smiled as he shook Mr. Morgan's hand.

"I am sorry I did not have better news when I last saw you," Dr. Hawthorne said. "But I wanted to stop by and tell you your prospects have changed."

"Dr. Hawthorne, you are always welcome," Mr. Morgan said, gesturing to a nearby chair. "Please have a seat. We are eager to hear some good news."

"I met a widow by the name of Mrs. Mildred Wolfe in New Bern." Dr. Hawthorne sat as requested. He set his bag on the floor by his feet and scooted to the edge of his chair, placing his elbows on his knees and linking his fingers. "Unfortunately, she recently lost her husband to the war. She did not take the news well and lost her baby soon afterward. She has no other family in the area and no means of support."

"The poor woman." Charlotte fumbled with her ivory shawl. "Have you spoken with her? Is she willing to travel?"

"I did take the liberty of speaking with her about your situation. She is willing to travel and nurse the baby in exchange for her personal care." Dr. Hawthorne scratched his temple. "Although I feel compelled to inform you she is in a terrible state of grief. You must see she gets proper rest and nutrition. Mrs. Wolfe is pale and has grown quite thin."

Conrad suppressed an inward groan as he rubbed his eyebrows in an attempt to hide his expression. The last thing he needed was another grieving person to deal with on this long journey. Guilt crushed him. How could he be so cruel at the woman's plight? She had been through more than he could imagine, and her troubles were much worse than any of them—for they all had one another—she had no one. Fresh remorse washed through him, cleansing his thoughts.

"Then we would be helping her as much as she would be helping us," Charlotte said, showing genuine interest for the first time.

"Indeed," Dr. Hawthorne said. "There is not a better solution than one to benefit all involved."

"When can we meet this young lady?" Mrs. Morgan asked, linking her hands in her lap.

"She will need a few days to get her affairs in order," Dr. Hawthorne said. "I would like to bring her by in three days."

"Splendid," Mrs. Morgan said, attempting a rare smile brightening her pale face. Thin lines appeared around the edge of her eyes and her mouth. "I would like to invite you both to dinner."

"Yes, I want to see how she reacts to the children, especially Ashlynn," Charlotte said. "I am concerned caring for an infant, so soon after the loss of her own little one, may prove too painful to bear."

"You have a good point," Mr. Morgan said, looking over at his daughter. "You surprise me, Charlotte. Such a wise statement from one who has never borne children of her own."

"A woman does not need to be a mother in order to have motherly instincts." Charlotte bristled at her father's comment and tilted her head with a questioning gaze. "Nor does one have to be a mother in order to be sensitive to other people's feelings."

Conrad shifted in discomfort as his earlier thoughts came back to haunt him. Why had he never seen this side of Charlotte before? Prior to Emma's death, he had never considered Charlotte as the marrying kind or a motherly figure. She had always been strong and independent, pushing away any man who attempted to court her. He liked this side of Charlotte and wished it had not taken a tragedy to bring it out in her.

"I had better be getting home," Dr. Hawthorne said. "I do not want my wife worrying about my long absence."

"Thank you for stopping by," Mr. Morgan said, standing to walk out with the doctor.

"Yes, we look forward to your return visit in a few days," Mrs. Morgan said, meeting Charlotte's gaze.

Once the front door closed behind them, David entered the parlor carrying Ashlynn. He cradled her in his arms as she slept. "Davie finally fell asleep. It took two of my navy stories about the high seas. The baby fell asleep as well. I think she likes my voice."

"Of course she does," Charlotte said, standing to hold out her arms to take the infant. "I will take her upstairs to her bassinet."

David kissed the top of Ashlynn's bald head and gave her over to her aunt. His chin trembled when he glanced up at them. "I have no idea how I will leave them behind when I go back to the ship."

"Well, the time is coming sooner than we realized," Conrad said. "Dr. Hawthorne just found a nursemaid for us. We will be leaving within the week if all goes well."

3

As promised, Dr. Hawthorne brought Mildred Wolfe over to meet them. She wore a faded black gown that had seen many washes, and her dark hair was styled in a bun with curls swirling around her oval face. Purple circles outlined her brown eyes surrounded in smooth pale skin. She looked as if she had not slept in days and grief consumed her.

Mildred kept her attention toward the floor and rarely looked up, but her actions did not prevent Charlotte from seeing the hidden intelligence in her eyes. She spoke with a soft voice, but the way she phrased her words indicated decent education and training.

While Charlotte's father said the blessing, Charlotte tried to concentrate on his prayer, but her mind kept lingering on Mildred. With a little meat on her bones and a new bloom in her cheeks, Mildred would be a beautiful woman. In spite of this insight to Mildred's potential, Charlotte identified with her despondency. Perhaps their kindred grief could build a bond of friendship between them. She would need female companionship while traveling with Conrad and David. Both brothers were good men, including Conrad in spite of his annoying habits, but neither of them could truly understand her perspective on things.

With the conclusion of her father's prayer, Charlotte's mother passed a platter of baked chicken to Mildred who was sitting beside her. Mildred selected the smallest piece and passed the platter to Dr. Hawthorne on her other side. Conrad elbowed Charlotte, shoving a bowl of mashed potatoes at her. She gave him a look of irritation as she accepted it and scooped two spoonfuls on her plate and passed the container on to David.

"Mrs. Wolfe, where did you grow up?" Mama asked before taking a few sips from her glass.

"Please, call me Mildred," she said. "I was born in New England. I met my husband, Frank, when he visited a friend from university. We courted during the summer and married in the fall. He brought me to New Bern. He heard land was more affordable in North Carolina."

"How long was he in the military?" David asked.

"Not long." She shook her head, glancing down at her plate. "Frank purchased a farm in New Bern, but he wasn't meant for farming life. He spent his days in restless disappointment. We struggled through the winter since we did not yet have any harvested crops. After Christmas, he sold the farm, rented a house for me in town, and registered in the military."

"How dreadful," Charlotte said, imagining how it must have felt for Mildred to know her husband was not content in their marriage—at least not enough to stay home and find work here.

"And what is so dreadful about the military?" Conrad turned to glare at Charlotte with a lift of his eyebrows. "A military career is quite respectable and a necessary occupation, especially now we are at war. Would marriage to a military man be so awful? If I recall, your sister was quite happy and content."

"Respectable, if it were not for all the killing. Mildred is now a young widow distraught with grief. I find the military an impractical career for families." Charlotte turned from Conrad, angry he could be so insensitive. She shoved a bite of potatoes into her mouth, determined to say no more lest she offend Mildred.

David cleared his throat as he laid his fork on his plate. "The military did not take my sweet Emma and cannot be blamed for ruining the family we had planned together. All of life is a risk it seems." David gave his full attention to Mildred. "Mrs. Wolfe, please accept my condolences for your recent loss. Although I must soon return to the military to complete my commitment, I go with a heavy heart. I am much obliged to you for agreeing to nurse my newborn daughter who must now grow up without her mother."

"It is the least I can do under the circumstances, sir." Mildred met his gaze. "If I can keep another child from dying and suffering the same fate as my little Franklin, perhaps my survival will have a purpose." Tears filled her eyes as she paused to swallow. "Otherwise, I fear I do not know why I am here."

Everyone grew silent around the table as they resumed eating. Forks scraped against plates, chairs creaked with movement, and glasses clinked against the table.

"When will you all leave?" Dr. Hawthorne asked as he pushed his plate a few inches away and folded his arms. He stroked his chin as he glanced from David to Conrad, waiting for an answer. "I believe a change of scenery will be good for Mrs. Wolfe, like a fresh breath of air."

"I agree. There is naught like sea adventure to cure one of melancholy." Conrad gave Charlotte a meaningful look and winked at her. "Charlotte and David are in need of it as much as Mildred." He turned to their guest with a grin. "To answer your question, Dr. Hawthorne, I have already taken the liberty of transporting Charlotte and the children's trunks aboard the *Victorious*. If Mildred is agreeable, we may leave tomorrow morning or the following day."

"Indeed, I am ready," Mildred said. "I have never been on a ship at sea before. The only regret I have is leaving my baby behind in his grave." She leaned forward as she pulled on a curl by her ear. "Mrs. Morgan, would you mind placing some flowers by my baby's grave at Christmas and on his birthday? Dr. Hawthorne can show you where he is."

"Of course," Mama said with no hesitation as she reached across the table and covered Mildred's hand. "It is the least I can do since you are saving my granddaughter. I would consider it an honor."

"I think I would enjoy a short trip into New Bern," Grandma Lauren said from the other end of the table. "It reminds me of the War of Independence when we had to flee to there and Hugh proposed to Tyra." Grandma's blissful expression shifted to sadness as she straightened in her seat. "I had just received news my son Scott had died fighting for our country. None of us are new to grief, but time will make the sting of it easier to bear. Do not waste time blaming the Lord—not when you need His strength the most."

"Mildred, would you like to go upstairs and meet Davie and Ashlynn?" Charlotte asked, scooting her chair back. "A servant has been watching over them during our dinner."

"Yes," Mildred set her napkin on the table.

"What about dessert?" Mama asked, her eyes wide with surprise.

"We shall come back for it," Charlotte motioned for Mildred to follow. She had no doubt the poor woman needed as much of a break from their reminiscent discussion as she did. Whenever one experienced a traumatic event, why did others feel the need to share their own experience? She didn't want to think about someone else's pain. Her own was enough to bear, and she feared it would never go away—this great big gaping hole in her heart—and in her life.

Conrad stood at the wheel of his ship breathing in the salt air, grateful for the soft breeze hovering over the ocean. The sails flapped in the wind as the bow glided through the water like a bird flying through the sky.

"If Miss Charlotte Morgan looks anything like her sister, I can see why David is so despondent," Mr. Higgins said, walking up to Conrad. "She is a beauty—that one."

"They were identical twins," Conrad said, thinking back to the first day he and his brother met them at a fall picnic. They had worn identical rose-colored gowns, their hair coiled in the same fashion with matching bonnets, and they carried white lace parasols. He and David loved the challenge of trying to tell them apart, fascinated by their beauty and wit. It seemed to be the perfect solution for two brothers looking for fun and entertainment. Neither of them would be left out or have to settle for a lesser beauty.

"Were they?" Mr. Higgins shielded his eyes as he looked down at the main deck where Charlotte held Ashlynn and Mildred gripped Davie's hand. The lad kept trying to jump up to see over the railing. A sailor took pity on him and swung the lad up on his shoulder so he could see the wide ocean. "Hard to imagine two of them with such perfection."

"Do not allow Miss Morgan's looks to deceive you, Mr. Higgins." Conrad chuckled, as he gazed in Charlotte's direction. She brushed back a strand of blond hair fallen from its clasp and into her eyes. Her profile was distinct, and she carried herself with confidence still drawing him as strong as the day he had met her six years ago. "She has a tongue that can wound a man's spirit deeper than a double-edged sword. It was the difference between Charlotte and her sister, Emma."

"Speaking from experience, are you?" Mr. Higgins grinned as he lowered his hand and regarded Conrad with a new expression. "I have never known you to be taken with a woman. Whenever we dock at ports and visit the taverns, you turn your fair share of heads and ignite giggles wherever you go, but an attachment has never been your way."

"Not when I have the sea calling me. An attachment would have been a huge inconvenience." The moment the words were out of his mouth, Conrad pressed his hand to his chest as guilt sliced through him. Her stubbornness might have been an inconvenience, but Charlotte herself could never be an inconvenience.

"She jilted you, did she?" Mr. Higgins rubbed his chin in thought, shaking his head and linking his hands behind his back.

"Actually, we would have had to be courting in order for her to jilt me. Sometimes I think we were merely chaperones for my brother and her sister." Conrad scratched the side of his temple, his discomfort increasing. He glanced up with a sigh and noticed a dark cloud in the distance. "I hope the weather holds up. I do not want the women and children to be frightened by a storm at sea."

"My friend, you are trying to change the subject," Mr. Higgins said with a grin, as he stepped forward and slapped Conrad on the back. "Are you trying to say you did not court Miss Charlotte, while her sister and your brother courted?"

"It is too complicated to explain," Conrad said, wishing he could distract Higgins from his personal life. "Charlotte and I have a history full of confusion."

"Ah, you do not know how she feels about you, but the fear of rejection was more than you could bear—or at least it is what you thought," Mr. Higgins said, as if he had already come to the conclusion. He lifted a dark eyebrow, and Conrad knew he enjoyed taunting him and wouldn't drop the matter until he heard some kind of confession.

"I had no intention of settling down." Conrad could not deny he had wanted more with Charlotte, but he had no wish to reopen old wounds. As much as he wanted her, he was not willing to give up his career in the navy to make a lasting commitment and have him landlocked with no way out. His thirst for adventure was too strong, but over time, he now realized the hold Charlotte had over him was just as strong. He figured it was too late to do anything about it. After witnessing the pain of his brother's loss, he wasn't sure he wanted to allow himself to be vulnerable.

"Ship ahead!" Dawson called from the watchtower. "British!"

Charlotte glanced up at Conrad and shaded her eyes. His sailors looked to him for direction. He couldn't risk Charlotte and the children. He pointed to the American flag. "Raise the British flag. Don your redcoats. Take the women and children below deck." Conrad turned to Higgins. "Get my telescope."

Once he disappeared, Conrad gripped the wheel tight in his hand as a sailor ushered Charlotte, Mildred, and the children below to his cabin. The dark cloud had grown larger. It would be imminent. A sailor brought him a British coat and took his away. Conrad shoved his arms into it and buttoned it up the middle. He took a deep breath. *"Lord, if you are listening, get us through the British blockade. If not for my sake, please do it for Charlotte, Mildred, and the children."*

Charlotte followed Mildred and Davie toward the steps leading below deck. If the tower watchman had seen a British ship, how far could it be? She scanned the horizon but saw no enemy ship. The deck exploded into chaos once Conrad shouted orders to the crew. The American flag lowered. What were they doing? Why would an American naval ship lower the flag?

Men rushed to their assigned duties. Two hurried past Charlotte and Mildred, disappearing below deck.

The babe whimpered at the unaccustomed noise. Gathering Ashlynn close to her chest, Charlotte moved with caution down the narrow staircase, her heart in her chest as her anxiety rose.

"I did not see an enemy ship," Charlotte said, glancing over her shoulder. "Will we soon be at battle? How shall I protect the children?"

"Captain Deaton already planned for this, Miss." The soldier behind her shook his head. "We will disguise the ship as a British vessel to slip through the blockades and avoid battle. He said he could not take the risk of battling another ship with you and the children aboard."

"The sun is still out." Davie whined below. "I do not wanna go to bed."

"You do not have to go to bed." Mildred promised. "We shall light some lanterns and you can play in the cabin."

Once they reached the door, Mildred turned the doorknob and pushed it forward. The hinges creaked. While Mildred lit a nearby lantern, Charlotte turned to the sailor escorting them. "Mr. . . ." She couldn't recall if he had told her his name or not.

"Just call me Vincent." Recognizing her awkward hesitation, he smiled.

"Thank you, Vincent." Charlotte swallowed her discomfort. "Please, how will we know when it is safe to leave our cabin again?"

"You should stay put until someone comes to tell you all is safe again." Vincent leaned forward and lowered his voice. "You will stay here, will you not?"

"Of course," Charlotte said. "I must do what is best for the children. Do not forget about us. We will be most anxious until we hear an update."

"Believe me, Miss Charlotte, there is no way the crew could forget any of you." He tipped his hat, turned, and disappeared into the dark hallway.

Charlotte released a deep sigh and strode into the dimly lit cabin. They would have to make do with their temporary confinement. For the moment, their biggest challenge would be entertaining a five-year-old boy who had lots of energy.

Ashlynn began to cry as Mildred went to the opposite side of the room and lit another lantern. The round window above the bed against the wall only provided a sliver of light. It was too high for Charlotte to see out. Charlotte shifted the babe over her shoulder and patted her bottom. Her crying subsided to tiny whimpers. She wished there was enough space for her to pace. At home, pacing calmed both herself and Ashlynn.

"What are we going to play?" Davie asked, looking around the cabin for something to spark his interest. His lips puckered in a disappointed frown.

"I believe she may be hungry." Mildred strode over and held out her arms. "If you will occupy little Davie, I will take care of Ashlynn."

Feeling bereft and inadequate, Charlotte cradled Ashlynn's head in her palm and gently lowered her tiny body into Mildred's arms. It frustrated her that only Mildred could provide what the child needed. How did she expect to raise two small children alone while their father spent his days in the military fighting a war? Perhaps her father was right when he indirectly insinuated she had no motherly instincts. Charlotte wrung her empty hands in despair, worrying she had taken on too much.

She should have known the child was hungry.

Charlotte lowered herself to the floor. At least the wooden floor had been cleaned. She couldn't imagine Conrad dusting his quarters and assumed he had ordered one of his crew to do it. She glanced over at a table against the wall. Various maps were laid out with rocks at each corner. An encased bookshelf layered three rows across was filled above the table. A stack of parchment paper sat on the corner held in place by a thick brown book. A case of several quills and three bottles of ink caught her attention.

"Auntie Charlotte, are these marching soldiers or sailors?" Davie held up three soldiers Conrad had carved for him.

"They can be whatever you want them to be," she said.

He wrinkled his brow and considered the matter. "Uncle Conwad said we will paint their coats blue so they can be American. I want them to be sailors like my dad." Davie lined the three soldiers in a row. "But I need some British soldiers so they can fight."

"Perhaps Conrad will make you some more," she said with a chuckle. No doubt, Davie would next want horses for a cavalry. Conrad would have his work cut out for him. Davie intended to collect a couple of troops for both the American and British soldiers.

She pulled a scrap of blue cloth out of the trunk at the foot of the bed and handed it to Davie. "You can pretend this is the ocean."

His eyes widened with excitement and a smile curled his lips. At least the idea appealed to him.

"And these can be your trees," Charlotte grabbed a few quills from the table and set them up in their cases. "Your sailors could be traveling through the woods on their way to the sea."

"Soldiers march, Auntie," Davie said with pride, puffing out his chest. His expression changed into a question as he wrinkled his brow and looked up at her with a sideways glance. "But where is their boat?"

"We will have to pretend it was lost at sea in a storm," she said.

"And I can pretend to be like God and make it thunder really loud." He lifted his hands high above his head, took a deep breath, and roared as loud as he could.

Startled by the noise, Ashlynn grew restless and kicked. Davie giggled and laughed. Charlotte laughed with him as she placed a finger to her lips. "We need to let Ashlynn eat and then sleep in peace. The thunder cannot be quite as loud." Charlotte kept her voice low as an example for Davie. He placed his thin finger to his own lips, copying her with a giggle.

"I am so thankful to be here with you, helping with Ashlynn." Mildred smiled down at Charlotte and Davie as she shifted the babe to her shoulder and patted her back to burp her. "Sometimes I wonder if my own little boy would have been like Davie."

"I am sure he would have been," Charlotte said. "All little boys love to play."

"True," Mildred said with a sigh. "I wonder if he would have looked like his father with light brown hair and brown eyes or if he would have been more like me with black hair. The children cheer me."

"Indeed, I feel the same way." Charlotte pulled her knees up so her skirt fell over her feet and then wrapped her arms around them. "I can only guess how much Ashlynn will be like her mother. I fear she will take on my personality from being around me so much."

"Sometimes children are not like anyone we know. They are a new creation from the Lord, unique in every way." A pensive expression crossed Mildred's face.

They lapsed into silence while Davie played with his toy soldiers. Ashlynn fell asleep, fed and content.

Charlotte glanced up at the circled window. All she could see was a slice of blue sky, but her mind kept going back to Conrad shouting orders up on deck. Could the danger be over?

4

Over an hour later, it was clear that the British vessel chasing them from the south had gained distance. It must be another frigate. Conrad had hoped it was a larger ship such as a ship of the line. If so, the *Victorious* could outdistance them in speed, but with the option no longer available, Conrad considered unloading some heavy artillery. He carried a shipment of supplies to the American military in Bridgeport. His superiors wanted to take advantage of his ability to maneuver through the British blockade. The idea of abandoning his mission so soon nagged him with unrest.

He glanced around the deck, pleased to see all his sailors had changed into British military uniforms. With the American flag no longer visible, he hoped they could pass for a British frigate without incident. Even above the order of transporting the artillery, he valued the safety of the women and children.

"British ship on the north side!" Vincent called from the tower, pointing ahead of them.

Traces of concern punched holes through the solid plan he had implemented. Conrad strode to the front rail and lifted his spyglass to his right eye. At first, he didn't see anything, and then he saw her, a frigate with a full set spread across three masts and a proud British flag flying high in the wind. He took a deep breath, determined not to panic or lose his head. No matter what, he had to make cautious decisions. Too many lives depended on him.

"Indeed, now we have two British vessels coming at us from both sides." Conrad lowered the glass and turned to look at his first mate. "I was not worried about one, but two present a new dilemma—entirely."

"What shall we do?" Higgins asked.

"Steer us closer inland. We know the waterways better than they. If our disguise fails us, we will sail like privateers and outrun them."

"Sir, if they were both behind us, I could see the logic in your statement. Right now, I don't know how we can outrun another frigate already ahead of us." Higgins's brow wrinkled in question, as he scratched the side of his head in confusion.

"I told you, Higgins, we know these inlets. I have been sailing up and down the Atlantic coast since I was a lad." Conrad handed the spyglass back to his first mate as his brother approached them.

"Captain, what is the plan?" David asked, saluting him and using his title out of respect for his position. "Where are my children?"

"Safe in my cabin below deck where they belong." Conrad pointed northwest toward the land in sight. "Higgins, look there and tell me what you see."

"The North Carolina coast, sir. And a ship heading our way." Higgins lowered the spyglass and gave Conrad a suspicious look. "Should I be seeing something else?"

"Indeed." Conrad nodded, unable to hide the slow grin crossing his face. He had an idea, but they wouldn't like it. All he had to do was convince them that his plan was better than trying to outrun a British blockade out to sea, or staying the course and risking a battle they didn't want, as long as the women and children were aboard. "There is a narrow inlet between the barrier islands leading into the Pamlico Sound up ahead. I believe we will reach it before the other frigate coming toward us. We are closer and can make the turn. The larger ship following us will not be able to make it. They will run aground."

"Conrad, are you mad?" David asked, abandoning the respect of rank between them and now speaking like a brother. "*We* could run aground. The Pamlico is too shallow and its masked shoals could wreck us and endanger my children."

"We have two battleships charging toward us that could endanger your children. If we sail into the sound, we could lose one of them without firing a shot."

"What about the other frigate approaching from the north side?" Higgins asked. "She is small and lightweight enough to follow us into the Pamlico. Do you plan to outrun her while trying to dodge shallow waters?" He shook his head and chuckled in disbelief. "Captain, you never cease to amaze me. Even while trying to dodge cannonballs, only you could manage to put us in even more danger."

"Captain, the British frigate is gaining on us!" Dawson called from the watchtower.

"If it works, it will be the best solution." Conrad pointed at Higgins. "Full speed ahead! Prepare for the turn. I will be at the wheel since I have sailed through the Pamlico before and know it best." He grabbed the wheel and inclined his head toward David. "Go below and tell them the captain commands the gunners to be ready."

"I thought you wanted to avoid a battle?" David asked.

"I do, but when we make the turn, we might be close enough for the British frigate to fire upon us, and if they do, we will stand and fight back before I allow us to sink or be taken."

Conrad wiped a puddle of sweat from his forehead as an image of Charlotte with little Davie and Ashlynn came to mind. "David, before you go below, promise me something."

"What?" David's dark eyes met his.

"Promise me if we end up in battle you will abandon ship with Charlotte and the children. Take a rowboat, swim to shallow waters, do whatever it takes to save them."

"I am their father. Of course, I will do whatever it takes." David came toward him and slapped him on his shoulder. "And I am trusting you to make sure things never get so far." David hurried down the steps to the main deck and disappeared below.

The *Victorious* increased her speed as the wind blew against Conrad's face. The inlet came into view, and he no longer needed his spyglass to see it. To his disappointment, the British frigate was also visible. Conrad swung the wheel, making a wide turn, careful to stay as centered as possible in order to keep the ship in the deepest part of the water. As they turned, a flash of light sparkled at them.

Conrad groaned. It was a signal of some sort that only the British would know among themselves. He had no idea how to respond. No doubt, they would give him ten to fifteen minutes to respond and then they would know the *Victorious* wasn't a British frigate. As he turned the ship into the small inlet, he cringed knowing their whole broadside would soon be vulnerable to possible cannon fire. Their only hope was to make the turn before the British captain decided they were American.

The light flashed again as the *Victorious* slid through the water, making a wide turn into the narrow inlet. Conrad gritted his teeth, hoping they would think him too busy commanding his ship to respond with a secret code. A few minutes passed and Conrad closed his eyes, saying a silent prayer for peace. A loud explosion burst through the air. Conrad opened his eyes to see a cloud of smoke spiraling above the British frigate. He gripped the wheel bracing himself for the impact.

An explosion rocked the ship as a wave splashed over the circle window. The contents in the room slid to one side. Charlotte and Davie lost their balance where they played on the floor. Mildred gripped Ashlynn tight in her arms and screamed as she lost her balance and fell into the floor.

"Oh dear, I fear a battle could not be avoided," Charlotte said, rolling to her knees and reaching for Davie.

"Was that real thunder?" he asked, his voice full of fear. He crawled into Charlotte's lap and clung to the arm she wrapped around him. "Are we going to sink?"

"I hope not," Charlotte kissed the top of his brown head and tightened her grip around him. More than anything she wanted to assure him they would not sink but couldn't utter the reassuring words since she had no idea what would happen. Too often she had hoped and prayed for something not to happen and it happened anyway. Emma's death was a bitter testament to where her faith had gotten her.

It wasn't as if she no longer believed in God or answered prayers—she had witnessed answers to other prayers in her short lifetime—but she now realized and accepted the fact that her prayers had not been in God's will. It was Emma's time to die and who was she to tell Davie that now wasn't their time to die when she didn't know it for a fact? What good would false reassurances do for Davie, especially if fate turned her into a liar?

"Davie, we do not know what is happening, so let us hang onto each other and hope we do not sink. Does this sound all right?" she asked. "One thing I can promise is to be right here with you."

"Yes." He bobbed his small head beneath her chin. "Do not leave us, Auntie. Is Daddy fighting?"

"Maybe."

More waves tossed the ship from one side to another. As things began to settle down, another shot burst upon them. One of the lanterns shifted off its hook and fell into the floor, exploding into flames.

"Davie, hold onto the bedpost. I have to put out the fire." She set him at the foot of the bed, and he did as she bid.

Charlotte swayed on her feet as the ship tilted again. She looked around for something to put out the fire. Like the bed, the wooden wash basin stand was nailed to the floor. She made her way to it as Ashlynn began crying. Mildred didn't move to console her, and fear drilled through Charlotte's heart. What happened to Mildred?

The fire spread across the square carpet. Charlotte grabbed the basin and poured the water over the fire, dousing half the flames. Charlotte pulled the quilt from under Mildred. Her unconscious body rolled, leaving Ashlynn exposed, kicking and screaming. Charlotte dropped the quilt and gathered Ashlynn in her arms. She handed the baby to Davie.

"Sweetie, I need you to hold the baby while I put out the fire. Can you do it for me?" Charlotte asked, gently placing the infant in his arms.

"Yes." He nodded. "No one ever lets me hold her."

"Just protect her head since she is too little to hold it up on her own." Charlotte placed Ashlynn in the crook of his arm. "Like this."

Once she was certain he had her, Charlotte grabbed the quilt and beat the fire until it dissipated. She turned and dropped on the bed beside Mildred and shook her shoulders. Blood dripped down her right temple. She placed her finger under Mildred's nose and felt the warmth of her breathing. Relief flooded her as she laid Mildred on her back and her head on a small pillow.

No more explosions erupted, and the swaying back and forth faded to the normal sensation of sailing through water. Charlotte brushed Mildred's brown hair back from her face and found a gash across her hairline above her forehead. It was about an inch long. She tapped Mildred's cheek, hoping to wake her. "Mildred, can you hear me?"

No response.

"Is she dead?" Davie asked. His voice sounded so alone and scared. Charlotte wondered if he thought about his mother. He was too young to be worrying about death, but how could he help it?

"No, she hit her head and it knocked her out, but she is still breathing."

"How will she feed Ashlynn if she does not wake up?" he asked, still holding Ashlynn's squirming body as if he would never let her go. Yet, his question was quite logical, in spite of being so young.

"Do not worry, Davie. We will figure out something. Can you hold Ashlynn a little longer while I clean Mildred's wound?"

"Yeah." He nodded. "But she likes to move a lot and keeps crying, and I do not know how to make her stop."

"I will hurry." Charlotte grabbed one of the square cloths and pressed it against the bleeding wound. Mildred moaned and tried to turn her head away, but Charlotte remained firm. "Shush." She coaxed her.

"Frank," Mildred muttered. "I lost the baby. I am so sorry." She sobbed and rolled over on her side, drawing her knees up.

"No, you did not," Davie said. "I have the baby."

Charlotte smiled at Davie, touched by his compassion. She hoped he would always maintain this part of himself even into manhood. Reaching over to console Mildred, Charlotte whirled in fright as the cabin door flew open and in rushed David.

Conrad steered the *Victorious* to the center of the Pamlico where he hoped the greatest depth would be. After the British frigate fired two shots, she took position and pursued them into the Pamlico. For the moment, they were safe. The sound was too narrow for them to swing wide and sail parallel with them. As long as she had to follow straight behind them, the British frigate could not fire her cannons upon them from the side nor could her crew prepare to swing aboard at this angle. All they could do was follow, but up ahead the sound would widen, and if the British captain intended to make his move, it would be then.

Higgins appeared on the main deck and climbed the steps to the quarterdeck. He paused in front of Conrad with a salute.

"Any damage?" Conrad asked.

"None, sir. I checked with the crew below and both shots missed us. Powder has been carried to each gunner, and they are prepared to fire when the order comes."

"Excellent." Conrad linked his hands behind his back and paced from one side of the quarterdeck to the other. "Higgins, I want your honest opinion. Why do you suppose a British frigate would fire upon another ship displaying a British flag? I have measured the distance in my head, and there is no way they could have seen anything aboard this ship to give them cause for suspicion."

"My only guess would be we did not respond in a timely manner to their secret coded light. With all the American privateers trying to sneak through the British blockade, perhaps they have devised some method of identifying each other."

"The same thought did occur to me." Conrad nodded. "It looked as though they were using the sun's reflection off a small mirror. If only I could have deciphered the message, I may have prevented this current situation. If we are to outrun them through the Pamlico, we will need to try and figure out this message system. No doubt, we will run into more British ships between here and Bridgeport."

"But how will we do it?" Higgins asked, stroking his chin in thought.

"We cannot, but next time we shall be the first to use the code. I have memorized the message they flashed at us. If the next British ship responds in a similar manner, we shall be safe and will know how to respond in the future."

" 'Tis worth a shot at least," Higgins said with a shrug. "In the meantime, we must find a way to lose the frigate trailing us. Any idea on what to do? She has better speed than we do. From what I can tell, she looks to be smaller with a lighter load. Are you prepared to dump cargo to increase your speed?"

"If it comes to it." Conrad nodded. "But I do not believe it will be necessary just yet. The captain has shown himself to be impatient, careless in wasting precious ammunition without proper distance and target range. If he makes enough mistakes, we will be able to outwit him." Conrad pointed north and grinned. "As you know, the Pamlico will soon widen, and when we come to the area, I anticipate he will be eager to pull up beside us and attempt to engage in battle."

"Indeed, it would be my guess as well." Higgins nodded, his dark curls protruding from beneath his hat. He gave Conrad a quizzical glance and lifted a dark eyebrow. "If it is the case, and we do not succeed in outrunning them, how do you propose to avoid battle?"

"Glad you asked." Conrad lifted a finger and began pacing again, while Higgins took the wheel. "Do you recall the British frigate which ran into shallow waters here in the Pamlico last year? It was most unexpected since the event occurred where the sound is at its widest."

"As you mention it, I do remember something about it." Higgins turned the wheel to steer around a small fishing boat. "But I cannot recall the exact details or where it actually occurred. Still, how does it help us here and now? It seems the British frigate is keeping pace with us." Higgins glanced behind them.

"Well, I do remember where the shallow part is, and if all works according to my plan, I believe we can guide them directly into it." Conrad rubbed his hands together as if he had just won a prize. "But we must be careful we do not stray too close to the shallow waters ourselves lest we fall into the same trap. Also, we will have to be careful we do not give them too much free room so they do not go around us."

"Ah, I see what you mean. Very clever." He stepped back and gestured to the wheel. "In this case, it would be best if you would take over steering the ship. How soon will we come upon the spot?"

"At this rate of speed, we will reach the area in about fifteen minutes." Conrad gripped the wheel with both hands and surveyed the water trying to make sure he had measured their bearings appropriately. "Of course, there are many shallow areas in the Pamlico, even when there is no shoreline in sight. The last thing I want to do is make a mistake in my calculations."

"True." Higgins walked away, his booted footsteps clapped against the deck floor where he paused in silence. "Uh, Captain, I believe we have trouble. The British frigate has swerved around on our left and is starting to catch us. If she gains anymore distance, her guns will be in position to fire upon us."

"Good. She is moving exactly as I predicted. Soon she will run aground," Conrad said.

"Her first gun is moving into position." Higgins strode back and grabbed Conrad's arm. "She is going to fire upon us before she hits the ground. We have to do something! Allow me to give the order to fire back."

"No, I refuse to waste ammunition when I am certain she will soon run aground. Even if she manages a shot before then, the damage will already be done if she hits her mark. We will need to concentrate our efforts in repairing what we can and moving out of the line of fire so she cannot get another shot at us."

"Sir, I fear you are taking too much of a risk." Higgins raised his voice in concern and gripped the rail.

"There is no adventure without a little risk. Higgins, you have sailed with me long enough to know that."

5

Another explosion rocked the ship, sending Charlotte into the floor. She cradled the baby in her arms, while her right arm and hip took the brunt of the force. Startled, Ashlynn cried and wiggled in distress.

Mildred sat up and pressed her back against the wall where she had been lying down taking a nap. Little Davie sat in the floor flipping through a book Charlotte had given him. The ship continued to sway back and forth. She whispered a prayer of thanksgiving that she had not fallen on Davie or hurt Ashlynn.

Charlotte's knees and elbows stung from the burns on her skin. She feared she might have suffered a splinter or two. By tomorrow, she would be discolored with bruises. At least the other lantern still hung on the wall, and there would be no fire this time.

"What was it?" Davie asked.

"I am not sure," Charlotte said. She suspected another cannon was fired at them, but she didn't want to scare Davie. "Mildred, are you all right?"

"Yes, but what do you suppose could be going on?" She brushed her dark hair from her face. "David left a while ago. Anything could have happened since then."

"If you will take her," Charlotte leaned up on her knees and held Ashlynn out to Mildred. "I shall go up on deck and find out something."

"But it could be dangerous. Are you sure you want to take the risk?" Mildred asked, as she accepted Ashlynn and laid back down, cradling the child against her side.

"I will be fine." Charlotte stood to her feet and walked to the door. "We cannot sit down here and wait forever. What if they forget about us?"

She pulled the door open and stepped out into the dark hall. Taking a deep breath, Charlotte crept up the narrow stairs, following the light above her. She ventured out on the main deck. The clean salt air refreshed her lungs and blew a gentle breeze against her face and neck.

"You need to go below where it is safe, Miss," a sailor called to her. He pulled on a thick rope and tied it into a knot, grunting with the effort. His gray hair was tied by a black ribbon at the nape. Sideburns layered his face with gray whiskers. Slight wrinkles circled his brown eyes.

"Please, were we being fired upon?" Charlotte asked, strolling toward him.

"Yes, but it is over now," he said. "You should go below until the captain says it is all right to come out on deck."

"If the threat of gunfire has passed, I do not understand why I must go below." Charlotte stood her ground and propped her hands on her hips.

"Because I said so." Conrad's deep voice spoke behind her. She could not mistake the warning edge in his tone, but she had no intention of backing down. If they were still in danger, she would do as asked, but if Conrad thought he could use his title as captain to boss her, he was mistaken. "We are sailing through hazardous, shallow waters, and I need to know you and the children are well and safe below. I do not need any distractions right now."

"I am not one of your sailors to be ordered about this ship." She whirled and lifted her chin as she met his hazel eyes. "And besides, I have never been a distraction. You managed to disappear after Emma and David's wedding and carry on with your career sailing the high seas as if we never met."

"You are so a distraction," he leaned close and lowered his tone through clenched teeth. "Then and now."

"I am sorry I am such a burden you would want me out of sight and out of mind." Her insides felt as if they were being squeezed by a printing press, branding her heart with words she didn't want to hear. At one time, she had hoped he could love her the way David had loved Emma, but his attempts to stop their wedding had convinced her otherwise. Today, he confirmed he had not changed.

"It is not what I meant and you know it," he hissed in an attempt to keep his voice low.

"At any rate," she cut him off, determined to change the subject before she suffered even more humiliation. "You could have warned me to douse the lanterns. I have never sailed on a vessel like this. How was I to know we would be tossed to and fro? It fell and caught the carpet on fire in your cabin."

"Are you all right?" Concern flared in his dark eyes as he searched her face. His lips twisted in dissatisfaction as he grabbed her hands and arms to look them over. The action caused her sleeve to rub against her sore elbow and she winced, jerking away from him. He stepped back and his gaze landed on the hem of her black gown. "Your dress is charred. Your legs could be burned."

Charlotte looked down. Indeed, one of her favorite mourning gowns was now ruined. Before she had time to bemoan the fact, Conrad stepped toward her. She stepped back. "I assure you. My legs are fine. I should know it if they were not."

"You could be in shock. You did not even know about your gown." He lifted a hand to brush her hair off her forehead. "Did you hit your head as well?"

"No, and the children are fine. I hurt my arm protecting Ashlynn, is all." She tilted her head away from his warm hand. His touch and everything about him brought back memories she had tried to forget. "Please, there is no need to pretend to be concerned over me."

"I do not pretend. As captain, it is my responsibility to ensure everyone on board this ship is properly cared for, including you." He stepped forward and held out his hand. "Come, I shall take you to the physician. I insist."

"Mildred will see to me." Charlotte looked down at his outstretched hand and backed up assessing his eyes. "I do not know your physician and prefer she take care of me."

His lips thinned, and he breathed out in frustration. Stepping toward her, Conrad bent and swept her into his arms. "I will see to you myself." He uttered the words near her ear as his warm breath breezed over her nape. Charlotte shivered, resting her injured elbow across the middle of her body. She tried not to concentrate on the strength of Conrad's arms as he carried her, but it was impossible. If she had been younger and naive as she once was, she could have mistaken his behavior as the actions of someone who cared deeply for her. This time she knew better, and she wouldn't allow her heart to be deceived.

Conrad chastised himself as he carried Charlotte across the main deck to the captain's quarters. She was right, and he should have warned her about the lanterns. Why did he not think of it? The idea she and the children could have been caught in a fire chipped away at the edges of his mind like a chisel.

"Where are you taking me?" Charlotte asked. "I thought we were going back to the cabin below? Is it not the captain's cabin?"

"I have installed you and the children in my private cabin below where I prefer to get a good night's sleep, but I have the captain's quarters up here where I meet with my men, make plans, and sleep on a cot when I need short naps," he said.

"What are your men to think of you carrying me like this?" Her cheeks flamed as she looked over at several men watching them.

Conrad grinned, unable to quench the possessive feeling rising inside him. He would not admit it to her, but if his men happened to think she was off limits, he could not pretend it didn't suit him. It would make it much easier to keep her safe, and he would not have to think about her with anyone else. In fact, it pleased him when he had returned for Ashlynn's birth to find Charlotte still unattached.

"They would think nothing, especially since it is none of their concern." He turned sideways to fit her through the doorway, crossed the red, black, and gold printed carpet, and set her on a carved wooden chair by a table covered with maps and charts. Conrad was sorry he did not have time to clear it off before he brought her inside.

What was left of the afternoon sunlight filtered through the front windows. It wouldn't give him as much light as he would like to view her wounds, but it would be better than any of the other cabins below deck. He walked over to the front windows displaying a beautiful scene of the ocean and pulled the gold drapes wider, tying them with red cords on each side.

"So is this where you have been staying?" she asked, her gaze wandering over to the other wall with three rows of shelves filled with various books. Beneath it sat a cabinet with glass-encased doors containing bottles of wine and goblets.

"Yes." He strode back, pulled up a matching chair, and sat facing her. "Roll up your sleeve and tell me how it happened." He pointed at her injured arm, while she glared at him with a frown. Conrad knew that defiant look, but to his surprise, she obeyed.

Her elbow was severely bruised, and the skin on top of it rubbed raw. He stepped outside the room and called to one of his sailors, motioning him over. "Tell Dr. Garrett to bring up some ointment for a burn."

"Yes, sir!" He saluted Conrad, turned on his heel, and strode away.

Conrad returned and bent to his knees beside Charlotte. He touched the scorched hem of her gown, and she slapped his hands away with her good arm. "I told you, my legs are fine! I should know whether or not I suffered any burns." She shoved her feet under her chair and gave him a daring look. "I cooperated and allowed you to see my elbow, but naught else."

"Fine, I will take your word, but we do have another matter to discuss." Conrad sat in the chair across from her and crossed his booted foot over his knee. He rested his elbows on the arms of the chair and linked his fingers as he studied the curious expression on her face.

"Which is?" she prompted, straightening her back and stiffening herself on guard.

"I realize you are not one of my sailors, but I cannot have you disrespecting me in front of my men and in obvious disobedience. It undermines my authority to everyone else on this ship. You may not agree with me, but could you set aside our past and your personal dislike of me long enough to wait and discuss them in private?" He lifted an eyebrow, hoping she would be reasonable.

"It depends." She tilted her head at an angle, and he had to ignore how adorable she looked, her wide green eyes baiting him.

"Now see, Charlotte? That is exactly the kind of attitude that gets you into trouble." He pointed at her. "You need to be more agreeable, so we can get along."

"You mean . . . let you have your way." She pursed her lips and scooted to the edge of her seat. "It is not going to happen, especially if I know you are wrong."

"Captain Deaton, please excuse me for the interruption, but the previous blast splintered the rudder. We have no steering capabilities at the moment." Higgins stood at the threshold and waited for Conrad's response as he glanced from Conrad to Charlotte and back. "Since we are in shallow waters, I thought you should know as soon as possible."

"Can it be repaired?" Conrad asked.

"Vincent believes he can repair it, but we will need to set anchor and keep the ship stationary while he climbs outside to make the repairs," Higgins said.

"We have no choice. Repairs must be made, but we could be vulnerable in the meantime." Conrad stood, his mind already at work processing the possible consequences. "Do we have a status on the British frigate?"

"Last we saw of her, she had run aground. We do not know the extent of her damage or how long they will be stuck." Higgins straightened and squared his shoulders, ready to receive his orders.

"Drop anchor," Conrad said. "Have the crew bring in the sails. Choose a few men to row back to report on the British frigate's progress and location." He glanced at Charlotte. "Please forgive me, but I must see to the crew. We will finish this discussion some other time. Wait here for Dr. Garrett to bring the ointment I asked for and then go back to the safety of the cabin." With mixed feelings, Conrad turned and left her alone in the captain's quarters, wishing he could stay and bait her more.

For the rest of the afternoon they worked on repairing the rudder. The constant hammering echoed through the walls of their cabin causing Charlotte to develop a headache. The following day, they raised the anchor and set sail before the British frigate came after them. Charlotte enjoyed a picnic on the deck with the children, David, and Mildred as they passed between two islands and left the Pamlico and ventured into the sea. Over the next few days, they sailed by Virginia and dodged two more British vessels.

Once the children were down for a nap, Mildred agreed to stay with them while she read one of Conrad's books. Charlotte came up to the main deck and joined David where he leaned on the rail. The water lapped up against the side of the ship as they plowed through the water. The afternoon sun slanted over the ocean, making the surface sparkle like crystal lights.

David sighed and rubbed his face with trembling hands. Whiskers shadowed his face, and his long sandy brown hair lay over his shoulders like strings. He usually wore his hair brushed neat and tied back by a ribbon. His unkempt appearance concerned Charlotte, but not as much as the dark circles around his red-rimmed hazel eyes. Over the last few days she had noticed him going through the motions of his duties but not really connecting with anyone. He hugged the children and came to see them, but he no longer teased and played with them.

"You need rest. I can tell you have not been sleeping well," Charlotte said, resting her elbows on the top rail and linking her fingers. The breeze felt wonderful in the heat of the sun.

"I am fine." His tone held a hard edge and his despondency broke her heart. It would have pained Emma to see him like this. Charlotte's raw emotions ran deep, especially her loyalty to her twin. For a moment, she felt a heavy burden of responsibility for David as much as for the children.

"It is hard to accept the fact she is gone, and I shall never see her again. I miss the talks we had, touching her . . . loving her . . ." Emotion clogged his throat. He turned away and gripped the rail as if it was a lifeline.

"I still dream of her at night. The dreams seem so real, as if she is still here with us. A few times I have awakened, eager to tell her what she did or said in my dream, only to be reminded I cannot." Charlotte allowed a sarcastic chuckle to escape her. "Sometimes I lay down at night and pray I will dream of her again, just so I can see and speak to her once more."

"I suppose it must be different for you, but each time I look at you, I see Emma. Not only do you remind me of her, but when I am near you, I feel as if I am near her." He shook his head and wiped his tired eyes and chuckled. "I suppose I sound as if I have lost my mind."

"Of course not. You are merely grieving over the loss of your wife. And believe me, I am used to being compared to Emma. I was always the troublesome twin. Everyone, including my parents and my brothers and sisters, would lose patience with me and ask me why I could not be more like her." She shook her head, aware of fresh tears filling her eyes as the view of the sea grew hazy. "To tell the truth, I never understood why I was so different. I always wanted to be more like her."

Silence lengthened between them. A spray of saltwater splashed up and Charlotte welcomed the cool relief on her hot skin. She forgot to bring her parasol with her and hoped her bonnet would protect her face from the sun.

"Charlotte, I know you admired Emma's reserved behavior and her ability to be the peacemaker, always willing to give something of herself in some sacrificial way." David turned and met her gaze, leaning his right elbow on the rail. "But I fear it wore her down and became the end of her too soon. She didn't have your fiery spirit and determination to fight. For if she did, I cannot help wondering if she would have lasted through the ordeal of Ashlynn's birth and survived. Do not look on your temper and passionate nature as an annoying weakness when it may be your greatest strength."

She opened her mouth to respond but realized she had no idea what to say. No one, other than Emma and her mother, had ever offered to see her persistent traits as a positive reaction to life. The way David had stated it gave her much to ponder.

"David and Charlotte!" Conrad stood at the door of the captain's quarters and waved them to come in. "I need to speak to both of you."

"I daresay," David held out his hand ahead of them with a grin, "our presence is in demand."

With reluctance, Charlotte strode toward Conrad, loath to leave the sun and fresh air. As she walked by Conrad, his warm presence alerted her senses, making her aware of the scent of sandalwood and soap. His brown hair was combed to the side and pulled back at the nape by a blue ribbon. Unlike his brother, he had shaved earlier in the morning.

"Let us view the map on the table," he said, pointing toward it.

"Good day, Miss Charlotte, David." Mr. Higgins nodded to them both where he stood at the end of the table with his hands folded behind his back.

"Tonight, we will be leaving the coast of Virginia and crossing the entrance to the Chesapeake Bay, not far from Washington D.C." Conrad came to stand beside David and trailed a line from the coast out to sea. "Along here is the area where the British come and go. In fact, they have so much traffic traveling through here, they do not even bother stationing a ship in the area like they do everywhere else."

"Do you mean to say we are going to be in greater danger?" Charlotte asked, looking up at Conrad's expression for confirmation.

"Not necessarily in greater danger, but possibly at more risk." He tilted his head as he looked down and met her gaze.

"Is there a difference?" she snapped.

"We are only in danger if we are discovered." He motioned to his first mate. "Now, Higgins and I have been discussing a plan. Our goal is to cross the area during nightfall. We will not light any lanterns anywhere on the ship. There will be no reading, card playing, or sewing, naught to require light. We will sail through the water by the quarter moonlight and what stars shine around the clouds."

"Conrad, it could be risky if this area is as high in traffic as you say." David crossed his arms and shook his head. "We cannot risk running into a British frigate."

"Keep in mind they will not have all their lights off like us. If anything, we will be aware of them before they are aware of us." Conrad touched David's shoulder. "But I have one other favor concerning the children."

"Yes?" David gave him a sideways glance, and Charlotte's attention piqued as she waited and listened.

"I realize Davie is still afraid of the dark. I spoke to our physician, and he has some chamomile tea we could give Davie to put him at ease and help him sleep longer. He assures me it will have no lasting effects on him and will be fine. We will keep the lantern light low until he falls asleep, and then we must put it out completely."

"It will be fine." David nodded, relaxing and unfolding his arms to lean his palms upon the table. "The lad could use a good night's sleep, and so could I."

"Then I will see that Dr. Garrett brings both you and Davie some of the tea." Conrad slapped him on the back with a satisfied grin. He leaned around his brother to look at Charlotte. "Do you have any questions? Any criticisms?"

"Only one observation." Charlotte stepped around David and smiled up at Conrad, lifting her pointer finger straight up. "I must admit I am impressed you know your nephew is scared of the dark."

"Well, perhaps you should observe more often, Charlotte. I am not as shallow as you think; in fact, I happen to know a lot more about my niece and nephew than you realize." He leaned forward and whispered in her ear. "And you."

His warm breath tickled her skin and sent shivers throughout her body. His hazel eyes sparkled as bright as the shining sea through the window behind him. She could feel her face warming in embarrassment. Without taking his eyes from hers, he said, "I would like to invite you all to dine early. Right here within the hour." He pointed to the floor. "And bring my niece and nephew."

6

Conrad could not say if dinner was well prepared or not, since his concentration was on Charlotte. She wore a radiant gown to bring out her green eyes, and she remained in high spirits the whole time. Of course, most of her buoyant behavior must have been due to his officers' attention. They were all taken with both Charlotte and Mildred.

Davie talked with anyone who would listen, while David stared down at his plate and brooded in silence. Once in a while, he glanced up and gave Charlotte a rare smile. On one occasion, he leaned over to Conrad and mentioned how much Charlotte reminded him of his Emma. It was the first time Conrad feared Charlotte's presence in David's life could be a hindrance to him getting over the death of his wife. It posed a problem, since Conrad enjoyed having Charlotte around, and he believed his niece and nephew truly needed her.

Once they arrive in Cleaveland and boarded their designated battleship, David would spend less time with Charlotte. Perhaps then, David could begin to heal. As his superior officer, Conrad could limit the time David spent away from the ship. On the few times when he did return home, Conrad could schedule outings for Charlotte.

Higgins approached Conrad at the wheel and stopped beside him. "I have walked the perimeters of the entire ship and checked every cabin on each floor. All lights are out. The sails are up. Dawson is in the watchtower. We are ready to increase our speed if you wish."

"Yes, I want to make it through tonight," Conrad said.

"I shall give the order," Higgins stepped down to the main deck and shouted out the orders to the sailors on duty. A few moments later, he returned.

"Is little Davie asleep?" Conrad asked.

"Indeed, the lad is sound asleep," Higgins said with a chuckle, shaking his head. "While David is snoring in a nearby chair, I offered to take him to his own cabin, but Miss Charlotte said to leave him be and let him sleep. I daresay, the two ladies may need some chamomile tea themselves if they are to get any rest tonight. David's snoring is echoing off the small walls within the cabin."

"A couple of years ago, Charlotte would have hunted me down and demanded I have David removed. Lately, she is not acting like herself. I fear Emma's death has changed my brother and Charlotte in more ways than I care to think on."

"Well, I have seen her demonstrate grit in defying you," Higgins said, and Conrad knew him well enough to hear the smile in his tone.

"I seem to be the only exception," Conrad said. "Charlotte would find the courage to defy me, no matter what the circumstance. The woman enjoys vexing me."

"If you do not make a move soon and reveal your intentions, you may lose her to some gallant hero who takes it into his hand to court her. Miss Charlotte would make a fine match to any of our officers determined to pursue her favor." Higgins slapped Conrad on the back in a friendly manner, sobering his tone. "And with all due respect, sir, I witnessed plenty of interest tonight at dinner. You must have seen it as well."

Conrad didn't bother to respond. Although he knew Higgins words to be true, they irritated him just the same. How could he declare intentions he did not have? He still did not want to settle down, but even if he did, Conrad doubted Charlotte would have him. The idea of her rejecting him would be more than he could bear, especially if he gave up his career and made certain sacrifices for her.

Footsteps came toward them through the dark, approaching up the steps to the quarterdeck. The outline of a man paused before them. "It is me, Vincent. I thought you would like to know I noticed a light on the backside of the ship."

"Do you mean a light from our ship or another approaching ship?" Conrad asked.

"It is too close to the water and our ship to be from some other ship. I waited to see if he would extinguish the light, but instead, he flashed several times, almost like a coded signal."

"Higgins, stay here at the wheel." Conrad turned to Vincent's silhouette. "You lead me to where you saw the light. I intend to find out if we have a disobedient rebel or a traitor masquerading as one of us."

Conrad followed Vincent to the main deck to the left side of the ship between a stack of two rowboats and a couple of barrels fastened by thick ropes. He leaned over the rail and surveyed the distance from the deck to where the ship met the water. As Vincent had said, a small light came from one of the round windows and projected onto the water. It would be easy for someone to cover the window with a piece of cloth to cause the blinking and set the coded signal.

He studied the message and a sting of betrayal sliced through him as Conrad recognized a similar code he had seen from the other British frigate more than a week ago. Who had he taken into his confidence as a traitor? Whoever it was, Conrad needed to catch him in the act before he cut out the light. It looked as if the light came from the cannon level.

"Come on," Conrad said. "You are coming with me."

With no lights, Conrad felt his way along the walls and descended the narrow staircase with caution. They passed several large cannons, the gunners sleeping in their hammocks nearby, and found the hallway leading to lower-ranking officers. As they drew closer, a faint light appeared under the door. Conrad shook his head at the audacity of the sailor in spite of the order to turn out all lights after nightfall.

When they reached the cabin, Conrad tested the doorknob. It was locked. He stepped back, lifted his booted foot, and slammed his heel into the door. The impact burst it open. Andrew O'Malley dropped the cloth he had been holding up between the twelve-inch whale oil lantern and the circle window.

"Captain Deaton!" Surprise registered in his young, brown eyes. He held up his hands, palms outward. "I was about to put out the light. This is not what it looks like."

"Other than you disobeying a direct order, what else does it look like?" Conrad asked, walking toward him. "Perhaps you are a traitor trying to alert the enemy of our whereabouts?"

"No, I would never do so. I am loyal." Andy stepped back, fear apparent in his expression as he kept looking from Conrad to Vincent.

"Oh, we intend to find out just how loyal you are," Conrad said, grabbing him by the collar.

The days passed from May into June, and Charlotte felt relief at how the hot and muggy weather grew milder the further north they sailed. She held her parasol over Ashlynn in the crook of her right arm. The sun shone bright, but a set of clouds approached from the distance. She wanted to get in as much sun and fresh air as she could before the rain caught them.

Davie bounced a small ball and tried to pick up a stone, playing a game of knucklebones with Conrad and Dawson. David sat on a barrel in the corner, watching with a brooding expression. He looked up and gazed in Charlotte's direction. The intensity of his concentration made her heart ache for him. At the moment, she couldn't tell if he stared at her or Ashlynn. If her, she had no doubt he imagined Emma. Charlotte could not blame him. If she had to look at herself all day, she would be reminded of Emma as well. Still, his behavior unsettled her.

The ball bounced and rolled over toward David's booted feet. Chasing the ball, Davie laughed and ran toward his father. He slapped his little hands on his dad's lap. "Daddy! Come play with me."

"Not now. Maybe later," David said.

"You never play with me," Davie said, twisting his lips into a frown. Disappointment and confusion filled his wide eyes as he patted his dad's knee trying to gain his attention. "You did not play with me when we had the picnic and Auntie Charlotte and Mrs. Mildred always have to read to me."

"Sorry, Davie. I do not feel like playing right now." David pushed his little hands away and stood. "I am going to my cabin to take a nap."

Davie stood and watched his father's back as he disappeared below. He sniffled and wiped his eyes, but he didn't turn around for a few more minutes. The ball forgotten, Davie hung his head and sat against a barrel. He propped his knees, wrapped his arms around them, and hid his face from sight.

He was too young to feel so rejected and alone. Unsure if she should comfort him or leave him alone, Charlotte watched for a sign, but he did not look for her. How could she make a five-year-old child understand his father's grief and depression was not a personal rejection?

Conrad cleared his throat and scratched his temple with a deep sigh. He gathered the stones in his hand and shook them as if rolling a pair of dice. Dropping them on the wooden deck, they rolled in scattered directions until one by one they came to a stop.

"Davie, why not come over here so we can finish playing?" Conrad asked, lifting an eyebrow and watching Davie's reaction.

Dawson sat in silence beside Conrad. He met Charlotte's gaze, and she was certain the sorrow on his face matched her own.

"No!" Davie shouted. He glanced up and blinked tears from his eyes as they streamed down his cheeks. His complexion held a pink hue, his bottom lip swollen and dark red where he had been biting it. "I do not wanna to play."

"What would you like to do, Davie?" Charlotte asked.

"Nothing!" Davie covered his ears and rocked back and forth, puckering his bottom lip.

"Lad, do not talk to your Aunt Charlotte that way," Conrad said, his tone a warning. He stood and walked over to Davie, bent down on his haunches, and pointed at Charlotte. "You need to apologize to her, right now."

"No!" Davie sobbed. "She is not my mama."

"It does not matter. You need to treat her with respect," Conrad said, shaking his head in disbelief. He shifted his weight to his right leg and rubbed his left knee. "Now apologize, Davie."

Davie wiped his eyes with the back of his hand and sniffled. He took a deep breath and swallowed before looking up at Conrad through watery eyes. His lips trembled as he started to speak, but his voice failed him. Davie paused and tried again. "My mama left me."

His words scratched her heart raw. She couldn't let him think Emma deserted him. It would have broken her sister's heart. Davie didn't understand, and he was confused and grieving. They would have to overlook his bad behavior. It would be too cruel to discipline him while he is in the midst of so much confusion and pain. The words of 1 John vibrated through her mind. *Whoso hath this world's good, and seeth his brother have need, and shutteth up his bowels of compassion from him, how dwelleth the love of God in him?*

"Conrad, leave him alone," she said, creeping forward, hoping Davie wouldn't reject her comfort.

"Stop, Charlotte." Conrad held up his hand, and his voice held a note of authority she had rarely heard. On impulse, she paused in obedience but gave him a glare of defiance. Once she got Conrad alone, she would have her say. Right now, she didn't want to cause Davie more confusion by quarreling in front of him. "I realize Davie is grieving and cannot understand what happened to Emma, but he must learn he cannot take his anger out on other people, especially innocent souls who have done naught against him." Conrad looked back at Davie and pointed at Charlotte a second time. "Davie, do what I asked or there will be consequences."

"What is . . . con-se-kenses?" he asked, tilting his head and scrunching his nose.

"Punishment," Conrad said. "Do you want to be punished?"

Davie shook his head.

Charlotte relaxed, silently thanking the Lord Davie had finally decided to cooperate. She glanced down at Ashlynn now asleep in her arms. At least, the baby could sleep in spite of all the noise.

"I am sorry, Aunt Charlotte."

Conrad pointed to a crate of ropes and looked at Vincent. "Sort through these and pull out the ones frayed and needing repair."

"Yes, sir." Vincent bent to his knees and opened the lid. It creaked as the hinges rotated.

"Captain, I need to speak with you, sir," Higgins approached from behind.

"What about?" Conrad asked, glancing over his shoulder. Higgins carried a piece of paper with a perplexed expression piquing Conrad's interest. He had sailed with his first mate long enough to know something was up when he wrinkled his brows and twisted the left side of his mouth, as Higgins did now.

"We have questioned Andy and searched his cabin for clues as to why he betrayed us. We roughed him up a bit, but he still maintains he is innocent and was not trying to betray us." Higgins held out the paper. "We found naught to condemn him, but we did find this suspicious letter. And after questioning some of the men, we discovered his family were Tories during the Revolutionary War. His father served with the British."

Conrad unfolded the letter and read the scrawled handwriting. *Dear P. K., It is done.* A. O. The message sounded mysterious, indeed. He waved the note. "Did you ask him about it?"

"I did, but he says it is naught to do with the navy, and he refused to reveal P. K.'s identity." Higgins leaned forward and lowered his voice. "He presents quite a dilemma with suspicious behavior and our lack of proof. What should we do with him?"

"Write up a report on what we caught him doing with the light and document this note. When we dock at the harbor, we shall turn him over to the authorities there. Someone may have knowledge as to whose initials Andy might be referring to on the note." Conrad refolded the paper and handed it back to Higgins. "Put this somewhere for safekeeping with your report."

"Yes, sir," Higgins said. He took the note and walked away, passing Charlotte as she strode toward Conrad, a look of determination in her expression. Higgins greeted her with a brief nod, and she responded in kind.

"I was hoping to find you," Charlotte said. She wore a dark blue gown with short sleeves and black ribbons fastened to each. Since the fire had destroyed one of her black mourning gowns, Charlotte often wore other dark colors to replace it and managed to find other ways to show she still mourned her sister. He admired her perseverance and loyalty to those she cared about. There were times when he wished he could be one of those lucky souls.

"There could only be one of two reasons you would take the time to seek me out." He gestured in front of them, and she stepped beside him to stroll across the main deck. "Since there is no major emergency, I can only assume you have a complaint."

"I do." She brushed her blond hair from her eyes and tucked it under her black bonnet. "I believe you were too hard on Davie yesterday. He is only five years old, and you expect him to be able to set aside his feelings of pain and confusion to apply reason and logic as if he was twelve."

"Charlotte, I realize how you see it, but it is our responsibility to teach him to think before he reacts and to be logical. He cannot use those skills when he turns twelve if we do not guide him in developing those skills now." He rubbed his hand through his hair and massaged the tense muscles behind his neck. "Davie needs a father figure, and my brother is too mired in his own grief to be there for him. I am only doing what I believe is right. I want the best for him."

"And so do I," she snapped, her tone growing in agitation. "And I believe Davie needs more time to grieve before you start hammering him with discipline he is too young to understand. You could crush his spirit and cause him to resent us." She stopped walking and poked him in the chest. "And I will not allow you to do it."

"Davie is as much my nephew as yours, and in spite of what you must think about me, I love him and would never harm him." He tried not to let it bother him that she thought so little of him, but the knowledge kept digging at him like a mole burrowing a hole. A rising tide of anger ripped through him, close to stealing the self-control he had managed to achieve in the navy. "Davie has to be disciplined. If you had your way, the lad would be coddled into believing the world is eager to please him when naught could be further from the truth. I would appreciate it if you would refrain from hurling damaging insults and false accusations, especially in front of him and undermining my authority. I will not have it."

"I do not coddle him!" She blinked several times as if she couldn't believe what he had just said. Her lips thinned and her skin flushed to a beautiful hue. "Nor do I . . . hurl . . . insults at you in front of him." Charlotte waved a hand in the air. "Why do you think I sought you out while Mildred is watching Davie?"

"I meant it as a warning. If you remember, I am quite aware of your antics when your temper gets the best of you." He grinned, hoping to lighten the tension between them, and linked his hands behind his back. "Charlotte, let us not quarrel. I am certain we both have the best intentions for Davie. You will see to his early education and safety, while I will ensure he has a father figure and appropriate discipline when I am around—at least until my brother is better."

"Where discipline is concerned, it is apparent you and I will not agree on the matter." She started walking again and looked ahead with a deep sigh. He hurried to catch up with her, wishing she would look at him again. "I doubt it will matter once we arrive in Cleaveland. You will go to your ship, and I will settle in and raise the children. You will not be around to quarrel with me on how to discipline Davie. If you recall, I am quite aware of your disappearing acts."

The truth of her words wounded him, but this time things were different. He had two children counting on him. "This is where you are quite wrong, Charlotte." He lowered his voice and deepened his tone to gain her attention. "Once we arrive in Cleaveland, I intend to be involved in the children's lives, and therefore, yours."

7

Charlotte strode away from Conrad, wondering what he meant by saying he intended to be involved in the children's lives as well as hers. The sea and Conrad's military career had always taken first place in his life, and she refused to believe he had changed so much those facts were no longer true. She would not be fooled by him again.

She searched for David and asked a few sailors if they had seen him. One of them finally told her he was on the level with the cannons. Charlotte rarely went to that part of the ship but took a lit lantern and followed the directions he had given her. David lay against the base of a cannon snoring with an empty flask of what she could only assume had been whiskey. He reeked of vomit and stale alcohol. She wrinkled her nose in disgust, thankful he wasn't awake to see her.

A memory of Emma wearing her white wedding gown and smiling up into David's face as they exchanged vows flashed across Charlotte's mind. Her sister's green eyes were filled with love and hope. The image came to a grinding halt as another followed with Emma lying on her bed, pale and weak after giving birth to Ashlynn. She had squeezed Charlotte's hand with what strength she had left. "Promise me . . . promise you will take care of them for me."

Closing her eyes on the painful sight of David, Charlotte allowed the memories to consume her. She would not forget her promise. Resolve filled her heart with renewed determination. Emma would not want her to leave David down here in such an awful condition. She walked closer and kicked his feet. He jumped and his eyes popped open in obvious confusion. A groan escaped his lips as he rubbed his face and blinked several times.

"Get up, David." Charlotte kicked the bottom of his heels again. "You have two children who need you. Now get up and be the man I know you can be."

"Leave me alone!" He rolled over and hid beneath his arms, hiding from the lantern light. "I need sleep."

"I am not going anywhere." Charlotte walked around him and bent to hold the light up at his face. He backed away until his head hit the base of the cannon and he could no longer escape her.

A sailor walked by and tipped his hat to her.

"Pardon me, sir." Charlotte motioned to the lad. "But would you bring a bucket of water?"

"Indeed." He gave her a brief nod and disappeared into the hallway.

Charlotte straightened and hung the lantern on a nearby wall peg and rubbed her hands together. Once she had David wide awake, she would have to convince Conrad to let him have a bath. He couldn't walk around the ship smelling like this. His uniform needed a good washing. It was one of the things she missed being on land—baths and clean clothing. Water needed to be reserved for drinking, but during the last rain, Conrad ordered his men to put out barrels to collect fresh rainwater. She hoped they had gathered enough.

She paced around the floor and studied the cannons. Most of the men had gone up to eat, while others took over topside duties. She walked up the aisle, glancing at each cannon on a wooden carriage platform. Conrad had said each side had fifteen eighteen-pound cannons and six twenty-four-pound cannons. A total of forty-two cannons. She paused to touch one of the cast-iron guns and wished the war would soon be over. A few months ago, she had prayed it would be over, just as she had prayed for God to spare her sister's life. Neither one of those prayers were answered. Her twin was gone and the war still raged on.

The sailor returned with a wooden bucket of water he carried by the attached rope and grinned at her as he walked down the aisle. "Here it is. What do you want me to do with it?"

"Pour it on his head . . . all of it." She pointed at David, unable to hide a mischievous smile.

"I was hoping you would say so." He lifted the bucket and dumped the water on David as she had requested. The lad stepped back out of reach as David sat up sputtering and yelling expletives Charlotte had never heard from him.

"Go!" Charlotte pointed in the opposite direction. "He will get mad at you but will do naught to me."

"I cannot leave you. He is drunk. What if he hurts you?" The lad asked, his eyes wide in concern.

"I will be fine," Charlotte said. "He is my brother-in-law and would never hurt me. Now go! I do not want anyone to see him like this."

"It may have already happened," he said.

"Argh! What is the meaning of this?" David demanded, leaping to his feet. He paused, squinted, and gazed at Charlotte. "Emma?" He stepped closer. "Is it really you? I must be dreaming."

Charlotte glanced over her shoulder to ensure the lad had left and then turned back to David. "No, it is me, Charlotte."

David blinked several times as if waiting to see if she would disappear. He shook his head and rubbed his temples as if trying to clear his mind. "Emma, I thought you were dead."

"I am not Emma. I am Charlotte." She stepped forward and evened her tone in an attempt to reason with him. "David, you need to snap out of it. I came to give you a miniature of Emma."

"Why? You are Emma." David swayed as he came toward her. "Come here. I have missed you."

"No, David. I am not Emma." Charlotte backed away, but he grabbed her and squeezed her in a tight hug. She tried to hold her breath to avoid the stench clinging to him, but her breath gave out. He leaned back and slipped both his hands around her cheeks as if he intended to kiss her. Panic shot through her stomach, and she fought the impulse to keep from kicking him since she didn't want to hurt him.

"Stop, David!" Conrad shouted as he ran toward them. "Let her go!"

Conrad pulled his brother from Charlotte, a sick feeling rushing to his throat. He resisted the urge to slam his fist in his face. Instead, he opened his hand and popped his brother on the side of his head. "What are you doing? You cannot attack Charlotte. I do not care how much she looks like Emma."

"I do not know what came over me." David rubbed his hand over his face, making his skin look red and raw. "Charlotte, please forgive me. I had too much to drink, and I mistook you for Emma, because I miss her so much."

"It is no excuse, and you know it," Conrad said, his obvious anger pulsing through the veins in his neck.

Eager to bring peace between the two brothers, Charlotte laid a hand on each man's arm and turned to David. "Of course, I forgive you. I have never been one to hold grudges, and I realize it was not your intention to behave as you did." She turned to Conrad, knowing her tone held a plea of cooperation. "Do not worry on my account. As Emma's identical twin, it was easy for David to mistake me for what his heart longs for—especially in the state he was in."

"And I had better not catch you in this condition again." Conrad turned to his brother and poked a finger in his chest. "Nor disrespecting Charlotte like that. Ever since we boarded this ship, you have been a drunk, ignoring your responsibilities and not carrying your weight around here. I tried to give you enough time to grieve, but now I realize I was too lenient with you. I cannot continue showing partiality between you and the other sailors. You have to be punished for neglecting your duties."

"Conrad, is that really necessary?" Charlotte asked, turning to face him and laying a hand on his chest. "Do you not think you are being a little hard on David? It is my fault. I should not have provoked him by having a bucket of water poured on his head while he was sleeping. Anyone would have been upset and disoriented afterward."

Mixed emotions rushed through Conrad as he looked down at her hand on his chest. He didn't want to push her away and hurt her feelings, but he could not concentrate with her so near, begging for mercy for his brother. Could she not see how hard it was for him to witness David's downward spiral? If he did not intervene now, things could get worse. He had to remain strong, even if Charlotte believed the worst of him.

"Yes, it is necessary. The rest of the crew will start resenting him if he continues getting away with what they cannot." He covered her hand with his and gripped her fingers tight. "Please understand, Charlotte. I have to do this for David. Trust me."

"Could he at least have a bath? He smells awful." She pulled her hand free of his and stepped back. "What kind of punishment are you going to give him? I do not want Davie to see anything and be upset."

Her words pierced him as he tilted his head and regarded her in disbelief. He blinked as he took a deep breath. "If you think I would do aught to hurt my nephew, then you do not know me at all. In fact, I doubt you ever did." His tone sounded harsh, but he didn't care. Conrad had grown weary trying to placate Charlotte and convince her that he was a fair and reasonable man. Let her assume what she pleased. "Charlotte, you may go, while I see to my brother. And yes, he may have a bath. I have no intention of making the rest of us on this ship suffer from his stench."

"Conrad is right, Charlotte," David said. "Go to my children, and I promise, I will do better from now on."

Charlotte backed away, leaned over to the adjacent cannon, and grabbed a flat, square object. Until now, Conrad had not noticed anything lying on the black iron gun. She walked toward David and held it out. "Very well, but before I go, I want to give you this."

David accepted the gift and stared down at it in silence. Tears filled his eyes.

"I am not much of an artist, but I tried to sketch a miniature of Emma you could always take with you wherever you go. That way if I am not around, you will not forget what she looks like." Charlotte clasped her hands together in front of her as she waited for David to respond. "Do you like it? I set it in a wooden frame so the edges would not wrinkle and fray."

"Indeed." David nodded. "I will always cherish it."

"Allow me to escort you to the stairs." Conrad stepped between them and gestured his hand ahead of them.

"No need." Charlotte glared at him, straightening her shoulders and stepping around him. "I can find my way," she snapped, lifting her chin and striding past him.

"Even so," Conrad rushed to catch her, "but I have one other matter we need to discuss." He caught her at the stairs and grabbed her elbow, forcing her to turn around. "I wish you had not given him the image of Emma."

"Why?" Confusion marred her smooth skin with a wrinkled expression between her eyebrows.

"It will only serve to remind him of what he has lost." Conrad lowered his voice. "Now he has had some time to grieve, he needs to let go of his pain so he can heal, not constantly remind himself of his memories and dwell on them. David must keep living. He did not die with her."

Charlotte paled as a stricken look crossed her face. Unshed tears filled her eyes. She blinked, staring up at him in silence. In a flash, she lifted her hand and swung her palm against his face. The slap echoed, ringing through his ears. His cheek stung worse than a bee and lingered long after she lowered her hand.

"I will always be thankful Emma had enough good sense to choose David and spared herself the heartache of loving you. I wish I could have had the same common sense to protect myself."

Over the next few days, Charlotte did her best to avoid Conrad. She had no idea what David's punishment consisted of and she chose not to ask. A few times, Conrad came to the cabin to pick up Davie, and they went for a walk around the ship. On one occasion, the lad returned with a new wooden soldier to add to his collection. He had been so excited and proud of what his Uncle Conrad had given him, Charlotte did her best to smile and share in his enjoyment.

Charlotte stood at the rail with Ashlynn, enjoying the morning sea. She glanced up at the white clouds hovering in the blue sky and wondered about heaven. What was it like for Emma? She looked down at her niece as she cooed and blinked, sucking on her fingers. Why would God allow this baby's mother to be taken from her if He was a loving and merciful God? It didn't make sense. Perhaps she didn't understand God's role in people's lives here on earth.

"I have not spotted a British ship in days," Dawson said to Vincent as he climbed down from the watchtower. "The Captain says the British blockade is hovering near the coast and by sailing around them further out to sea, we have a better chance of making it past New Jersey without being detected."

"Well, if there is one thing I know, the captain will get us safely through the blockade." Vincent lifted a cup of coffee to his mouth and sipped the steaming brew. He swallowed and chuckled, shaking his head. "We might find a bit of adventure since our captain is not afraid of taking risks. Think about it. The man has gotten us up the coast from the Carolinas with only one slight incident through an entire British blockade. The feat in itself is just short of a miracle."

"True." Dawson nodded as his hair flipped sideways in the breeze. "What about the traitor? Have they gotten any information out of him?"

"Naw." Vincent wiped his mouth after he took another sip. "But he took a good beating. I imagine he is wishing he had behaved."

Who had taken a beating? Why were they calling him a traitor?

Another young sailor greeted them and climbed up to take Dawson's post. For a moment, Charlotte envied his view from the sky. She cuddled Ashlynn close and strolled over to Vincent and Dawson. "Did I hear you say we are near New Jersey?" she asked.

"Indeed, we are." Vincent nodded, taking another sip of his black coffee. "I suspect we shall be heading inland toward Bridgeport in a few days. Then we could run into more Brits. They are doing their level best to keep Americans from going in or coming out. Do not worry. The captain knows what he is doing."

"Here comes the captain now," Dawson said. He pointed over Charlotte's shoulder. Out of curiosity, she glanced behind her to see Conrad striding toward them with a purposeful look on his face. His square jaw set at an angle and his dark eyebrows narrowed, creating a tiny dent between them. Something was on his mind, and it did not please him.

Charlotte had no desire to speak to him if she could avoid it. She turned back to Dawson and Vincent with an appreciative smile. "I am sure you have much to discuss with the captain, so Ashlynn and I will take a little stroll around the deck before I must return her to Mildred for another feeding."

She stepped away, hoping to escape before Conrad reached them. To her disappointment, Conrad's stern voice reached her ears.

"Charlotte!"

Pretending not to hear him, Charlotte hurried in the opposite direction. She couldn't risk going any faster with the baby in her arms. Ashlynn whined at the discomfort of being jostled in Charlotte's arms. Booted footsteps came closer, increasing in pace. Charlotte's heart skipped in panic. There was nowhere for her to escape him on this ship.

"Charlotte, I know you heard me." His tone deepened in frustration with a slight growl rumbling under his breath. "Now stop this instant. I have something to discuss with you."

"Well, I have naught to discuss with you," she flung the words over her shoulder. Determined to avoid him, she rushed toward the stairs leading below deck. Only a few more steps and she would make it. Charlotte had no idea what she had done to anger him, but she would rather not know, especially after their last heated discussion. What had he done to David? Surely, he would not have ordered his own brother to be whipped or beaten as he had the traitor in their midst? Fear pulsed through her as her breath hitched in her throat.

"Stop!" Conrad gripped her shoulder, his fingers curling into her flesh. "I have known you to be many things but never a coward. Why are you running from me?" He lowered his voice at her ear.

The sting to her pride twisted through her like a tree root with a blade. She paused and slowly turned to meet his determined gaze. "I have never lacked courage, especially when it comes to challenging you. I merely wished to avoid a quarrel, since all our discussions tend to end in one." Ashlynn began to cry. Charlotte moved the infant over her shoulder and rubbed her tiny back to comfort her. "What is so important you insist on making a scene in front of your sailors?"

"David."

"What did you do to him?" Charlotte held onto Ashlynn with one hand and gripped Conrad's shirt in the other. Tears sprang to her eyes. "Did you have him beaten?"

"I did no such thing!" He shoved her hand away, while his questioning eyes swept over her in disgust. "The only man who has taken a beating on this ship is a traitor we have contained in the hold. I wanted to ask you not to give David any more keepsakes to remember his wife by. The miniature drawing you gave him of Emma is consuming him. I cannot get him to do anything. All he wants to do is sit and stare at it—and remember."

"Is it so bad for him to remember her?" Charlotte's voice rose. Anger and confusion poured through her tone. How could he deny David such a small comfort?

"Only when it keeps him from living." Conrad rubbed the back of his neck as he looked down at the wooden deck and took a deep breath. "Charlotte, I am so sorry your sister is gone, but my brother is still alive, and he needs to keep living."

8

Conrad gripped the wheel on the quarterdeck with Higgins standing next to him. They had sailed as far north as they could and had to turn inland to Bridgeport. What they hadn't planned was to arrive in the midst of battling ships. The night sky lit with orange fire as the American and British frigates fired upon each other and floating smoke drifted around them, hovering over the surface of the water.

"Since they are locked into battle and have to be side by side to shoot at each other, we could try to sail around them," Higgins said, propping his elbow over an arm and rubbing his chin in thought. "They would be too engaged to attack us."

"Possibly," Conrad nodded, tilting his head as another thought struck him. "Or we could risk being fired upon from the other side as we go by. They have cannons set up on both sides of the ship."

"We could cut out all the lights as we did once before," Higgins said.

"Those two ships are blowing each other up and one of them are our American guys." Conrad pointed in front of them. "I do not want to risk running over any swimming survivors. My other concern is other ships could be on the way to help, since the battle is viewable from the shore. In fact, I had hoped to send a rowboat ahead so those onshore would know to expect us and not confuse us with the enemy."

"Captain!" Dawson called from the watchtower. "A British frigate is heading toward us from the north."

Conrad whirled to scan the dark sea. Faint lights shone in the distance, but he could not tell how far away they were in the fog or how fast they approached. He watched for a moment and determined she sailed at full speed as the lights drew brighter and clearer. Either she intended to help the British frigate already engaged in battle or she had spotted the *Victorious* and intended to attack.

"I think it might be a little too late to cut out the lights," Conrad said. "Higgins, give the order to man the guns, rouse the sailors to take their stations, and tell my brother, David, to join Charlotte and the children. They would be in no better care than with their own father." An image of his brother in a drunken state came to mind. What if he had managed to sneak a bottle? What good would he be then? "Uh, Higgins, allow me to be honest, but discreet. If you notice my brother has been in his cups again, do not give him charge of the women and children. Have a man sober him up and give the duty to someone else more trustworthy."

"Yes, sir!" Higgins saluted him before taking off to the main deck to bellow out the orders to the rest of the crew.

More gunfire boomed. The cannonballs missed their mark and dropped in the water but shook the entire ship as the swells grew and tossed them about. Even though he had hoped to avoid battle, if they had to face it, he preferred it to be now at the end of their journey. Since they were near the Bridgeport shore, they had a better chance of being saved if the *Victorious* suffered damage and sank.

The crew snapped into action following his orders. The sky lit with an orange glow as the other two ships continued to battle. Conrad ordered the *Victorious* to sail wide around the battling ships. He lifted the spyglass to his eye and scanned the distance ahead of them. Lanterns and torches lined the shore where people watched the battle, ready and prepared to defend their domain. Somehow, he had to make sure his ship wasn't mistaken for the British, while out-maneuvering the British.

"Hoist the American flag!" Conrad called to his crew, determined not to be misidentified. If they go down, it shall be as Americans.

Waves splashed over the deck as another cannonball landed nearby. Were they aiming for the *Victorious* or was it an unfortunate coincidence? As they grew closer to shore, the ship became a target, and everyone on board was in greater danger. The sound of cannon fire grew louder.

Higgins returned to the quarterdeck and clasped his hands behind his back. "The gunners are ready and prepared to fire upon your command, sir. The masts are set at full sail and we have increased in speed, but the one chasing us seems to be catching us."

"Indeed." Conrad lowered his spyglass and met his first mate's gaze. "What about David and the children?"

"I ordered Vincent to find him, while I saw to the gunners. He will stay with them himself, if David is drunk."

Conrad nodded, knowing he would have to accept Higgins's word on the matter. At the moment, he had a British fleet to face if he intended to make it to shore. "Have one of the sailors cut the rowboats loose. I want them ready in the event we need them. We are going in and there will be no turning back. We cannot hover out here in the sea waiting for the British to disappear. Our supplies are running low and soon we will be out of food. The time to act is now."

Another ball shot through the mainmast sail and landed on the other side of the ship and into the water. The force splintered the wood from the mainmast and flew against a lantern that caught fire. The fire spread to the torn canvas hanging down and spread through the rest of the material like a torched bale of hay. A large piece ripped away and fell on a sailor. He screamed as another man ran to his aid. A second piece of burning canvas fell and caught the rope around a barrel on fire.

Conrad shouted orders to regain control over the loud chaos. Several soldiers formed a line passing down a bucket of water to put out the fire. By the time they managed to contain the fire, the British ship from the north had caught them as the *Victorious* pulled level with one of the other battling ships. With allies on one side, Conrad ordered his first line of cannons to open fire on the other side where the British approached. The entire ship lurched with each boom.

At the same time, the enemy ship fired and an explosion hit the main deck. Shattered wood splintered and flew in every direction. Men shouted, some from pain and others from shocked fear. A wave whipped over the side and splashed onto the main deck, washing a sailor overboard.

"Fire the cannons again!" Conrad yelled. Anger gripped him as determination spiked through Conrad. This wasn't how he intended to arrive in Bridgeport. He would save the souls on his ship, if he had to blow the enemy to pieces before they had time to launch a full attack.

After being tossed about the cabin, Charlotte and Mildred began to fear for their lives in spite of David's constant reassurances. It had been a while since Vincent had checked on them and they were left to wonder about the terrifying noises above them. When an inch of water seeped into their cabin, his words faded to an awkward silence.

"I do not wish to alarm you, but it appears as if we have been hit," David said, looking down at the floor as the water crept across the cabin. "I believe we shall go up on deck and see what damage has been done and determine what we shall do. If we are sinking, I would rather try a rowboat or swim for it and not wait down here for the worst to happen."

"I agree," Charlotte nodded, picking up Ashlynn from her wooden bassinet.

"Indeed." Mildred stood and grabbed Davie's hand. "If the ship is taking on water, I do not wish to be caught below deck."

"Can you swim, Mildred?" Charlotte asked as David took his son from Mildred and swept the lad onto his hip.

"No, I never had the opportunity." She shook her head as her eyes widened with fright and her skin paled. She gripped David's shirt sleeve in her fist. "Please, are we truly sinking?"

"I do not know. I will be able to better judge our situation once we are above deck." David pulled away from her and rushed up the dark narrow stairs. "Come on. Hurry!"

Charlotte covered Ashlynn's head with her blanket and set the baby on her left shoulder, cradling the back of her head for protection. Ashlynn kicked and screamed in protest, but Charlotte held her close, determined to keep her safe.

As they emerged, the sound of gunfire exploded from every direction, almost hurting her ears. The smell of gunpowder and burning smoke layered the air with the stench of rotting fish.

"Be careful!" David warned, pushing out his free hand to keep them from falling through a gaping hole in the main deck, exposing the gunners below. Blood soaked the deck in various puddles. Charlotte clutched the collar at her neck as her mind flew to Conrad. Was he hurt? Her heart pounded as loud as the cannon blasts around them.

"Daddy, will they shoot us, too?" Davie asked, clinging to his father with a mixture of awe and fear on his face. David bent to speak into Davie's ear, but Charlotte couldn't hear what he said. It must have satisfied her nephew since he nodded and rested his head on David's shoulder.

The American ship beside them took another hit. Three men screamed in agony and were blown into the water. A severed leg flew in the opposite direction from its body. Tears sprang to Charlotte's eyes. She touched her throat as her breath hitched in a moment of panic. It would only take one cannonball and they could all be gone in an instant. The realization clawed at her conscience, seizing her mind, and stealing her ability to concentrate.

"Lord, please save us from this madness," Charlotte whispered. It was the first heartfelt prayer she had uttered since Emma's death. Her other prayers were mumbled out of a sense of obligation fused with a mixture of anger and confusion. This time she feared for her and the children's lives. Only the Lord could help her now.

"David!" Conrad called from the other side of the main deck. He and a sailor were tugging on the rope around a small rowboat. He waved them over. "Bring the women and children."

David guided them over debris, around the large hole, and through sailors rushing by to follow orders. The men fought hard to keep them afloat, helping the wounded, and firing back. Her gaze slid over to Conrad as he pulled a rope from its knot and slung it to the side. He had pulled off his jacket uniform, rolled up his sleeves to his elbows, and worked beside his men. While soot and dirt covered his white shirt and pants, relief filled her at seeing his strong arms and his blooming health. "Thank You, Lord, for keeping him safe." The whispered words were out of her mouth before she realized she had thought them.

"Help us turn this boat over," Conrad said to David, pointing at the rowboat they had just freed from the ropes.

David set his son on his feet, and Mildred grabbed the lad's shoulder. She pulled him to stand in front of her safely out of the way.

"You are going to take the women and children to shore. We are close enough and you can make it," Conrad said, bending to lift one side of the rowboat. All three men grunted and flipped the wooden rowboat right side up. David turned and lifted his son inside on the bench then held a helping hand out to Mildred.

Conrad reached for Charlotte, but another blast hit them and she stumbled into his arms, still cradling the baby. Charlotte's left palm rested against his chest where his heart beat fast and furious.

"I am so glad you are all right." She breathed heavily from fear and anxiety.

"Be careful, Charlotte," Conrad lifted a brown eyebrow. "I might get the impression you actually care for me." A mischievous grin tipped his mouth.

"I do care." She blinked up at him searching for a sign in his expression to give away his thoughts. His unshaven jaw showed faint lines more prominent under his eyes. The way he kept staring at her, as if committing her image to memory, increased her concerns. Conrad carried a heavy burden for the lives of his men. "Though you make me want to box your ears at times, I have never wished you any harm." A moment of fear pierced her heart at the thought of anything happening to him through this battle.

Conrad gazed into her eyes as fire raged and cannons boomed around them. He took a deep breath and touched her arm as heat radiated through his skin. "Stay safe."

"Are you not coming with us?" she asked, disliking the panic threatening to rise within her. Somehow being in his presence made her feel safer. She trusted David but not as much as Conrad. He possessed an air of authority and mature judgment she had recently come to depend on. How could they leave without him? He was part of the family. Yet, she understood his responsibility to the men on this ship.

"No, I cannot leave my ship or the souls upon it who are in my care. As captain, I will adhere to my duty and be the last man to leave my ship." He took the baby from her and gestured for Charlotte to climb into the rowboat. "Now off with you before we are hit again. You must think of the children."

"Of course." Charlotte settled inside the boat and sat on the bench across from David and Davie. Conrad leaned down and gently placed Ashlynn in her arms. Charlotte admired his self-discipline and integrity, as she wondered why she had not seen this side of him before.

Conrad motioned for two other soldiers to join them and handed the paddles to them. "Swing wide and try to stay out of firing range."

"Yes, sir," a sailor answered, giving Conrad a salute.

He motioned for the sailors standing by to lower the ropes. His gaze met Charlotte's one more time. Something flickered in his hazel eyes, and warmth pooled in her stomach like swallowing warm tea. He leaned forward, maintaining her gaze as his men lowered the rowboat over the side.

Ashlynn squirmed in Charlotte's arms and screamed as the sailors rowed them away from the *Victorious.* With a heavy heart, she glanced over her shoulder, keeping Conrad in her sight where he stood at the rail watching them. Another cannon hit the ship, rocking them sideways and igniting small waves in every direction. Conrad gripped the rail until the shaking subsided and turned to bellow orders to his men.

Tears streamed down Charlotte's cheeks as fear clawed around her heart. She looked toward land where a row of fiery torches lined the shore. She wished they were closer. "Please, Lord, keep him safe." She whispered the prayer as she kissed the top of the baby's head.

"Do not worry. We can make it," David said. "Conrad is smart and strong. He will survive this battle. He has been through worse."

"What if he is captured by the enemy?" she asked, blinking back tears as she looked away. A hot tear dripped and slid down her cheek. Mildred slipped an arm around her shoulders but remained silent.

"He is a man and not as invincible as we all seem to think," Charlotte said, wiping her face. "Perhaps it is what made him so against a marriage commitment."

"Nonsense." David slapped his thigh. "Conrad has never been against it; he is merely committed to his career and the adventure he is able to seek out of life. Unlike me, he has never been a family man."

"Uncle Conrad is part of our family," Davie said.

"Yes, it is true." David swept his son on his knee. "But I was talking about a wife and children of his own."

"He does not need children when he has Ashlynn and me," Davie said. "He can play with us."

"Charlotte, forgive me, but are you and my brother forming another attachment?" David asked. "Watching the two of you a moment ago brought back memories of when you both courted at the same time as Emma and I. If so, I hope you remember what happened last time. Conrad will never settle down. I do not wish to see you hurt."

Glad the darkness hid her expression, Charlotte cleared her throat. "I assure you, I do not need reminding. Conrad was my sister's brother-in-law and remains the children's uncle. He is part of the family, and I care for him as a member of our family. I have known him these past six years, and I know he could never give up his love for the sea." Her voice lowered with sorrow, but she couldn't hide it. "Believe me, I realize marriage to Conrad would be like his own personal prison, something worse than being landlocked as he calls it. I have heard him say it often enough, I could never forget it."

No one spoke for a time as the cannons boomed in the distance and the darkness lit up in flames with a British frigate burning. The sound of the paddles pulling through the water helped Charlotte relax and made her think of home when she would go fishing with her brothers. As they drifted closer to shore, the roar of the waves grew louder and the murmuring voices from people standing on shore became audible.

"I cannot swim and the waves scare me," Mildred said, anxiety clear in her tone.

"I will take care of you, miss," one of the sailors offered. "If you will trust me."

"It appears I must," she said.

"Charlotte, will you be all right with Ashlynn?" David asked. "I could have one of the other sailors assist Davie and I could take her."

"No, I shall be fine." Charlotte cuddled Ashlynn to her chest, thankful the child had finally settled down and stopped crying. "I would not be parted from her for the world. Besides, you know my brothers taught Emma and I to swim before we were even ten. I grew up playing in the waves when I could get away from household chores."

The boat lifted with a rising swell. Charlotte held onto Ashlynn with one hand and gripped the edge of the bench with the other, waiting for the wave to break over them. Instead, it carried them closer to shore and finally broke beyond them. Charlotte braced herself, expecting the next wave to crash into them. She wasn't disappointed. A moment later, water poured into the boat, smacking against the side of her head and body. It startled the baby and she began to cry. Davie yelled in fright as he clung to his father.

"Who is out there? Identify yourselves!" a man's voice called.

A yellow-orange light glowed nearby, but it was hard to answer as another wave crashed over them. The men set the paddles on the floor of the boat. "I think we can touch bottom here," one of them said. "It might be best if we try to guide the boat to shore on foot."

"Good idea," the other one answered.

"Daddy, the water is burning my eyes," Davie said, rubbing his knuckles over his eyes and taking deep breaths.

"Hold on! Here comes another one," David warned, grabbing Davie close to him.

This time a five-foot wave slammed over them. Charlotte gasped for air as the drenching water rolled over her and clung to her hair and clothes. She had leaned over Ashlynn and tried to shield her as best as she could, but the child gave a wrenching scream. Mildred shrieked in surprise.

"There are women and children out there!" a man shouted from the shore.

Wave after wave hit them, but Charlotte kept a protective grip on Ashlynn. Each time Charlotte held her breath, waiting for the baby to sputter and cry so she would know the child was all right. To her relief, extra hands joined them around the boat and they were hauled to shore and surrounded by torchlight, lanterns, and unfamiliar voices. Even the gritty sand did not bother her, since she was so thankful to make it to shore.

"Welcome to Bridgeport." A tall man in a dark blue uniform came toward them and cocked a pistol. "Now the battle in our harbor is over, we need you to identify yourselves. Which ship did you come from?"

9

Thankful that Charlotte and the children were no longer in danger on the ship, Conrad reorganized the uninjured men on the main deck and ordered the gunners below to fire and reload. The frigate from the north ceased pursuing them and concentrated on their engulfing flames. Waiting for the onslaught of return fire, Conrad turned in a slow circle, feeling dizzy and sick to his stomach. At the moment, he couldn't tell if the *Victorious* would ever set sail again.

Vincent came toward him. His brown hair hung loose around his shoulders, and his soot-stained uniform was ripped and burned from putting out the fire in the sails. In spite of his obvious fatigue, he walked with assurance and strength. "Vincent, find Dr. Garrett and tell him I would like a report of all injuries and all deaths," Conrad ordered.

"I cannot, sir." Vincent shook his dark head, pain etched in his eyes. "He was killed in one of the blasts."

"Then you must check on everyone below and bring me a status report," Conrad said, knowing that the number of lives to be saved would now be less since they had no physician. "I need to know the number of dead, severely wounded, and those able to help us fight off further attacks and make it to shore."

"Yes, sir." Vincent saluted, turned on his heel, and strode away to do as he was told.

Higgins approached from the opposite direction, a grim expression on his weary face. "The ship is in a sorry state. We are lucky to be this close to shore, otherwise I doubt we would make it another night. She's taking on water in the hold, but it looks like we shall be able to seal it closed within the hour. We will have to drift to shore. Most of the sails are gone. I do not know the exact count at this time, but judging by the looks of it, we have lost half our crew."

"May God have mercy on their souls." Conrad shook his head and closed his eyes as he rubbed the growing whiskers on his chin. "To make matters worse, we are now without a physician. We will have to help each other and do as best as we can."

"By the way, two of our cannons were destroyed," Higgins said. "One was a twenty-four pounder and the other an eighteen-pounder. The gunners who manned them are gone as well."

"I wish there was some way we could have prevented all this." Regret weighed heavily on Conrad's heart, but he had no time to dwell on things that could not be undone. He sighed deeply. "Dump what is left of the inoperable machinery. No need in trying to force this broken ship to carry more weight than she can tow right now." Conrad scratched his temple, deep in thought. If they could time their descent at the same time as the flowing tide coming onshore, perhaps he could manage to steer them toward the docks, or at least closer than they were at the moment. "Higgins, do you happen to know if we can still steer the ship?"

"Yes, sir, the steering mechanisms seem to be intact," Higgins said, wiping a drop of sweat from his forehead. "During my inspection of the ship, the rudder appeared to be fine."

"Very good, I shall be on the quarterdeck." Relief flowed through Conrad as he digested this one piece of good news and started walking there. "And be sure to send Dawson to me." Conrad paused, glancing over his shoulder at Higgins. "Dawson is all right, is he not?"

"Indeed, he is." Higgins nodded with a broad grin. "The lad climbed down from the watchtower as soon as we were fired upon. I gave the order myself."

"Excellent. And it is why you are the best first mate I have ever had." Conrad linked his hands behind his back and walked on. "I am glad the lad's life was spared. Indeed, I wish we had been able to spare more."

Over the next hour, Conrad put Dawson in charge of feeding the wounded after their injuries were bound and dressed. The British frigate finally sank, while the other British ship limped away with severe damage. Relieved there would be no more attacks, Conrad concentrated on saving his ship and caring for the wounded.

The other American ship looked to be suffering as much as the *Victorious*. A few of their sailors were climbing into small rowboats. One side of the frigate appeared to be leaning into the water more than the other. Conrad wondered if he should offer them some assistance, since it was now apparent that the *Victorious* would remain afloat.

Conrad left the wheel and leaned over the rail. "Higgins, have the American flag hoisted as high as possible, so no one at Bridgeport can mistake our identity."

"Yes, sir." Higgins turned to a young sailor and gave the order.

Conrad returned to the wheel and steered them closer to the sinking ship as they drifted toward shore. Once they were close enough, Conrad stepped down to the remaining part of the main deck and leaned over the side. "Hello! I am Captain Conrad Deaton of the *Victorious* with the American Navy. May we be of assistance in bringing some of your survivors to shore?"

"I am Lieutenant Forbes of the *Guardian* from the American Navy," said a man in a battered uniform. "Our captain was hit and is unconscious. I have assumed command. We need to get him to a physician as soon as possible."

"Of course." Conrad motioned to Higgins. "Drop temporary anchor and prepare to set up a boarding plank. We will accept as many as possible. I doubt their ship will stay afloat much longer."

Higgins turned and carried out Conrad's orders. They ended up accepting twenty-two new souls aboard, including Lieutenant Forbes and their unconscious captain. Having the extra hands aboard made makeshift repairs and sailing much easier to replace the manpower they had lost during battle. An hour later, the ship made it to the wooden dock where an army of American soldiers waited to greet them. Lit torches and scattered bonfires guided them safely.

Vincent and Dawson threw the ropes on the dock and a couple of them caught them and wrapped the ropes around the posts, securing it into tight knots. Higgins ordered the anchor to be dropped. Four men wearing decorated uniforms approached the ship and saluted Conrad.

"Please identify yourselves."

To Charlotte's relief, David spoke up and explained who they were and why women and children accompanied them. With her clothes soaking wet, gooseflesh popped up on her skin and seemed to multiply each time the breeze blew. Ashlynn continued to scream in her ear. If the child was as uncomfortable as she, Charlotte couldn't blame her.

"I am Colonel Vernon," said the tall man who had aimed the rifle at them when they first arrived. "We have evacuated most of the homes around here and prepared Bridgeport for a possible attack. We saw the English ships arrive earlier and have been watching the battles. Therefore, I can offer yourself and the other men dry clothing, but I am afraid I have no dry clothes appropriate for the women or children. I am sure one of our men will know someone in town who could spare a couple of dry gowns, and hopefully some children's clothing."

"I think she may be hungry." Mildred held out her hands for Ashlynn. Knowing she was right, Charlotte gave her the baby and tugged on her long hair, wringing the water out. "Sir, is there a private chamber where we could dry our clothes by the fire, and I could feed the baby?" Mildred asked.

"Indeed, I will have one of my men prepare a chamber for you." He motioned to a soldier who strode over. "Go ahead to the Windshore House and prepare a chamber for the women and one for the men. Build a fire and order a bath for both rooms."

"Yes, sir," he said, saluting Colonel Vernon.

"Do any of you require a doctor?" The colonel asked, looking around at each of them and meeting their gazes.

"No, thank you," David said, shaking his head. "With the exception of our disheveled appearance, we are all in perfect health, and I pray we remain that way."

"What happened with the battle between the ships? Do you know the outcome? Have any survivors made it ashore?" Charlotte asked as images of Conrad and his sailors came to mind, and her heart ached with worry.

"I have stationed my troops throughout the shore along the bay, so we will be sure to help any survivors." He lifted a finger as he led them to a building. "But to answer your question, based on what I could see from my spyglass, one of the British frigates caught fire and sank. It looked like the other one sailed away. The two remaining ships are American, so we have men we need to save."

"My brother is Captain Conrad Deaton of the *Victorious.* Would you let us know if he makes it ashore?" David asked. "We are most anxious to know his condition."

"Uncle Conrad is coming?" Davie asked, lifting his wet head off David's shoulder. "He has to. He promised."

"I am sure he will," David said. "Right now we have to give you a bath and get you dressed in some warm clothes."

"Aunt Charlotte, I do not wanna bath!" Davie whined, turning to look at her.

"She will not be giving you a bath. I will," David said. "Aunt Charlotte and Miss Mildred will be tending to their own needs tonight, and I am quite certain their hands will be full dealing with your baby sister."

"I am hungry!" Davie rubbed his belly.

Colonel Vernon laughed. "Now this is what I like, a good lad with a hearty appetite. As soon as you have had your baths and are ready, I will have our cook provide a hearty meal."

"Sir, we are so thankful for your kind hospitality," Charlotte said, wrapping her wet shawl around her shoulders and feeling no better. She would welcome a warm fire. The summer nights were cooler here than she was used to at home. It made her fear how difficult the winter months would be this far north. She would have to inquire about a warmer wardrobe for herself and the children in the coming months.

They arrived in front of what appeared to be a three-story brick home. Colonel Vernon lifted his lantern as he turned the knob and pushed the front door open. He swung it wide and held it with his booted foot as he waved them inside. "Come in.

This is Windshore House where I have established my quarters and where you shall be staying the night as our guests. Do not fret about the sailors from the other vessels. We shall find room for them in the barracks, and our infirmary will assist as many of the wounded survivors as we can."

"We are much obliged, Colonel," David said with a nod. "I hope you will not lose sleep over having us here. My daughter is still young and often cries during the night. We hired Miss Mildred to nurse her after my wife's demise. She still takes nightly feedings."

"I am sorry for your loss." Colonel Vernon glanced at Charlotte. "I confess, I had assumed you were the children's mother."

"My twin sister was," Charlotte said, unable to hide the sadness in her voice at the reminder. Would the pain never go away? "David and his brother are being transferred to the Great Lakes, and I promised my sister I would be available to my niece and nephew."

"I see." Colonel Vernon's gaze slid over to David. "Perhaps at a later time, we can discuss the arrangements. I should like to help if I can."

"Colonel," a soldier descended the stairs. "The chambers are waiting and the lady's bath is ready."

The front door swung open and another soldier came in out of breath. He wiped a lock of brown hair off his forehead as he took another breath and saluted the colonel. "Sir, the *Victorious* has arrived at the docks. They have many wounded, and the ship is in a sorry state. The other American vessel sank and the captain of the *Victorious* brought their survivors aboard." He rubbed his chin. "I am told they lost their physician. The captain is asking if we have a doctor we can spare."

"See, I told you, Charlotte," David grinned. "My brother not only made it, but he saved others in the process."

"Sounds like a man I am most eager to meet," Colonel Vernon said.

"Our prayers have been answered," Charlotte clutched her stomach in relief, her heart already feeling lighter.

Conrad tried to ignore the exhaustion pressing against him as his sailors called to him for guidance, help with their pain, and confirmation they would live. He lacked the ability to assess their wounds, to determine which ones were mortal and which ones were not. Still, he did his best to offer encouragement to anyone he had the opportunity to speak to and prayed he did not offer them false hope. When he brought the traitor up from the hold, the lad had suffered a head injury and didn't survive. Conrad ordered his body to be disposed of with the rest of the crew who didn't survive.

He refused to leave the ship until the last man had been carried away. He ordered Vincent and Dawson to load the trunks belonging to David, Charlotte, Mildred, and the children, including his own. The first thing he wanted was a hot bath and then a warm meal.

"Higgins, the *Victorious* and her crew are yours to command." Conrad followed Higgins over the wooden plank to the dock. "What is left of her at any rate."

"She will be patched up soon and back out at sea. There is still some sailing life left in her." Higgins turned and held out his hand with a wide grin. "It has been a pleasure sailing under your command, Captain."

"Indeed." Conrad gripped his hand in a tight shake and let go. They turned and walked toward the row of buildings where the others headed. "I have no idea what the Great Lakes will be like, but I am curious and look forward to the adventure."

The sound of waves rolling to shore and lapping against the dock poles greeted them with a quiet breeze as he walked across the wooden boards. He stepped down into the sinking sand, his boots crunching against broken shells. They made their way by lantern light between two sand dunes topped with patches of grass. Conrad couldn't help wondering if there would be waves and sand like this on the Great Lakes. While his sailors were sent to the barracks nearby, Conrad and Higgins were led to the Windshore House.

Dim light greeted them, from the bronze chandelier hanging in the foyer behind the young soldier who answered the door. "State your names, please," he said.

"I am Captain Conrad Deaton," Conrad pointed his thumb to his chest.

"And I am Lieutenant Stanley Higgins."

The soldier stepped back and opened the door wider, motioning them inside. A wooden coat rack stood in the left corner and a portrait of an elderly gentleman hung on the wall. "Colonel Vernon is waiting for you in the parlor to the right." A wide archway revealed another room with blue interior walls.

Conrad walked across the foyer and into the parlor. A dark fireplace was on the other side of the room with a white mantle. Sitting in a chair with carved wooden armrests was a middle-aged man wearing a dark blue uniform with shiny gold buttons. He looked up from his book and grinned.

"You must be Captain Deaton," the man said and then glanced over at Higgins. "And you are?"

"Lieutenant Higgins." He saluted him, as his gaze slid to the colonel's stripes on his uniform.

"None of that." The colonel waved his hand and motioned for them to sit down. "You have both been through a lot tonight. You have watched your comrades die, others tortured with injuries, and now I cannot even offer you a bath. The two we have are already taken by the ladies and your brother." He pointed at Conrad before gesturing to a chair. "Please, sit down."

"We are dirty and will ruin your furniture," Conrad said, looking around the room. He held out his hands and frowned at the dark soot all over them. "May we have a wash basin?"

"Of course, but sit down in comfort and do not worry about your current condition. We have much to discuss. Your brother has told me of your transfer to the Great Lakes and how you are to captain a ship for the war there. By the way, I am Colonel Vernon." While he talked, Conrad exchanged a glance with Higgins and shrugged. He walked over to a chair by the window and sat. Higgins took his cue, looked around, and settled on a chair by the wall under a portrait. "Do you have the orders you received?"

"I do," Conrad nodded. "Among the personal belongings in the trunks we brought here."

"May I see them?" Colonel Vernon asked, raising an eyebrow.

"Why?" Conrad was perplexed as to why the man would want to see his orders. Did the colonel suspect him of lying about his travel arrangements? What possible motive would he have to leave the domain of the great sea and his own ship, if not to take orders from his commanding officers to go out to the middle of nowhere?

"I should like to help you, but to do so, I need to see your orders for myself and verify their accuracy. You are of the navy. I am of the army. My connections in your world are somewhat limited, but I hope we will be able to benefit each other." He closed his book and set it on the small table beside him. "After all, we fight for the same country."

"Indeed, we do." Conrad nodded, hoping the skepticism flowing through his mind did not show in his expression.

Colonel Vernon had already helped them, by hosting them for the night. "Let us speak in plain truths. How can I help you?"

"Ah, but first let me tell you what I can do for you." He held up a finger as he leaned forward and set his elbows on his knees, linking his fingers. "I will provide a sturdy military wagon for you, complete with two horses and a gun each for you and your brother, David."

"In exchange for?" Conrad tilted his head and watched the colonel closely.

"In exchange for a weekly letter regarding my son's whereabouts, his condition, and activities." He paused and sighed deeply, rubbing his mustache. "I dislike admitting it, but I was hard on Avery when he was a lad, and it seems he cannot forgive me. When he decided to enlist, I am certain he chose the navy just to spite me. He will not return or acknowledge my letters, but he does write his mother at times. His letters are too cheerful and content to be the truth. It is my belief he chooses to spare her worry and to keep her from informing me about the life he has chosen to keep from me."

Conrad thought about David and Davie. He considered the idea of what it would be like if he had a disagreement with his own son. In no way would he want to be shut out regardless of his mistakes as a parent. Yet, he could not agree to violate the privacy or confidence of a man he had yet to meet.

"Colonel, I cannot agree to write you a weekly letter. Things may get hectic as they often do during war. However, I will agree to write when I can."

"It is reasonable," he agreed.

"I do not know your son and therefore do not know intimate details of his life. Even if I am introduced to him and we become good friends, I will not betray his trust. If I become aware of which ship he is sailing, the name of his commanding officer, his position, rank, and health, I will forward the information to you. It is no more than what would be on his roster. As much as I would value the offer of your military wagon, these are my terms as a gentleman and as a naval officer. Will it suffice?"

"I suppose it will have to." The colonel sat back and crossed his booted foot over his knee, keeping a level gaze on Conrad. "I admire your honor and integrity. Few men possess such characteristics these days."

"In my opinion, a man who lacks integrity has a grave fault, and it will quickly bring his downfall," Conrad said.

10

For two weeks, they traveled through woods, crossed streams, and in the last few days, began climbing mountains. As the wagon rocked and rolled over uneven ground, Charlotte found herself feeling grateful Colonel Vernon had provided a sturdy wagon. For once, she agreed with Conrad, sailing the seas was much better than this grueling travel over land. In spite of the sticky July heat, the annoying insects, and wild creatures, Charlotte would not give Conrad the satisfaction of admitting it.

They sat around the fire after an evening meal of beans and a bowl of blueberries they had picked earlier in the day. Mildred had taken Ashlynn to the wagon to nurse her. Conrad slapped his neck at a fly buzzing around him. His mouth twisted in disgust. "I wish I had never left the sea. These Great Lakes had better be as broad and vast as I have heard."

"And what shall you do if they are not?" David asked, gazing at the miniature Charlotte had given him of his wife. He squinted in the dim firelight and leaned closer toward it.

"I shall put in a request for another transfer," Conrad said. "Even if I have to give up command of a ship."

"I doubt it," Charlotte scoffed, not caring how unladylike she sounded. Out here in the middle of nowhere seemed ridiculous to worry about certain rules of society.

"What do you mean, Charlotte?" Conrad turned a sharp eye toward her, his tone deepening in obvious displeasure.

"You like ordering people around too much to give up the good fortune of such authority," Charlotte snapped, thinking back to how his attitude and behavior had grown worse the further they traveled away from the sea. He had gotten angry over Ashlynn's crying during the night, hurt Davie's feelings by refusing to carve another soldier toy, and harassed his brother for still grieving over his wife. As for Charlotte, she could do nothing to please him. He complained about her coffee, for encouraging his brother to remember her sister, claimed she coddled Davie too much, and criticized her for bringing all the trunks she had packed.

"In your case, it is necessary. Your judgments of late have not been as prudent as I would have liked for the person dedicated to raising my niece and nephew." With a twisted grin, Conrad leaned forward and settled his elbows on his knees, meeting her gaze over the dancing flames between them. "You must face it, Charlotte. You need me."

"What I need is to be free of you," she said, leaning over to pick up a few sticks and tossing them into the fire. "As soon as we arrive in Cleaveland, I shall be relieved to know you will be leaving for your ship, and I shall be mistress of the entire house."

"Can I go on the ship with you?" Davie asked, patting Conrad's arm to gain his attention.

"Maybe some other time." Conrad ruffled the top of his head, making his brown hair stand up in every direction.

"Conrad, you are much too arrogant for your own good," David said, rubbing a hand over his stubbled chin as though he was in great distress. "I have always told you so."

"I have to be." Conrad rubbed his hands together and stared into the fire. "Someone has to take care of you, do they not? When you decide to fall apart, who will be around to make decisions and ensure your children are well cared for, if I am not? I do not have the same luxury as you."

"That is uncalled for," Charlotte said. "You know he is still grieving over his wife. It has only been a couple of months. Some people grieve for years over loved ones they have lost. You have only had to be the responsible one for a short time. While he settled down with a loving wife, had two beautiful children, and provided well for them these past five years, you were the one doing as you pleased. You docked at one harbor town after another, enjoyed the taverns, and left broken hearts everywhere you went. You have no right to criticize your brother for being a decent family man with such a big heart to love deeply in spite of the pain it has caused him."

"If you had your way, he would never forget your precious sister," Conrad said, his voice rising in anger. "The two of you would be so deeply mired in a state of your own make-believe world enshrined in Emma. You both must face the reality she is gone and will not be coming back."

An awkward silence followed. Conrad squeezed his eyes shut and dropped his head back on his shoulders as if realizing the mistake of his words. He clenched his fists. "Charlotte, I am sorry. I did not mean for it to sound the way it did."

Charlotte's face grew hot. She repeated the words he had said in her mind, trying to make sure she had not misunderstood him before reacting. A tiny ball of fury began to burn in her chest, and as each second passed, it grew larger, scorching every coherent thought into irrational pieces.

"Emma was precious to those of us who loved her and still love her. My twin's memory will always be precious." Charlotte gulped, taking a deep breath. "And you are right about one thing, as long as we live, neither of us want to ever forget her and no lecture from you or any passage of time will ever change it." Charlotte stood and crossed her arms. "Perhaps if you knew what it was like to truly love someone, you would understand you do not stop loving someone simply because the person is dead. Instead, we have to learn to accept the fact they are gone."

Charlotte turned and strode through the dark toward the wagon.

For several days Conrad thought about what Charlotte had said about grief and his inability to love. Since then his mind swam in more confusion than ever. When they traveled on the wagon, if she looked in his direction, she glared at him over Davie's head.

His brother had stopped talking to everyone but Charlotte. All he wanted to talk about was Emma. Charlotte was more than happy to oblige. If they continued to wallow in so much grief, Conrad feared the two of them would be lost to him forever. Charlotte may have accused him of never loving anyone, but she was mistaken. It was because he cared about them he hated to see the two of them hurting and in so much emotional pain.

It was mid-morning and they stopped the wagon to stretch their legs and relieve themselves before climbing the next mountain. He missed the roads from back east. Now they had to carve out their own path, and he hoped he had chosen the route with the least amount of dangerous obstacles.

David took another sip from his cup and smiled, closing his eyes as if savoring the taste. Conrad sipped his own black coffee and grimaced. Nothing about it was great, only tolerable. He stood and dusted off the back of his pants before walking over to his brother. Mildred and Charlotte watched him in silence, while Davie happily chewed his beef jerky. Conrad bent and grabbed David's mug from him. He brought the rim near his nose and sniffed the distinct odor of whiskey infused with coffee.

"Give it back!" David yelled as he scrambled to his feet. "You had no right to take it."

"I have every right! It is *my* whiskey you poured into your coffee." Conrad swung the mug, tossing out its contents. "You went into my trunk and took what was not yours. You wasted it, David. I brought the whiskey along for an emergency."

"No, *you* just wasted it." David pointed at Conrad, as his breath came out in short gasps. He blinked and turned away as if trying to decide what to do.

"I need to go to the privy," Davie danced from one foot to the other.

"I will take him." Charlotte stood and held a hand out to her nephew. The lad gave a hesitant glance at his father and then at Conrad. Realizing Davie needed to know he and his father would be fine, Conrad nodded. Davie placed his hand in Charlotte's outstretched palm and off they went.

"David, you have got to do better. Find a way to grieve without letting your whole world fall apart. The decisions you make now will affect Davie and Ashlynn as they grow older. If you will not think of yourself, at least think of them." Conrad ran his hand through his hair and paced back and forth. He had never seen his brother like this. In the past, if he grew depressed or upset over something, we would snap out of it after a couple of weeks, but this was different. Conrad feared it could go on forever if it took root in his life.

"I am thinking of them!" David rushed at Conrad and pushed him from behind. "And you tried to make me look like a fool in front of my son."

Anger boiled through Conrad as he squeezed his fists by his side, willing his temper to cool. He could punch David back for his insolence, but what would it accomplish? The two of them would end up in a fight, and in his disheveled state of distress, David was in no shape to defend himself.

"You are doing it all on your own, David. I am tired of making excuses for you. This time when we board ship on Lake Erie, you will work as hard as the rest of the crew or you will be punished. Do I make myself clear?"

"You love lording your authority over me. You are worse than Father." His dark eyes blazed as he stared at Conrad. "Perhaps I shall put in for a transfer."

"Go ahead," Conrad said, working hard at keeping calm. "At least you will finally realize how lenient I truly have been with you."

A scream ripped through the woods. Conrad glanced around, trying to determine where it had come from.

"Back there!" David pointed behind Conrad as he shook his head and shoulders, determined to shake himself out of his sluggish stupor.

Conrad realized his brother wasn't so inebriated he had lost his sense of direction and sprinted toward the cry. He shoved leaves and branches aside, dodging trees and roots in his path. A tree trunk lay in the way, and he leaped over it. Charlotte's soothing voice reached his ears, along with Davie's crying. Had the lad fallen? He hoped the child had not broken any bones. Fearful scenarios sped through his mind as his heart beat like lightning.

"You are safe, Davie. I have you now," she said.

Charlotte swept him into her arms and turned to run, slamming into Conrad. She grunted and stepped back. Fear and tears were in her eyes as her lips shook when she looked up at him in relief. "He said a snake bit him. I did not see it, so I do not know what it was."

"Were you not supposed to be watching him?" Conrad snapped, taking the child from her.

"Give him to me," David said, sobering up. "We need to find out if it was poisonous."

"Unfortunately, we will know soon enough," Conrad said, handing Davie over to his father. Davie's cries subsided to whimpers as he reached his small arms around his father's neck.

"Take him to the wagon where he will be more comfortable. We cannot do much of anything here," Conrad said. "Davie, where did it bite you?" he asked, hurrying to keep up with his brother.

"My . . . ankle." He touched his hand to his right foot. "Hurts."

"I know, but try to stay awake, son," David said. "What color was it?" When Davie didn't respond, David's tone grew in desperation. "Davie? Answer me, please."

"Conrad, I think he is unconscious," David said as they left the covering of the trees.

"I suppose it answers our question." Conrad sighed, unable to hide disappointment and worry. "It was poisonous. Probably a rattlesnake. The next twenty-four to forty-eight hours will be critical."

Charlotte burst into tears behind him. Sudden guilt shot through Conrad. He should not have insinuated she was not watching him. She never lets the child out of her sight unless he is with one of them. He had no doubt her love for the lad was just as strong as his, but right now he did not have time to comfort her. He had to help David save him . . . if there was anything they could do.

"Wait, David, let me set up a pallet out here on the ground. We will need the sunlight to assess his wound and watch his symptoms. We can move him into the wagon later at nightfall. We will not be going anywhere anytime soon." Conrad climbed into the wagon and rummaged through piles to find the thickest quilts available, while he listened to the conversation outside.

"What happened?" Mildred asked.

"Davie was bit by a snake. We think it was a rattler." Anguish carried in his brother's tone.

"Oh my Lord, I pray he will live," Mildred's voice faded into shocked silence.

Charlotte's weeping increased. She wasn't the sort of woman to carry on in a crisis like this. Between her two sisters, she had always been the first one to react sensibly, wiping away blood, sewing stitches, and figuring out how best to ease a headache. Emma was there after the crisis, nurturing and feeding everyone, while Melanie fell apart and managed to pull herself together well enough to assist Emma.

"Here we go." Conrad emerged from the wagon and laid out the quilts. David dropped to his knees and laid his son down as gently as possible.

Conrad pushed up Davie's pants leg. A fang mark appeared on the bone of his ankle where the swelling had already doubled the size of his foot and lower leg. Conrad pulled off the shoe. The area had already turned to a dark red color. The poison was spreading quickly. David closed his eyes and turned away at the sight.

"David, it is not as bad as it could have been," Conrad said. "The rattlesnake only managed to get one fang into him, which means less poison was put into his body. We must have faith. I have heard of people surviving rattlesnake bites. It is not impossible."

"Were any of them small children?" Tears filled David's eyes. "First, his mother and now him."

"How could he only have one fang bite?" Charlotte asked, wiping tears from her face and placing one of Davie's favorite pillows beneath his head.

"The snake must have been at an awkward angle, but in my opinion a blessing. It may be what saves his life," Conrad rubbed his chin in worry.

After a few hours Davie finally woke, but Charlotte's relief didn't last long when he rolled over and vomited onto the ground. Charlotte eased his head onto her lap with the pillow and let him weep as he curled in a ball and wrapped his arms around his stomach.

"Hurts. I want my mommy!" Tears streamed from his eyes and soaked the pillow. He groaned in obvious pain and drew one knee up. His injured leg seemed to be paralyzed.

"I know. I am sorry, Davie." Charlotte stroked his short brown hair. She had gotten him to sit still long enough for her to cut his hair after his bath at Windshore House. Now she feared she might never get the privilege of cutting it again.

Conrad was right. This whole ordeal could have been avoided if she had been paying better attention to Davie. Ever since they left home, Davie had spent so much time around his father and Conrad he had come to identify with them. After Ashlynn was born, he had asked lots of questions about girls and boys. He had seen her and Mildred change her nappies and knew he was different.

She closed her eyes and thought back to the morning when he had surprised her by saying, "Aunt Charlotte, you have to stand over there. You cannot look because I am a boy and you are a girl." Amused, Charlotte had agreed. She stood a few feet away, by a different tree. He was within hearing distance, and she could still see him if she peeked over her shoulder. Her biggest worry had been Indians. It never occurred to her a snake could be lurking in a nearby bush where Davie would choose to stand. If he didn't live through this, she had no one to blame but herself. She should have been more assertive.

To Charlotte's relief, Davie finally cried himself back to sleep. She hated to see him in so much pain and prayed the next time he woke, the poison would pass through with little consequence. Nightfall came and still Davie slept, but at least he still breathed. It meant he could possibly survive this ordeal.

Conrad made a pallet for him in the wagon and moved him inside. They all agreed Charlotte should be the one to stay with him in case he had any complications or woke and begged for his mother once more. Charlotte didn't disagree with them, but she knew what they were all thinking. If he was delirious and wanted his mother, only she could pass for the likes of Emma. As many times as she and her twin switched places as children for fun, never had she felt like more of an imposter than now.

A dim lantern spread light throughout the covered wagon. Conrad placed a pillow beside Davie's head and motioned for Charlotte to lay beside him. Mildred and Ashlynn lay in a horizontal position at her feet with the trunks around them. David kissed the top of Davie's head and crawled out, but Conrad remained.

"I owe you an apology." He looked at Charlotte and rubbed his temple. "I said something implicating you and I was wrong. I know you did the best you could and you would never leave Davie unattended." He paused, ran his hand through his hair, and sighed as if regrouping his thoughts. "What I am trying to say is, I am sorry. What happened to Davie is not your fault. It could have happened whether or not David or I was with him."

"Thank you, but it does not matter at this point, does it?" She tilted her head to the side to regard him. "I tried my best to protect him and still this happened. It was so fast. The snake came out of nowhere and struck with lightning speed. I cannot change what happened, but I will always bear the responsibility of what happened—especially if he does not make it." She looked down and shook her head with a sarcastic expression as she bit her lower lip. "I appreciate your apology and concern. The worst thing I could do is break my solemn word to Emma. And I am afraid I may have already broken it by allowing Davie to get hurt."

"This is exactly what I was afraid you would think. You take on too much. He is as much mine and David's responsibility as yours. I did not mean to add to the burden of guilt you are already feeling." He shook his head and lifted his palm.

"I must admit, you have a talent for doing it, but I am learning to overcome it," she said. "Besides, you have already said what you think of me. I need no reminders." She slid under the quilt he had provided and turned away from him. "Now, please leave. Davie and I need rest."

Conrad crawled to the opening and climbed out with a sigh of frustration. He threw another log and a few limbs into the fire to keep it going a while longer. Unrolling a blanket, Conrad made a makeshift bed at David's feet. Conrad couldn't remember the last time he prayed fervent prayers, but tonight he fell asleep, begging for little Davie's life. By the time sleep overcame him, he felt a renewed hope and confidence in the Almighty. No other options were available to him, other than a blind faith in what he could not see or explain. His thoughts faded as exhaustion claimed him.

11

After a few days, the swelling in Davie's foot and leg stayed the same, but parts of his skin turned from a deep red to a dark purple. They took turns staying with Davie, coaxing him to eat and calming him when the pain and fear became too much.

Conrad brought Charlotte a cup of coffee while she sat with Davie in the wagon. "David and I have been talking, and we believe now is the time to start traveling again. Davie survived the first two critical days and seems to be improving. The sooner we can get to the next town, the sooner we can have a doctor look at him."

Charlotte sipped her coffee without saying anything. She looked down at Davie where he slept in blissful peace, finally escaping the pain if only for a few hours. Brushing his brown hair to the side of his forehead, she sighed.

"He is so tiny. I cannot believe how close we came to losing him," she said. "Life is so fragile. We spend most of our lives taking it for granted until a tragedy comes along to remind us of our weaknesses. I prayed such fervent prayers for Emma to live, but after she died and my prayers went unanswered, I thought I would never pray hard again." She brushed her knuckles across

Davie's cheek in a tender path and blinked back tears. Her nose turned pink and her lips trembled. "I was wrong. I prayed just as hard for Davie. Once again God has humbled me and showed me I did not know myself as much as I thought I did."

"Do not be so hard on yourself, Charlotte." Conrad thought back to the moment he had snapped at her and all but accused her of not watching Davie the day he was bitten by the snake. He had tried to apologize before, but she had been too willing to blame herself, much to his increasing distress. He took a deep breath. "I meant what I said the other day. I know you watched Davie as well as any of us could. The snake could have bitten him no matter who was with him. They lurk in shadows and strike so fast when we least expect it. I want you to know it was not your fault."

"It is my fault. I should have sensed the danger even if I had not seen the snake." She brushed a lock of Davie's hair behind his ear. "It is my responsibility to protect him, and I failed."

"Nonsense." Conrad shifted his weight where he leaned through the door of the covered wagon. "In that case, no child would ever get hurt or sick. I am certain your childhood was not completely injury-free, and I know your parents are caring and thoughtful. They love you and are protective of you even now as an adult."

"True, but it is different. Being a parent comes more natural to those who have children born to them. Emma trusted me."

"Yes, but I doubt she intended for you to blame yourself for whatever happens to them." He shook his head. "I did not mean what I said. I was only upset, and I spoke in haste."

She smiled as she looked up at him, her bright green eyes shining, but tired with circles under them. "Now who is taking more upon himself? I feel this heavy burden of responsibility, but it is not due to anything you have said or not said."

"Conrad, are you ready?" David called from outside.

"It is time for us to go. Mildred has decided to ride up front with us, and she will carry Ashlynn. Would you like for me to stay with Davie while you break your fast before we go?"

"Indeed." She nodded. "Please give me a few moments, and I will join the others outside the wagon."

Conrad straightened and stepped back, bumping into David.

"Has Davie awakened?" David asked, hope lingering in his voice and in his dark red eyes.

"No, but he stayed awake longer yesterday, so there is no reason to think today will be any different." Conrad gripped his brother's shoulder in an effort to encourage him. "We must give him more time. The swelling did not go beyond his knee. I believe it is a good sign, and he will recover."

"I hope you are right. I will feel better once a doctor has seen him." David shoved a hand through his hair. "We have clouds approaching from the west. We need the weather to hold up long enough for us to climb the next hill. When will Charlotte be ready?"

"I am coming," she called, climbing out of the wagon and patting her hair where it now curled on top of her head in pins.

"Charlotte, I saved you a couple of pieces of bacon and a biscuit," Mildred said, bouncing Ashlynn on her shoulder. "It is not as soft and warm as it was when I first baked it this morning but still edible."

"Wrap it up and bring it with you," David said. "We have to leave now if we are going to make some distance before the rain overtakes us."

The sound of a roar echoed through the trees. Something large and black ran at them. Charlotte and Mildred screamed as they turned and ran toward the wagon. David went after his gun while Conrad stood in front of the wagon, hoping he would not have to fight a black bear before David returned with the rifle. Instead, the animal made his way over to where Charlotte's plate sat on a stump.

"Uh, Mildred, what did you put on Charlotte's biscuit?" Conrad asked, realizing they were not in as much danger as he originally thought. David returned with the rifle, but Conrad motioned for him to wait.

"Only a bit of honey," Mildred said.

Conrad leaned through the wagon flap to deliver the bad news. "Charlotte, I believe your breakfast is gone."

Charlotte held her breath while Dr. Jacobson continued to examine Davie. For three days, they had cared for Davie in this boarding room, where she and Mildred took turns watching over him. The town of Williamsport was smaller than Wilmington but looked to have promise with a tavern, a post office, a school, and a jail. Conrad and David continued to sleep in the wagon outside, but she appreciated having them both here now, especially if Dr. Jacobson gave them bad news.

Even though she and Mildred alternated sleeping by Davie's side, it was blissful to have a bed with a feather mattress again. The nice bath and warm meals were heavenly. This town and the boarding house reminded her of civilized life and made her long for home. She even missed sailing on the *Victorious.* Charlotte took the opportunity while in Williamsport to write letters to her family and gave them to Conrad to post.

"After monitoring Davie for three days, I must say he is doing remarkably well considering he received no bloodletting or treatment with leeches to draw out the poison in his blood." Dr. Jacobson closed his black bag and handed Charlotte a small brown bottle. "Give him this for the stomach upset, and it will also help him sleep."

"What is it?" Davie asked.

"A mixture of ginger and cloves. It will help you feel better." Dr. Jacobson leaned over and touched him on the tip of his nose with a playful grin. "I promise."

"My leg looks like a monster, does it not, Daddy?" Davie asked, holding it up for everyone to see. "I told you I am feeling better. I have not thrown up at all."

Charlotte's insides lifted in hope as she smiled down at her nephew. To see him awake and talking, sounding more like himself again, made her want to sing praises to the Lord out in the street the way the Bible says King David did back in his time.

"I know, and we are all grateful." David leaned forward and rubbed his son's arm in a fatherly gesture. He turned back to the doctor, his expression shifting to more sobering thoughts. "Doctor, what about the discoloration and swelling? When can we it expect it to go away or will it?"

"The swelling will take some time but will eventually disappear. The discoloration will fade as well, but there will be some scars to remind him of the incident. At this time, I cannot tell how long it will take for the purple color to go away or how deep and big the scars will be. It is too soon to tell. The important thing is, he will live." Dr. Jacobson smiled and met everyone's gaze around the room. "You can all breathe a sigh of relief. He is over the worst of it."

Charlotte thought about how hard it had become for Davie to get out of bed and walk. He could not put any pressure on his leg without severe pain. His father had carried him here to the boarding house, and Davie had spent most of his time in bed. "What about walking? Will he be able to walk without pain? Will he have a limp?"

"Ah, good question." He lifted a finger as he gazed down at Davie, contemplating his next words. "In truth, he may have a slight limp, but he may also have a full recovery. It is a good sign Davie can still wiggle his foot and toes."

In response, Davie lifted his leg and moved his foot to the right. "See I can move it this way, but not this way because it hurts." Davie leaned his head to the left as if willing his foot to do the same.

"It is because of the swelling on the left side." Dr. Jacobson moved toward the foot of the bed and grabbed his big toe. "Do you feel this?"

"Yes." Davie nodded, pleased with himself. "See, Auntie Charlotte, I will walk as soon as it is all better."

"I believe you shall, Davie." She linked her hands in front of her, feeling her own excitement grow with his, as relief poured through her.

"What about this?" Dr. Jacobson slid a finger on the tender region on the underside of Davie's foot.

"Yes, it almost tickles." Davie giggled. "But feels a little heavy."

"Sounds like there is still a bit of numbness by the heaviness Davie feels, but the feeling is coming back. This means the nerves were not damaged and there is no reason why Davie should not be able to walk." He shook his gray head in disbelief and picked up his bag. "It is nothing short of a miracle. Considering the alternative, I believe Davie is in divine hands. Your prayers have been answered. Your family has good reason to celebrate."

"Will it be all right if we continue our journey?" Conrad asked. "David and I are expected to report to our commanding officers in a few weeks, and we are only halfway to our destination in Cleaveland, Ohio."

"Keep him off his leg for another week and then let him begin to test his weight on it," Dr. Jacobson said. "He is young and small. I feel it would be no trouble to carry him to and from the wagon since he will be riding most of the time. You may leave as soon as you wish." He placed his black hat on top of his head. "I will see myself out. Good day." He dipped his head in a quick nod of departure and walked out the door.

"See? I can play now!" Davie scooted to the edge of the bed, ready to jump down.

"Not yet, the doctor said to wait one more week." Charlotte ran to his side and kept him from leaping off the bed. Davie gave her a pouting look and popped his lower lip out. How would she manage to keep a young lad full of energy like Davie from bouncing around since he felt better?

Over the next week, Conrad tried to make up for lost time. He pushed them to leave earlier in the morning than normal, gave them shorter breaks during the day, and forced them to make the most of daylight before they settled into camp for the night. By the glaring looks Charlotte sent his way, and the snide comments she made, Conrad sensed she would soon lose patience with him.

He looked up at the sky and marveled at how the rising sun cast a purple glow across the morning clouds. Here, the days were much cooler than back home. He liked it better.

To his disappointment, they were not yet on the road. Conrad had already fed and watered the horses, while Davie and David broke their fast. He glanced down at Charlotte sitting on the stump drinking her coffee. Dark circles framed her eyes. Usually her hair was swept on top of her head under a bonnet, but this morning her blonde hair fell in long waves around her shoulders.

He liked this wild and disheveled look about her. Unfortunately, it brought back the desire he had always had for her.

With Davie feeling better and no crew to manage, inviting thoughts of Charlotte were getting harder to ignore. He sipped his second cup of coffee and continued to pace, determined to bring his thoughts into submission and concentrate on something else.

"We should have left over a half hour ago." Conrad tossed the rest of his coffee into a nearby bush, allowing his pent-up frustration to show. "What is taking Mildred so long with the baby?"

Charlotte looked up and narrowed her gaze upon him, thinning her lips in obvious disapproval. "Did you sleep under a rock last night?" She sat up straight, her back as rigid as the mainmast of his ship. "Ashlynn screamed for hours and kept the rest of us from getting any sleep. Mildred and I took turns trying to console her, but nothing we did calmed her. How could you be so ignorant of her distress?"

"Of course I heard her crying, but what does it have to do with us moving on in a timely manner this morning?" Conrad strode over and paused in front of her. "We have a schedule to keep whether or not a baby is upset." He pointed a thumb over his shoulder. "Go tell her to hurry up."

"No." Her green eyes sparked with defiance and her lips twisted in anger. "You do it."

"If she is feeding the baby, you know I cannot interrupt her." Conrad shifted his weight to his other foot and rubbed his chin. "Why are you being so obstinate? I am only trying to ensure we keep to our schedule. We lost a lot of time with Davie's illness."

"The better question is why are you being so unreasonable?" She lifted a blond eyebrow and took another sip of her coffee, as if determined to continue relaxing and carrying on with her usual morning routine. "The rest of us have hardly had any sleep, and we need more time before we begin the day's journey. What does it matter when we arrive as long as we make it? I declare, Conrad, you act as if we are a ship of sailors to command."

"Charlotte, I promised my superiors we would be there in a fortnight." Conrad shoved his hands on his hips. "I intend to keep my word."

"Well, it is your misfortune." She stood and faced him, tilting her head back. "You should not make promises for other people. Did you forget you are not alone on this journey? We are traveling with two small children and the consequences can slow you down, rob your sleep, and wreak havoc in your plans." She pointed toward the wagon. "Right now, you have to be Uncle Conrad, not Captain Deaton. The children are not little sailors to be ordered about."

"This is absurd." He looked away and took a deep breath as if mustering patience. "I am one and the same. You cannot split a man in halves. It is like saying a woman cannot be a mother and wife at the same time. I do not know where you come up with these crazy ideas." He shook his head in disbelief and pointed to his chest. "We are the adults. We make the decisions, and they do as we say. It is plain and simple."

"Davie's snake bite should have been proof enough it is not so simple. Instead of concentrating on the days we lost due to his illness, you should be thankful he survived." Charlotte stood and jabbed a finger against his chest. "Where are your priorities, Conrad? It does not matter when we arrive, but it matters we must all arrive safely." She poked him again. "That should be your number one concern."

"You presume too much, Charlotte." Conrad leaned forward, lowering his voice to a dangerous pitch at her ear. "I love my nephew as much as you, and I resent the implication that I do not."

"Then act like it." The anger in her clipped tone scalded him, rousing his own defensive temper. Her accusing eyes blazed up at him like green prisms hiding a secret. What was wrong with her? Just because he wanted to keep to a traveling schedule did not mean he cared less for his niece and nephew than she.

"Charlotte!" Mildred hurried from the back of the wagon, carrying Ashlynn. "I think I know why she has been crying and refusing to eat or sleep."

"What is it?" Charlotte went to her.

Conrad followed, his gut tensing with unease. Of course, he knew the baby had been crying off and on during the night, but no one had mentioned she refused to eat—at least not to him.

"I believe she has a fever," Mildred said, lifting the blanket from Ashlynn's face. At the moment, the child was not screaming, but she writhed in discomfort and whined.

Charlotte leaned forward and brushed the blond hair beginning to grow on the top of her head for the last couple of months. It was now clear Ashlynn would have the same color hair as her mother and Charlotte. Her facial features were already beginning to favor her mother. She would be a constant reminder to David of what he had lost.

"What does this mean?" Conrad asked.

"I do not know." Mildred shook her head. "Right now, her fever does not appear to be high, but sometimes they start out low before climbing to a higher temperature."

"I wish we had two wagons." Charlotte inclined her head toward their only wagon. "I fear Davie may not be strong enough to fight off another illness right now."

"Is it so serious?" Conrad glanced from Charlotte to Mildred. He had little experience with small children and did not know what to expect. At least Charlotte had been around her other nieces and nephews. Conrad had never even held an infant until Davie was born.

"Is what serious?" David approached from behind, holding Davie's hand.

A moment of silence passed between them as they all searched for the right words to break the news to David.

"Ashlynn is sick with a fever," Charlotte said. "We do not know what it is or how serious it might be, but we all agree Davie should not be around her right now. He may not be strong enough to recover from another illness so soon."

Shock absorbed into David's expression as he bent to sweep his son into his arms, settling the child on his hip. He rubbed his eyebrows in worry as if contemplating what to do. "I will keep Davie with me, if you all will do everything in your power to save Emma's baby."

"We will take care of her," Conrad said, slapping his brother on the back in a show of support. He met Charlotte's gaze. Regardless of how insensitive she thought him, Conrad had not missed his brother's choice of words. He had referred to Ashlynn as Emma's baby, distancing himself from her as if she was not his own.

12

Charlotte and Mildred took turns staying up with Ashlynn. Throughout the night, her fever increased and she refused to eat. David and Conrad paced outside the wagon, while Davie fell asleep by the fire on a small pallet his father made for him.

A lantern burned on a trunk beside Ashlynn. She had finally quieted and succumbed to sleeping on her side. Charlotte watched her tiny chest rise and fall with the rhythm of her breathing. Her blond hair was matted with sweat against her scalp due to the rising fever. As the hours passed, her breathing grew more labored.

"I do not know what else to do." Mildred rubbed her palm against her eye. "She has not eaten all day. I am afraid she will grow too weak to fight this illness, whatever it is."

"Me too." Charlotte brushed Ashlynn's hair to the side. Her skin was too pale and so smooth. "I keep asking myself, what would Emma do? And I do not know." Charlotte lifted her empty hands into the air and dropped them. In truth, she had no idea what her sister would do. Perhaps her sister would be as perplexed as she, but they would never know since Emma was not here and she was . . . and their lives depended on her. "I remember the doctor saying Emma would die if she did not drink enough water. He feared she would become too weak after Ashlynn was born when she refused to eat or drink."

"So what can we do?" Mildred asked, her brown eyes wide with hope.

"He suggested we tilt Emma's head and slip a bit of water down her throat each hour. Her muscles automatically constricted and swallowed. I assume it would be the same way with a baby. If Ashlynn is too weak to suck the milk she so desperately needs, perhaps we could give her a few drops of water each hour to keep something inside her."

"We have to try. I cannot stand the thought of losing another baby." Mildred gave an uneasy glance at Charlotte. "I mean, I realize Ashlynn is not mine, but I have come to love her as if she was my own."

"I understand. How can you not love her? She is so innocent and sweet." Charlotte dug in one of the trunks and searched for a spoon. "Here it is." She lifted it out and poured a few drops of water from a flask onto the spoon. Leaning over her niece, she tipped the small spoon, wetting Ashlynn's lips. The baby smacked and licked her lips before twisting her mouth and puckering up as if she wanted more. Charlotte smiled, more than happy to oblige.

They gave Ashlynn as much water as she would take. She fell asleep for a couple more hours and woke up again before dawn. It was Mildred's turn to repeat the process, and to their delight, this time Ashlynn swallowed more.

A while later, Charlotte woke and rubbed the sleep from her eyes. She sat up on her elbow and glanced at Mildred still sleeping on the other side of Ashlynn. A surge of thankfulness at having Mildred's help with the baby swept through her. She had no idea how she would have coped without her friend. Even though David was their father, he hardly understood the needs of children, and Conrad was even worse. Charlotte could confide in Mildred and seek her good opinion on things.

Charlotte scooted to her knees and leaned over, touching Ashlynn's forehead with the back of her knuckles. The baby's smooth skin was cool. Relief flowed through Charlotte, and she touched her stomach as happy tears filled her eyes. While she knew it was not uncommon for infants and small children to develop illnesses, she had little experience with such matters. She had naively assumed the first time either of the children became sick, they would be able to recover in the comfort of their own bed, in the peaceful surroundings of their own home, and a doctor would be available. The idea they would be out here in the middle of nowhere with no civilized town in sight, never occurred to her. Even on Conrad's ship they had a decent bed and a doctor with access to a few medicines.

Low voices rumbled outside near the campfire. Conrad and David were already up rebuilding the fire for their breakfast. Charlotte grabbed her brush and ran it through her hair, wishing she could have a bath. She crawled to the flap and climbed out the back. Once her feet landed on the ground, she straightened her dark gown as best as she could. Charlotte took a deep breath and marched toward the men, eager to share the good news.

Smoke lingered from the small flames David stoked with the kindling he had gathered. Davie sat up and coughed, blinking and waving a hand in front of his nose. Conrad pulled the lid off one of the barrels attached to the wagon and dipped the iron coffeepot, filling it with water. Her foot stepped on a fallen branch, snapping it in two. They all turned to look at her.

"Good morning," Charlotte said, clasping her hands in front of her as she approached.

"Morning." David nodded and turned back to his task, blowing on the flames as they set sparks onto more twigs.

Conrad grunted in response in the midst of a wide yawn. The scene almost made her yawn as well, but she managed to fight the impulse.

"Auntie Charlotte, I am hungry." Davie swung his blanket to the side and sat up. "Can I have a warm biscuit?"

"I have to make them first." She rubbed the top of Davie's brown head. She walked around the fire pit so David could see her better. "I have good news. Ashlynn's fever broke." She waited, but David didn't respond. Instead, he lifted a log and set it on the burning fire.

"David, did you hear me?" she asked, leaning closer to view his expression.

"I did." He nodded, staring into the fire with a blank expression. He settled his elbows on his knees where he bent on his haunches. "Emma would appreciate all you did to save her."

"What about you, David?" Charlotte stepped closer. "Are you not glad your daughter is better?"

"Of course I am, but what I wanted most was for my wife to live." He gestured toward Davie. "These children are the only link I have left of her, and not long ago, I almost lost him. I cannot allow myself to get attached to her. She is too little, too fragile. I cannot take any more pain."

Over the next few days, Conrad contemplated David's response toward his daughter's recovery and continued to watch his behavior. He had wanted David to heal and get over his wife, but not this way. Pretending Ashlynn didn't exist would only create future problems and pain. He didn't want his niece growing up and feeling neglected or unloved. Was David now blaming Ashlynn for Emma's death?

"Conrad, I thought we were coming to live in a town on the lake. This place looks hardly big enough to qualify as a town." Charlotte leaned forward, cradling Ashlynn in her arms, where she sat beside Conrad on the front wagon bench. "Where are all the buildings and people? I did not want to be alone when you and David leave for duty. I thought I would have neighbors around us, if we needed anything."

"You will not be alone. You will have Mildred." Conrad tipped his hat further over his head to hide his disappointed expression as he surveyed the narrow dirt road. He pointed to a cleared lot where several timbers lay stacked. "Looks like they are building something there."

"It shall be a lonely building. Do they at least have a doctor? I need a doctor for the children." She laid the baby on her lap and smiled, allowing Ashlynn to grip her finger as she made funny faces and noises. The baby cooed and Conrad grinned, enjoying this playful side to Charlotte.

"As a matter of fact, there is a Dr. Long," Conrad said. "It is my understanding he arrived here about a year ago." He breathed a sigh of relief. "So you and the children should be in good hands."

"I am not worried about myself, only Davie and Ashlynn." She bent to kiss the baby's cheek, and something inside him sparked a longing he had never had. He liked seeing her with the children and appreciated this caring and nurturing side of Charlotte. He didn't want to leave them here alone. What if she needed him?

"I worry about you." The words slipped off his tongue before he could stop them. He held his breath, waiting for her stunned reaction. Part of him hoped she would let the comment go unnoticed, but not Charlotte; she laughed.

"Now this is something I refuse to believe, Captain Deaton. You forget . . . I know you too well." She crooked a finger as if to scold him. "I know I vex and annoy you more than I delight and pamper your male ego." Charlotte sighed and looked away as she lifted Ashlynn to her feet and placed her on her lap. "In a few days you will be well rid of me." She smiled her winning smile and leaned toward him. "But I daresay, you shall miss the children."

Unable to trust himself, he let the awkward moment pass between them. It didn't matter if he would miss her as much as he would the children. She wouldn't believe him regardless of what he said and it was his own fault. Years ago he had hurt her when he refused to allow their courtship to grow as serious as David and Emma's, and since Emma's death, he had managed to insult and belittle her judgment even when he intended to do the opposite. He deserved what she believed of him, and the knowledge of her thoughts only increased his regret.

"You were able to secure us a house, were you not?" she asked, sudden fear igniting her dark green eyes as she sat Ashlynn back on her bottom. "The sight of so few homes is beginning to distress me more than I care to admit."

"I do not know." He pretended to be perplexed and touched a fingertip to his chin. "Perhaps I was so involved in my career and being captain of my own ship, I neglected the security of a home for my niece and nephew."

"Do not tease me!" She slapped at his arm. "I am perfectly serious. Were you able to find us a house or merely a boarding room?"

"Being in the navy does have its advantages." Conrad gave her a mischievous grin. "My superiors have wives who are already living in the area, and they arranged everything for us. You will be living in a white house. I know naught else until I see it."

"They have wives who follow them through their military career rather than staying home where it is safe? What a novel idea." She glared at him, and her voice turned hard. "Too bad you could not have been so open-minded. I should like to meet these couples."

"I was heading out to sea where it is much different and definitely not safe," Conrad gripped the reins tight in his hand as he shifted on his seat. He wished they would soon arrive. He feared their temporary truce was about to come to an end. They passed a few more scattered buildings and homes.

"It does not matter." She shrugged. "You have chosen your path, and I have chosen mine. We shall live with our decisions and make the most of it. Besides, I must think about the children now. Do these ladies have social activities? Do they ever host any balls?"

"I thought you hated such activities?" He gave her a curious glance, wondering what brought on such a question.

"In the past, I did. I was childish and immature. I have learned a lot from Emma. She always knew how to be happy and do what was expected of her. While I was out chasing dying dreams and a fantasy world which never existed, she grew up and left me behind." She hugged Ashlynn tight against her. "But since Emma's death, my life has changed, and I have changed as well. No more silly dreams. I have two children to raise, and I want to do what is best for them. I will become involved in the community here, make friends, go to church, be involved in society, and build a life for the children and myself."

"What about David? Do you intend to leave their father out of this life you intend to build for them?"

"Of course not!" Her scolding tone crawled over his nerves as he tried to interpret what she meant. "I am no fool. David will eventually remarry and move on. With my involvement in society, perhaps I can help introduce him to suitable women."

"And what about you?" Conrad scratched the side of his temple. "If David remarries, there will be no need for you to raise the children."

"I will still be their aunt and part of their lives." She laughed. "My goodness, Conrad, I have no intention of disappearing. I could live nearby and take them on outings. I promised my sister I shall always be here to take care of them and I shall."

"Ah, I see. You intend to live the spinster life." The unease rising inside him dissipated as he better understood her intentions. After their courtship, Charlotte had always claimed she would never marry, and to Conrad's delight she was still single when he returned home from the sea. If he ever found the courage to settle down, Charlotte would be his choice. No one else understood him or stirred his passion as much as she.

"It is not what I said." She shook her head. "I stated I intend to live near the children so I could continue to be part of their lives. Whether I am married or single does not matter. If God intends for me to marry, He will bring the right man into my life who will understand my wishes."

"I thought you said you would never marry?" Conrad rubbed the back of his neck, disliking the sweat now wetting his skin.

She laughed. "I said lots of childish things, Conrad." Her tone sobered. "I never thought I would be living the rest of my life without Emma, but here I am." She sighed. "I am beginning to think plans are foolish. None of us know our future or how much time we have. We must make the most of what God gives us."

"It is bigger than I imagined and right on the lake." Charlotte stood with her hands on her hips and surveyed the large white house in front of them. Mildred stood on her right, and David held his son's hand on her left. Conrad walked up behind them carrying Ashlynn, as if a baby in his arms was as natural as his spyglass when on his ship. Of late, Ashlynn looked more content in his arms than in the arms of her own father. The last time Charlotte could recall David holding her was weeks ago.

"Are you not satisfied?" Conrad asked. "I thought you would be pleased."

"You had no idea what to expect. You told me so yourself." She glanced at him over her shoulder. Charlotte refused to allow him to take credit for their lodgings. She didn't know who to thank just yet, but she would find out soon enough. "And, of course, I am pleased. For the first time in months, I will not be swaying back and forth over water in a small cabin or rocking against the contents of a wagon over rough terrain and roads."

"Indeed." A grin toyed at his lips, "But you did say you would much rather sail on a smooth ship than be hauled over land in a rickety wagon."

"How did you hear me?" If she recalled, Charlotte remembered thinking she would not give him the satisfaction of knowing her true feelings on the subject. She feared he would gloat for a month. The man loved the sea so much he should have been born a merman with fins. "I do not believe those were my exact words."

"Perhaps, but close enough." He leaned toward her and whispered, "You do realize the covered wagon does not have wooden walls, do you not?"

"Of course, but perhaps a *real* gentleman would not have imposed himself on the conversation between two ladies." She tilted her head and stared at the outside paint. "The color is more of a cream, but the window frames are white."

"And there are plenty of windows." Mildred nodded. "Two on the first floor on each side of the front door and five more on the second level—a total of nine windows. I do not think I have seen a house with so many windows."

"I daresay, we will have plenty of sunshine streaming inside. There will not be a dreary room in the house." Charlotte nodded as she stepped forward.

"Can I see my new chamber?" Davie reached out and grabbed her hand.

"Wait, Davie, someone is coming down the road," David said, shielding his eyes from the sun as they all turned to see four horses pulling an approaching black carriage. Dust scattered in the air as the wheels rolled over the dirt road and pebbled rocks.

"I think it may be Commodore Evans and his wife," Conrad said, walking toward their visitors to greet them.

"Have you met them before?" Charlotte asked.

"No." He shook his head without turning around.

"Then how do you know it is them?" she asked, lifting a hand in question.

"Because there is no one else who would be expecting our arrival, unless they themselves are the ones who spread the news, and since I can think of no reason why they would, it must be them." Conrad waved toward a gray-headed man who hung out the window, waving as the carriage rolled to a stop behind their wagon.

The door opened and out popped an older man wearing a blue uniform with gold stripes and symbols on his shoulders. He stepped back and reached a hand to his wife. A bark echoed through the air and a brown cocker spaniel leaped out of the carriage around his two owners. The animal ran toward Conrad, leaping up to his waist.

"Daddy!" Davie dropped Charlotte's hand and hurried to his father who swept him up in his arms with a good laugh. "Will he bite me?"

"No, no. You do not have to worry about Georgie." The elderly man helped his wife down from the carriage as he turned to look at Davie. "He merely wants to play. We brought him because we knew you would be coming." He pointed to himself and looked around at everyone. "I am Commodore Jacob Evans, and this is my wife, Mrs. Lucille Evans. We hope you will like the Durham House. We have been sorry to see it empty these past months. I am sure the walls will enjoy the sound of children's laughter again."

"The walls can hear?" Davie's brown eyes widened.

"Of course not, my boy, I was merely joking." Commodore Evans and his wife laughed. Hers had a ringing pitch that could irritate if she was to laugh for too long. Like her husband, she had gray hair, and slight curls peeked beneath the blue turban wrapped around her head. She wore a floral print dress of blue flowers on white with a gathered neckline. The corded sleeves reached to the elbows.

"What is on your head?" Davie pointed at her, tilting his neck and squinting to observe her. "It looks like a funny hat."

"Well, I suppose it is." Mrs. Evans touched the blue material above her ear. "This is called a turban." She glanced at Charlotte and Mildred. "The First Lady wears them. I met her a few months ago when my husband was called to Washington D.C. to meet with President Madison. Mrs. Madison is a delightful woman. Lots of other women are now wearing them as well."

"I have not seen any of those," David said, staring at her in the same way as his son.

"I suspected as much." She smiled and turned to her husband, who now leaned on a cane, but as far as Charlotte could tell, he carried it for fashion and didn't appear to need it. "I believe we need introductions."

"My dear, I have never met these officers. We only corresponded through courier letters," Commodore Evans said.

"Pardon me, but I am Captain Conrad Deaton, the one you corresponded with." Conrad introduced everyone else.

"Excellent." Mrs. Evans rubbed her hands together and smiled as if in anticipation. "Now, let us go inside. I am eager to see how you like the house I picked out for you." She looped her arm around Charlotte's. "And we shall discuss how best to introduce you to everyone in town."

13

"Captain Stallings liked the area so much he had this house built for his family when we were commissioned to Lake Erie last year." Commodore Evans stood in the study staring out the window. He linked his hands behind him as if reluctant to face Conrad. "His wife spent most of her time filling it with these excellent furnishings." He touched the ruby red drapes tied to the side by a gold-cabled rope. "When he received the summons to command a ship on Lake Huron, they were loath to leave it."

"I cannot blame them." Conrad sat in an armchair carved from gilded beechwood upholstered in an interlaced curved pattern matching the color of the drapes. The chair was most comfortable with an enclosed concave back circling around to the arms. Another identical chair faced him, positioned in front of a fireplace with an oak mantle and carved lions' heads on each side. Conrad noticed on his earlier tour of the house all the fireplaces in each room matched this same design. "It is obvious great care was given to the details of the architecture and the selection of furniture throughout."

"Indeed, the rent is modest, and I assured Captain Stallings I would only rent it out to a respectable family who would take exceptional care of it. Do you know what their one stipulation was?" He turned and lifted a finger.

"I have no idea." Conrad shook his head as he crossed a booted foot over his knee and regarded Commodore Evans with interest. The man was different than any superior he had ever had. While Conrad sensed a firm authority with equal fairness in him, he also sensed a sensitive and compassionate nature few men ever displayed in the navy. His attempts at awkward humor with the women and children were more amusing and endearing than anything else. Conrad could tell the commodore won Charlotte's heart by her warm smile when he said her sister must have been a beauty, if she herself was the standard to judge by.

"Their one condition was a family with children should live here. When I received your letter about your family's recent loss and learned your niece and nephew would be coming with you, I knew the Durham House would be perfect."

"Why did they name it Durham House?" Conrad asked.

"It is my understanding Stallings's wife was a Durham before she married, originally from the City of Durham in England. The war between our two countries has not been easy on her."

"I imagine it would not, much like so many families during the War of Independence. Charlotte's family still talks about it." Conrad thought back to the tales her grandfather used to share after dinner when he courted her before David and Emma's wedding.

"They still have ties back in England?" Commodore Evans asked.

"No, they were originally from Argyll, Scotland." Conrad shook his head. "Her grandfather, Malcolm MacGregor, settled in Wilmington, North Carolina, where he built a successful rice plantation called the MacGregor Quest. It took a lot of courage for Charlotte to leave it and her family behind."

"But she did," Commodore Evans walked across the wood floor, passing the desk to settle in the empty chair across from Conrad. "In my experience it means the good Lord has a quest for Charlotte to continue on the legacy of her ancestors, even if she does not know yet what the quest is."

Conrad braced his elbow on the armrest and rubbed his chin in contemplation as he mulled over the commodore's words. He thought back to what Charlotte had said about her life changing and it changing her. Discomfort clenched his gut. He had always felt secure Charlotte would always be waiting for him when he finished his career in the navy. In his mind, he imagined the time to be in another five or ten years, but now he was not so sure.

Even though she had been angry and hurt, he chose to remain in his career. She had never seemed interested in other men or determined to wed before she reached a specific age like other girls. Charlotte was more like him, eager to enjoy life and have fun. For as long as he had known her, she was content to live beneath her parents' roof, free to be herself, ride her horse in the countryside, and read about faraway places. She used to daydream about visiting Scotland, the birthplace of her grandparents, visiting England and Ireland, and traveling to distant lands. She was a dreamer, much like he.

"I think she knows what her quest is—to help raise her sister's children, and since their father brought them here to Cleaveland it meant Charlotte had to come here as well." Conrad shrugged, meeting the older man's gaze. "It is a noble cause to be sure."

"So she has won your respect, has she?" Commodore Evans grinned as he sat back in his chair and hung his cane over the armrest.

"Charlotte has always had my respect, even if she does go to great lengths to vex me at times." Conrad scratched his right temple, uncomfortable with the way the commodore seemed to be staring right through him. He shifted in his seat and switched positions, crossing his other foot over his knee. If only he could stretch his legs and go for a long walk to explore the grounds and see the lake. Idle restlessness filled him with frustration. He wanted to talk about the war, not Charlotte, not when things seemed to be so out of focus with her.

The man threw his head back and laughed. "A woman who knows her own mind, is she?"

"Not at all, she keeps changing it, and it is what causes most of our arguments." Conrad wished he had bitten his tongue as Commodore Evans laughed even harder.

"Captain Deaton, I believe you are a man who is smitten and in complete denial." Conrad opened his mouth to protest, but his superior lifted his hand to stop him. "Do not bother to deny it. Time will tell if I am right. Either way, you will be quite busy sailing a ship, commanding a crew, and fighting a war. In the meantime, Miss Morgan will find the quest for which the Lord brought her here."

"But I already told you why she came," Conrad said, feeling a little more frustrated with each passing minute.

"You told me her quest, but I am referring to the quest the Lord has in mind for her. The one none of you yet know about."

"Forgive me, sir, but am I to assume you know what it is?" Conrad arched a suspicious eyebrow. "Are you also a chaplain in the navy?"

"No, but my father was a chaplain during the War of Independence. I merely have a feeling." He drummed his fingers on the armrest and sobered his tone. "Now, let us discuss your new orders. You will be taking over command of the USS *Larkspur*. She is a fairly new ship, only about a year old. Our ships are lighter and faster than those of the British. Their guns can outdistance us in shooting range, but if we sail better, we can turn the advantage in our favor. One of the reasons I chose you was because of your daring exploit in outsailing three British frigates off the coast of the Carolinas. It took courage, focus, and cunning manipulation since you were sailing a schooner. Is it when you received command of the *Victorious?*"

"Yes, and thank you, sir." Conrad gave him a brief nod.

"The British have one thing going against them," Commodore Evans shook a finger in the air, "their ego. For the most part, they have every reason to believe they will beat us. They have more manpower, ships, artillery, and experience. While a few of our sailors make careers out of the U.S. Navy, most of them are sailors by trade. They know how to build ships and how to sail them. When something is your livelihood, you become great at it. We started building ships right here in the wilderness on Lake Erie. We must get more ships into the water. They have to be strong, swift, and with courageous leaders like you sailing them."

"I am honored, but what is our strategy? I am used to the British blockade on the coast, and I know the Southern waters well, but I have never sailed the Great Lakes."

"Commander Robert Barclay is in charge of the British fleet on Lake Erie. Over the past year, he has lost a huge number of his squadron. He is not receiving reinforcements and supplies from the British as he had hoped. He has over thirty-five long cannons that can shoot up to forty-two-pound shots over distance. We need courageous leaders to get our ships close enough to penetrate his vessels and swift in getting out before being blown to bits."

"Blown to bits?" Conrad swallowed with difficulty. "May I ask, how sturdy are our ships?"

"We have more ships, but they are lightly built with short-range cannons. Our hulls are only two inches and cannot withstand a cannon blast from one of Barclay's ships. In fact, even a musket shot could penetrate it."

"I see." Conrad rubbed the aching muscles in the back of his neck. What had he signed on to do? It sounded like a death sentence. He should have asked more questions, but what choice did he have? If the U.S. Navy wanted to order him to do something, he had to follow orders or face a dishonorable court martial. He looked up at his superior officer. "How much time do I have before I am expected to join the USS *Larkspur*?"

"One week."

Some parts of the Durham House reminded Charlotte of the MacGregor Quest at home. The furniture here was a little more elegant, which surprised her for a place out in the middle of the wilderness. While Commodore Evans and Conrad were in the study discussing war, David took his son outside to explore the grounds. She and Mildred remained inside conversing with Mrs. Evans in the parlor. Ashlynn had finally fallen asleep in Charlotte's arms. She longed to unpack their wagon. Bending her elbow where she cradled Ashlynn's sweet head made her arm ache, and she would have loved to lay her down in the safety of her bassinet.

"You will enjoy church on Sundays. We have a young pastor who arrived here about six months ago, and he is a bachelor. Since we have more sailors in the area than anything else, eligible women tend to get married off as soon as they reach a marriageable age or catch the eye of some dashing hero," Mrs. Evans said with a rosy glow highlighting her cheeks.

"We have not come here for the purpose of finding husbands," Charlotte said, searching for a polite way to steer the conversation in a different direction without offending this sweet woman who had gone to such lengths to welcome them. "Even though we lost some of our mourning attire on our travels, Mildred is a widow and still grieving over her husband and the loss of her infant son. And I feel my twin sister's loss just as deeply, I assure you. My responsibility is to her children, not a courtship, but I am open to whatever the Lord brings."

"Of course, I never meant any offense. It has only been four months and it is customary for a woman to mourn her husband a least a year. Although I have never thought it fair that a man is not expected to mourn his wife nearly as long. I told my dear Jacob that he had better mourn me as long as I am required to mourn him."

Charlotte exchanged a glance with Mildred. Neither of them knew an appropriate response. She cleared her throat. "Well, as soon as I am able, I intend to go to town and buy some more black material so we can be in mourning for the proper time. I cannot stand the thought of dishonoring the memory of our loved ones."

"Oh, my dear, you should not concern yourself with such sad thoughts." Mrs. Evans turned on the settee and took Charlotte's hands in her own large ones. Her skin was warm, and she wore a motherly expression. Charlotte gulped, missing her own mother. She blinked back the sting of tears hovering close behind her eyes. Mrs. Evans continued, "I realize it is customary to mourn for a sibling for three to six months, but I wish you would at least consider half-mourning. After four months, it is perfectly acceptable for you to attend social outings and to wear other dark-colored gowns." She patted the top of Charlotte's hand. "As loving and caring as you have led me to believe of your sister, she would want you to go out and make friends for yourself and her children. She would not want you to remain sad and depressed."

Charlotte didn't say anything but managed to nod. It was true. Her sister would agree. It was as if she could hear Emma's voice in her head telling her the same thing.

"Good." Mrs. Evans let go of her hand and turned back to the front. "Now we have that settled, I wanted to tell you about a few stores in town. If you turn down the street beside the corner where they are building the post office, there is a mercantile store, a general store, Dr. Long's office, and Mercy Community Church is at the end of the road. Pastor Luke Shaw lives in the small gray house beside the church."

"If the post office is not yet built, how will I send letters to my family?" Charlotte asked.

"We have a courier who arrives on Wednesdays to deliver and collect mail from folks. Until the post office is built, he will continue to make deliveries, but afterward, you will need to come into town to pick up your mail."

"How do you correspond with your husband when he is aboard ship on the lake? What if I have an emergency concerning one of the children, how do I reach Conrad and David?" Charlotte linked her fingers in her lap as she waited for a response.

She tilted her head with a sad expression. "Well, sometimes I go for weeks without hearing from him. At times, they send a rowboat to shore for supplies and it often contains letters. There have been times when I receive letters from a courier from neighboring towns around Lake Erie such as Toledo, Euclid, Fairport Harbor, and Erie itself where the ships are being built. Most of them come from Erie. They are a larger town, have more supplies, and sailors can exchange posts with those on land for a period of time."

"It sounds so different from Wilmington," Mildred said. "Sometimes I could go for months without hearing from my husband. It was so hard on my nerves, especially when I read news of a battle close to where his last letter might have been posted."

"For those of us who are left behind, we women have a support group and we meet each Thursday to pray and encourage one another. We share news, exchange clothes for our little ones who have grown out of clothing, and sew things for the sailors."

"It sounds like a wonderful opportunity. Are there any other widows in it?" Mildred asked.

"Yes, two are widows and you will be the third. There are three unmarried daughters. Charlotte, you will be the fourth in this group who has never been married. The rest are either married to sailors or mothers of young sailors." Mrs. Evans leaned forward and touched Mildred's arm on her right and Charlotte's arm on the left. "I have decided I will host a special dinner to introduce you both to our friends. If any of them have their husbands, sons, or brothers at home for a short visit, we will extend an invitation to them as well. Time is precious when their men are home, and they are more likely to attend if they do not have to leave them at home."

"Mrs. Evans, you do not have to do such a thing. Mildred and I can visit during one of your regular meetings," Charlotte said, her stomach fluttering at the thought of meeting so many new people so soon. She would not even have time to make a decent gown by then.

"Nonsense, I want to do this for you. Trust me, it will be fun."

Conrad stood on the narrow strip of the sandy shore at Lake Erie. He had never seen a lake where he couldn't see the other side of the shore. The fact small waves continued to lap against the rocks nestled in the sand at his feet surprised him. Granted, these weren't the large, white foamy waves he was used to at the ocean, but it was better than still water. He would miss the salty sea and the smell of it in the air. Perhaps once out in the middle of the lake where no land could be sighted, he would no longer feel landlocked.

Once Commodore Evans and his wife departed, Charlotte cornered Conrad and asked when he would be leaving, but he managed to avoid answering. He wasn't ready to talk about it yet. First, he wanted to discuss the details with David. They had a lot of unpacking to do, supplies needed to be bought, and there were safety details he wanted to address with Charlotte and Mildred.

What if neither he nor David returned? For the first time in his life, Conrad felt a real burden for those he would be leaving behind. No one had depended on him this much. Now, everything had changed. Charlotte wasn't the only one whose life had changed; so had his, and unlike before, he liked the idea of being needed—being missed.

"Uncle Conrad!" Davie ran through the yard and down the bank toward him. "Daddy said he would teach me how to swim when I get a little older."

"What a great idea." He held out his hand. When Davie reached him, he slipped his small hand into Conrad's. "Your dad learned to swim when he was about seven and I was nine. Our father taught us how to swim at the same time."

"Ashlynn and I cannot learn at the same time, because she is too young. Right, Uncle Conrad?"

"Right, Davie." Conrad squeezed his hand and swung it back and forth. "Perhaps Charlotte can teach her when she gets older."

"Because she is a girl?" He looked up at Conrad with wide, brown eyes.

"Maybe." Conrad chuckled and brushed the brown hair off his forehead. "By then you might be old enough to teach her yourself. You are five years older than Ashlynn, and she will look up to you."

"I am her big brother," he said with excitement, bobbing his head up and down. "I should be the one to teach her."

"Listen, Davie, I do not want you near the water if no adult is with you. Will you promise me?" Conrad looked out over the water and searched for a sign of a British or American ship. The entire scene displayed a peaceful and radiant setting as the afternoon sun began to fall, giving the moon its night of glory. Appearances were not always what they seemed. Somewhere lurking out there on the water was a brewing battle. Conrad bent and met his nephew's gaze. "Promise?"

"Yes." He nodded. "Will you take me fishing before you go?"

"I am sorry, but the lake is not safe right now. You cannot see them, but there are battleships out there and angry men who dislike Americans. You cannot trust them."

"You mean the British?" He gave Conrad a questioning look. "But you are a captain. You can fight them. It is your job."

"True, but even as a captain, I am only one man. I cannot fight a whole crew of men by myself." Conrad pointed to his head. "Sometimes fighting is not using our muscle or our weapons, but our brains. If I were to wait and attack them with my whole crew, I would have a better chance of beating them. Do you understand?"

"I think so, but you would not be alone. Daddy and I would fight with you."

Conrad's heart constricted at the thought of anything happening to Davie if he tried to be a hero. How could he make the lad see the danger around him without scaring him and wounding his courage? He gripped Davie's shoulders to ensure his attention. "Even the three of us would not be enough against so many men. If the enemy comes to the house, I want you, Aunt Charlotte, Mildred, and Ashlynn to escape into the woods and seek help from the neighbors. If you do not have time to escape into the woods, lock yourself in the cellar and hide."

"But I do not want to be a coward and hide." Confusion swam in his dark eyes.

"Davie, cowards are people who hide and do naught. Heroes are people who are smart enough to hide when they are outnumbered and have no weapons and live to fight another day when they do have help and better weapons." Conrad gave him a gentle shake by the shoulders. "Do you understand?"

"Now I do." Davie grinned. "Soldiers and sailors have to be smart, so they do not die and they can keep fighting."

"Something like that." Conrad chuckled, balling his fist up and holding it out. Davie balled his own small fist and punched his knuckles with a laugh.

"Davie! Conrad! Dinner is ready." Charlotte called from the house.

Conrad licked his lips and rubbed his belly. "Are you ready for some good food?"

"Yeah! I am tired of beef jerky." Davie ran off toward the house.

Conrad strode behind him, watching Charlotte stand on the small front porch and wrap her brown shawl tight around her. She greeted Davie with a smile and ushered him inside but paused at the threshold, looking back and waiting for Conrad. A pensive expression crossed her face. She leaned against the door frame as he climbed the two steps and paused in front of her.

"We need to talk," he said, noticing the rosy glow in her cheeks from where she had been in the hot kitchen cooking. He would have to hire a cook and manservant for them. He didn't want her and Mildred straining to accomplish certain labors while he and David were gone.

"Yes, I know." Her lips curled. "I have been wondering if your visit with Commodore Evans was as entertaining as ours with his wife. It sounds as if she has grand plans for us, and we will all be married off to new spouses by the end of the year, including you."

For once, her green eyes were not blazing at him in anger, but endearing and light-hearted. He wished their time together was like this more often. They could have been close friends, supporting each other through the hard times, and trusting each other to be honest about their faults even when it hurt, rather than baiting and attacking each other.

"Our orders are to leave in a week. I will be commanding the USS *Larkspur*."

"So soon?" Her eyes widened in surprise as she straightened and moved away from the door frame, stepping closer. "I had hoped you and David would be allowed to stay another fortnight while we settle in the new house."

"Me, too." A moment of silence passed between them. Could she feel the connection between them as strong as he? Or had she shut him out of her heart and mind, determined to leave him behind—in the past? He had been a young fool, and now he wasn't sure what he was—a family man or a career man. The idea of marriage was no longer as repulsive as it once was, but the thought of it still squeezed the breath of life out of him. He clamped down on his runaway thoughts and cleared his throat. "We need to discuss your safety and some backup plans if the British were to come to the house." He glanced at the beautiful water mirroring the setting sun like a glowing fountain. "I dislike the house being so close to the lake."

"Well, in the absence of a war, I think it is perfect." She stepped around him and strode to the edge of the porch, looking out over the magnificent view. "In fact, this is exactly what I would have dreamed of if I were starting a new family—a home right on the water."

"No," he chuckled, "it would be a ship at sea."

"Indeed." She nodded, not disagreeing with him. "But this would be the next best thing."

He didn't say it, but he agreed. The only thing missing was a larger front porch so they could set out two rocking chairs, one for him and one for her. Conrad shook his head and rubbed his tired eyes. What was he doing imagining such things?

"I want to go to the store tomorrow to buy supplies and get some black material to make some mourning gowns," she said.

"I wish you would not."

"What do you mean?" She whirled, lifting a blond eyebrow in confusion. "We need supplies."

He walked closer, set his elbow against the round pillar, and leaned over her. "Supplies are fine, but I wish you would not make more black gowns. I would like to see you happy and in bright colors again—at least before I go."

"You sound like Mrs. Evans." She crossed her arms and rolled her eyes. "Mildred is in mourning for a whole year since she lost her husband. She is in need of more gowns. As for me, I have agreed to start wearing a bit of color. I need a few new gowns as well. Mrs. Evans is throwing a dinner party for us in a week."

"I thought you disliked such events." He crossed his booted feet at the ankles, wondering if he and David would still be around to escort them.

"Not when they are in my honor." She grinned, and just as fast, her smile faded. "Besides, I am lonely and would like to make new friends." She took a deep breath. "Perhaps it is because I am so far away from my family or I miss Emma so much, but I am lonely. After a while, a person grows weary of being lonely."

14

It had been so long since Charlotte shopped in town. Excitement spiraled through her as she sat on the wagon seat next to Conrad. Mildred and David had stayed behind with the children so she intended to take her time once they reached Cleaveland. The morning weather was cool, but not so much it stung her nose and toes. She gathered her brown shawl tight over her charcoal gown. The black bonnet on her head blocked the sun out of her eyes, but she disliked the itchy ties under her chin.

"What did you mean yesterday when you said you are lonely?" Conrad broke the silence. "You have been surrounded by people since we left Wilmington. I daresay, between the children, Mildred, David, and myself, I doubt you have had a moment of peace to yourself."

"True, but it is not the kind of loneliness I meant. What I was referring to is the kind of connection and friendship my sister and I had. She understood me, and I could tell her anything without feeling judged or criticized by her. Even if she disliked my thoughts or something I had done, I knew I still had her unconditional love and friendship."

"You sound as if you are describing an ideal marriage." His dry tone made her wonder if he believed no such thing existed.

"I suppose I am." She laughed, thinking back to how Emma had described her marriage to David. "If Emma's feelings about her marriage are any indication, then it is how I would imagine it to be. I must admit things changed after she married. While we were still twins, devoted and loyal to each other, she now had this personal relationship with David she couldn't share with me. I suppose my loneliness started then. You and I ended our courtship and you went off to sea." She shrugged and lifted her palms up. "So I have been feeling this way for a while, but her death has deepened it even more."

"I am sorry. I did not realize . . ."

"No need." She waved a hand, dismissing his unspoken words. "Let us talk about something more cheerful. Will you and David still be here to attend Mrs. Evans's dinner party?"

"I intend to ask," he said, adjusting the gold lace-bound high-cocked hat on his head. It was complete with tassels on the side, a loop, silk cockade, and buttons. As much as she always resented Conrad's devotion to his military career, she could not deny how handsome he looked in his uniform. Charlotte looked away, determined not to allow herself to fall for him again. He would only end up breaking her heart, and with her recent grief, she wasn't sure her heart could take it this time.

"Good. You both deserve a little enjoyment before you go." She looked out at the trees as they passed down the lane. "And do not forget to write to us. The courier may only come on Wednesdays, but Mrs. Evans said her husband often sends a rowboat to shore with a stack of letters if they are near the shore. It is my understanding most of the letters come from couriers in the town of Erie, north of here."

"I will. Perhaps some of my letters will make you feel less lonely." He grinned, giving her a sideways glance.

"I doubt it." A dull ache lingered in her heart as memories from years ago crept into her current reality. She had waited for the courier, hoping and praying for a letter from Conrad, only to be disappointed when none came. "A letter is hardly a decent substitute for the absent person, but I still want news of you and David. Your nephew will be wondering about you both, and I would like to tell him the two of you are fine."

They came to the site where the post office would soon be built.

"Mrs. Evans said to turn down this street." Charlotte pointed left on Main Street. Conrad followed her directions until she gestured toward a brick building on the right. "Stop here at Grady's General Store."

"I am going to the Carriage House across the street," Conrad said as he set the brake.

"But why?" Charlotte scooted to the edge of the bench, preparing to climb down. "The wagon is fine."

Conrad leaped down and hurried to the other side, offering her his hand. "Not for Sunday trips to church. You and the children need a proper carriage—something to protect you from the rain and cold wind during the winter."

"You can be full of surprises, Conrad." She paused, looking at his hand.

"Are you referring to me helping you down or being thoughtful enough to even consider a carriage?" He lifted an eyebrow and met her gaze.

"Both." She placed her hand in his, trying to ignore the flutters in her stomach as he closed his warm fingers around hers. The strength in his arms as he assisted her was hard to ignore. She concentrated on the green sign with yellow letters in front of them. As soon as her feet touched the ground, Conrad pulled her close and leaned down at her ear.

"I have always been a gentleman," he whispered. "You cannot deny it."

"No, I cannot, but then you always ran off like a dandy." She jerked her hand away and stomped across the dirt road and stepped inside the store. The bell above the door rang to announce her arrival.

"Welcome!" A woman who looked to be in her early thirties called from behind a long counter. She had a stack of shirts she folded. She paused to glance up and smiled at the sight of Charlotte. "You must be new to town. My name is Pamela Grady. How may I help you?"

"I am on my fourth month of mourning for my sister, and my friend has eight more months for her husband. I brought her measurements, if you have a seamstress here in the store. If not, I shall hope I can find the time to sew a decent gown before Mrs. Evans's dinner party next week."

"We do have a seamstress. My sister is Miss Henrietta Falkirk, and she is in back working on a gown for another young lady here in town. I will take your friend's measurements." She held out her hand. Charlotte handed her the piece of paper, noticing the blue floral print dress she wore and the dark blue shawl. "What is your friend's name?"

"Mrs. Mildred Wolfe. We will both need warm cloaks. I imagine the winters here are much colder than we are used to in Wilmington." She glanced over at a table full of wool scarves, gloves, and hats.

"I am sure we can help you both. Will you be in half-mourning then?" Mrs. Grady asked.

"Yes, I promised Mrs. Evans I would make an attempt to discard my dreary wardrobe and attend her dinner party in dark colors."

The door opened and the bell rang. In walked a man wearing a black flat top hat and a sensible short waistcoat of the same color. He had light brown hair combed in waves, hazel eyes, and a long thin face with sideburns. Tipping his hat to Mrs. Grady, he bowed his head with a smile of greeting. His gaze slid over to Charlotte where he paused with interest.

"Good morning, Pastor." Mrs. Grady held out her hand toward Charlotte. "I would like to introduce our latest arrival, Miss Charlotte Morgan of Wilmington." She gestured to the pastor. "And this is Pastor Luke Shaw of Mercy Community Church at the end of Main Street."

"A pleasure to meet you." He strode forward and took her hand as she dipped into a polite curtsy. He bowed and bent to kiss the top of her fingers. Charlotte could feel herself blushing and forced herself not to pull back.

"Thank you," she said, as he held her hand a little longer than necessary, but finally released it with a handsome grin. Unsure of what else to do, she turned to rambling. "We have been traveling for a long time, but I am looking forward to attending services on Sunday. I know it will be a nice change for my nephew as well. I would like for him to meet some other boys his age."

"And how old is he?" Pastor Shaw tilted his head as he searched her face. She wondered what he thought of her. In truth, he did not look like any pastor she had ever seen. He was too young, tall, and handsome. "Is he in your charge?"

"He is five, and yes, my sister died in childbirth with his baby sister. Their father will soon take his place on board a ship somewhere on Lake Erie."

"Then it is a blessing they will have you to care for them," he said, his voice a silken timbre.

"I hope so, for I have never before been a mother. I am trying my best."

"It is in circumstances like yours the Lord will use us most. Take heart, Miss Morgan, you are not alone on this mission." He awarded her with an encouraging smile and glanced over at Mrs. Grady. "I will leave you two to finish your discussion, while I pick up a few things."

As he walked away, Mrs. Grady leaned forward on her elbows across the counter. "Is he not a handsome man? He is one of the few around here young enough not to need a walking cane, in no danger of a war, and morals to guarantee his future wife will never have to go fish him out of a house of ill-repute."

Stunned, Charlotte glanced up at her new friend and laughed. "I have never quite thought of a pastor in that way."

Conrad picked up his ax and swung at the wood, splitting it in half. He had been chopping wood for over an hour. While the early August air was much cooler here in Cleaveland than in Wilmington, he had already broken out in a sweat. David took the wagon to a neighbor's house to buy a few chickens.

Their next purchase would be a cow. If he could get a good price, he would consider a few hogs as well. Charlotte insisted she didn't want to have to take care of them. He planned to leave the two horses for her. He and David had no need for horses on board a ship. Each morning when he woke, he tried to think of things he should take care of before they left. The days were passing by quickly, and he feared he would forget something.

Charlotte carried a bucket of water toward him. A bit of it sloshed out onto her apron, but she paid it no mind as she charged forward. Sometimes she reminded him of a bull when she got something into her head and refused to let it go. Of late, she had been amiable, which concerned him. Why wasn't she working on something to irritate him? Now they were getting along so well, he didn't want to leave. Usually, he couldn't wait to get back on a ship, but this time things were different. He was content to watch the lake from the house.

"You have been working so hard, I thought you could use a drink of water." Charlotte set down the bucket, dipped the ladle, and handed it to him.

His hand brushed against hers as he accepted it. He met her gaze as he allowed the water to wash his thirst away. The way her green eyes glinted in the sun and her blond strands blew around her smooth face made her look like a portrait on a landscaped canvas. "When I finish this, we can work on your shooting. I imagine it has been quite some time since you did any target practice. I merely want you to be prepared if anything happens while we are away."

"Conrad, what has gotten into you?" She laughed and changed her stance as she shaded her eyes. "My mother was known all around Wilmington as the War Woman. Do you honestly believe she would allow me to grow up without knowing how to shoot a gun? Just let me know which guns you are leaving behind and make sure I have some ammunition. We will be fine. You were never this concerned before when you went off to sea."

"I never left you alone before. You always had a large family around you with plenty of protection and support." He brushed Charlotte's hair behind her ear. He dipped the ladle and drank more water. "Things are different now. And besides, I promised your father I would take care of you. I have written him a letter, updating him on our progress. I plan to give it to the courier this Wednesday."

"I will write him. He should not have asked such a thing of you, and I will tell him so in my next letter." Her brow furrowed and her lips frowned, causing a dimple in her chin. "He knows how you dislike this kind of responsibility. I am not your burden, Conrad Deaton, so whatever you promised him, just forget about it." Her voice hardened.

The sound of a horse riding toward them caught their attention, and both of them turned. "Who could it be?" he asked as the rider cantered toward them at a steady pace.

"It looks like . . ." Charlotte stepped forward as a slow smile crossed her face. "The pastor." Unexpected excitement filled her tone, alerting Conrad to an unexpected change in her behavior. All the tension in her body faded.

"The one you told me you had met in the general store?" Conrad asked.

"Yes." She wiped her hands on her apron. "I wonder what brought him out here?" She whirled, straightening her gown beneath her apron, and brushed the tendrils of hair around her face. "I wish I had known he was coming. Do I look all right?"

Conrad felt like someone had hit him in the gut with a cannonball. Charlotte was not a vain woman. She had never cared about her looks. Why now? She didn't wait for Conrad to respond as she turned with a bright smile and walked toward the pastor as he slowed his mount. The man dismounted with elegant grace and met Conrad's height of six feet two. He wore black breeches and hose with a white shirt and a short black waist jacket. His eyes never left Charlotte's, and the air in Conrad's chest seemed to thin all of sudden. She had told him about meeting the pastor, but she had conveniently left out his age, his looks, and her obvious attraction to him.

The pastor bowed and kissed the top of her knuckles. Color blossomed in Charlotte's cheeks. The only time Conrad could recall seeing her blush was when she was profusely angry at him. This was different. It was a blush of pleasure. Unexpected pain sliced through his heart with a silent echo over and over. How could he ever hope to compete with a godly man? Against another military man or a tradesman, Conrad had no doubt he could win Charlotte's heart back. He knew the thoughts of those kind of men and could anticipate where they would mess up before they even knew it themselves, but a pastor was a different matter entirely.

Confusion clouded his judgment as he tried to reason with himself. He had spent several years building his career in the navy. Did he want to change things now? Plenty of other officers had wives. Had he misjudged Charlotte? He thought she would never leave her beloved Wilmington and twin sister. Emma was gone, and yet, here she was in Cleaveland without any of the MacGregors or Morgans. She had committed to caring and loving the Deaton children, her sister's children. How much more loyal would she be to her own husband and children?

"I would like to introduce you to Captain Conrad Deaton. He will be commanding the USS *Larkspur.* Conrad was my twin's brother-in-law." She led the pastor over to Conrad and motioned to him. "This is Pastor Luke Shaw."

"A pleasure to meet you, sir." Pastor Shaw extended his hand. "It is always an honor to meet those who are serving our country. After meeting Miss Morgan yesterday, I wanted to stop by and meet the rest of the family, especially the little nephew she told me about." He grinned. "I hope you and your brother will have a chance to worship with us at Mercy Community Church before you depart."

"We will try to make it." Conrad nodded, hoping to keep his promise.

"Even if the men do not make it this Sunday, Mildred and I will be bringing the children," Charlotte said.

"Oh, you remind me." The pastor pulled out an envelope from his inside pocket. "This is from Mrs. Evans. I promised

I would deliver it safely. It is an invitation to her dinner party next Tuesday."

"Will you be there?" Charlotte asked.

"I will. Commodore Evans delivered my invitation yesterday evening," the pastor said.

"Conrad, I will take Pastor Shaw to the house and introduce him to the others."

He didn't bother responding as the pastor took his horse's reins and held out his elbow to Charlotte. With her bright smile feeling like a punch in Conrad's side, she slipped her arm through the pastor's and the two of them sidled off toward the house.

Conrad watched them go as he fought the urge to keep from being sick on his stomach.

Even though his visit was unexpected, Charlotte enjoyed having Pastor Shaw stay for dinner. He had an endearing way with Davie, and even David seemed to warm up to him. Conrad was the only one who hung back with an unusual reserve she didn't understand. Pastor Shaw was amiable, humorous, and didn't bother trying to preach sermons at them. She wondered if he stopped to welcome all the new neighbors to the community. Either way, she hoped he would stop by again in the near future.

David brought the pastor's horse from the stables and held out his hand to the pastor. They shook hands. David handed over the reins. The pastor mounted his horse and waved to them.

"David and Conrad, I want you both to rest assured in knowing that while you are away, I will stop by often to check on Charlotte, Mildred, and the kids."

"We appreciate it," David said, nodding.

Conrad didn't respond.

Pastor Shaw's gaze met hers, and she could feel herself blush. It was at least the tenth time today, but she couldn't help it. He was a charming and handsome man. He would never be Captain Conrad Deaton, but she would just have to be content with the knowledge Conrad didn't want her. He wanted his career. She wasn't looking for a husband, but if the Lord brought her a kindhearted and decent man, she would not complain, and she would make the most of it. Such a man would be a gift, and she would do everything in her power to cherish and love him and forget Conrad.

"Charlotte, he seems to be taken with you, and I would be surprised if he did not ask if he could court you soon." Mildred touched David's arm. "Do you not agree?"

"I do." David nodded, holding out his hand to Davie, who ran over and slipped his tiny hand into his father's. "He reminds me of me when I first met Emma. And of course, each time I look at you, Charlotte, I am still reminded of her."

"You all are teasing me." Charlotte waved a hand in the air to dismiss them. She couldn't help smiling though. It felt wonderful to receive compliments and for someone to look at her as if she were beautiful for being herself and not looking like her dead sister. No one here in Cleaveland knew Emma, and as much as she loved and cherished her twin, it was nice to escape the comparisons. "Although he is handsome and nice, I imagine he comes by to meet all the new families in the area to extend a personal invitation to attend church."

"Time will soon tell. I have witnessed enough courting couples to sense the difference." Mildred grinned at her as she carried Ashlynn. "I will be going to my chamber to feed the baby."

"So you think he is handsome?" Conrad asked, looking at Charlotte.

"I do." Charlotte smiled. "Did you happen to notice he has hazel eyes just like you?"

"No, I do not spend a lot of time looking into my eyes," he snapped. "Or the eyes of other men either."

Realizing how silly her question must have sounded, Charlotte covered a hand over her mouth and laughed. "I suppose not."

"Conrad is my brother, and I did not even notice it," David said, leaning around as if trying to peer into Conrad's eyes.

"Get away from me!" Conrad shoved David, who laughed even harder.

"Women notice details you men often miss," Mildred said, glancing behind her.

"I am going to be a handsome man when I grow up," Davie said, puffing out his chest with a wide grin.

"You will, indeed." Charlotte bent toward him and kissed the top of his head. "You are already a handsome lad, so it is only natural."

"Let us change the subject," Conrad said, a look of disgust on his face. "Tomorrow the courier will be coming. If you have a letter to mail, drop it on the table in the foyer." He touched Charlotte on the shoulder to gain her attention. "I plan to hire a cook and a manservant before we leave. We do not have time to advertise, so I thought we would call on Mrs. Evans tomorrow and inquire if she knows anyone she would recommend. Would you be willing to go with me?"

"Indeed. I think I would enjoy a visit with her. I wonder how many invitations she sent out for the dinner party? And you could ask Commodore Evans if you and David will be allowed to stay long enough to attend." Charlotte longed to grab his arm and walk with him as she used to do but refrained, linking her fingers behind her. "I shall go write letters to my family. I need to ask my father why he asked you to take care of me as if I cannot take care of myself."

"Charlotte, on his behalf, I can honestly tell you he was upset and grieving over Emma," Conrad said. "His concern was for your state of mind since his own was so distressed. Please, do not be so hard on him. You do not want to cause a long-distance argument. Time is too short and precious."

"Since when did you become so philosophical?" Charlotte paused and crossed her arms. She stared up into his hazel eyes as he stopped and faced her. She tried not to feel anything, but her aching heart betrayed her as it always had where Conrad was concerned. Hardening her resolve, she mustered the courage she needed to send him away. "Conrad, I commend you on getting us here safely, but now we are here, you will be gone in a few days just like usual. You will not be around to take care of any problems arising in your absence." She pressed a hand against his chest and could feel his fast-beating heart. "I must admit this time you seem more concerned at leaving me than usual, but I can only assume it is because of your niece and nephew. We will be fine. You have never bothered to worry before, so there is no need to start now."

"I am going to take Davie inside," David said, moving past them and joining Mildred.

"You cannot mean it." Conrad blinked at her, his face turning pale even as dusk fell around them. "I realize I do not deserve your trust, but give me some credit."

"I did. I gave you credit for getting us here safely. Now, I would never dream of keeping you from your precious ship. The sooner you depart, the better we will both be. You will be back on the water, and I will continue making a life here."

"I will win you back," he growled between his teeth.

"Why?" She shook her head in confusion and tilted her neck to look up at him. "Why would you want to win me back when the very idea goes against your principles and all you have strived to gain in the navy?" Charlotte stepped away from him. "No, I am only a challenge to you right now. You like the adventure of a challenge. The moment you win, your interest will fade." She pointed to her chest. "I am not a game, Conrad. I am a person with feelings—feelings you have no respect for."

"Charlotte, you said you have changed." He pressed a hand over his chest. "Well, I have changed as well. I am not the same man I was six years ago. You have to believe me."

"That is the interesting part, Conrad." She scratched her temple and took a deep breath, backing away from him. "I do not have to believe you."

15

The knowledge of Charlotte's resentment ate at Conrad like a shark devouring its prey. He recognized the fact he had brought this entire situation on himself, but he didn't know what to do about it. All he could do was get up the next morning, break his fast, and take her to Mrs. Evans's as he had promised. The trip into town was tense and silent. Charlotte was cordial but only spoke to him when it was impossible to avoid him. She knew how he felt, but she didn't trust him. What could he say to change her mind about their past?

One piece of news he was thankful to learn was that he and David would be allowed to attend the dinner party Mrs. Evans planned to host. They would leave the following morning.

Mrs. Evans recommended two people as a cook and three men as manservants. They visited the cooks first and struck a bargain with a Mrs. Cooper. She had gray hair and appeared to be in her late forties. With a deceased husband and four grown children, she was eager to accept a position providing stable housing.

By the end of the day, they chose Mr. Porter as their new manservant. For an elderly man in his late fifties, he was in good health and still robust enough to chop wood, hitch the horses to the wagon and carriage, and go into town for supplies and errands. Conrad felt better knowing a man would be around the house to assist the women with the harder tasks and provide a bit of protection if needed.

After dinner, Charlotte, Mildred, and the children retired to the parlor. David went to his chamber, and Conrad took refuge in the study. Most of his business transactions were complete. Conrad grabbed a copy of *The Swiss Family Robinson* novel and thumbed to the third chapter where he had creased a corner of the page to mark his spot. With his love of the sea, a novel about a family shipwrecked on an island would relax and entertain him for a while.

He read until he could no longer keep his eyes open. Rubbing his eyes, he closed the book and stood. Conrad grabbed the lantern to climb the stairs to his chamber. The rest of the house was quiet, and so he assumed everyone else had gone to bed. The stairs creaked under his steps. Once he reached the landing, Conrad tried to keep his boots from making too much noise as he strode by his brother's chamber. A dim light filtered into the dark hallway.

Curious to know if David had fallen asleep with a candle burning, Conrad stepped closer and pushed the door wider. David sat on the other side of the bed with his back to Conrad. Hunched over with his elbows on his knees, Conrad could not tell if he bowed his head in prayer or was reading. Conrad walked inside, knowing his footsteps would announce his presence. David did not move.

"David?"

Silent tears crawled down his brother's face as he clutched a gown that must have belonged to Emma. A single candle burned on the table in front of him where a miniature portrait of Emma was displayed in a frame. It was the same image Charlotte had given David on the ship. A lock of blonde hair lay in the crease of a Bible open on the table. Beside it were Emma's hair combs, a brush, and pieces of jewelry.

"I was just walking by when I saw the light in your chamber and wondered if you had fallen asleep with a burning candle."

"You are intruding, Conrad. This is my private time to remember and cherish her." David wiped his face and took a deep breath as he ran a hand through his brown hair. "Some things were never meant to be witnessed by anyone else."

A surge of compassion shot through Conrad, followed by a blast of anger twirling inside him. He expected David's grief to linger, but not a corner of his chamber decorated with her personal things as if he had built a shrine in her memory.

"How do you expect to get over her if you come in here each night and wallow in your self-pity and smother yourself in her things?" Conrad scoffed in disgust. He stomped forward and jerked Emma's gown out of David's hands before his brother had time to realize his intention. Conrad held it up in his hand, shaking it for emphasis. "Where did you get this? I did not see any of Emma's gowns in the trunks you and I packed."

David stood with his fists clenched at his side, his breath coming out in puffs as his anger rose. "Conrad, I put up with your bossy attitude on the *Victorious* out of respect to you as the captain, but coming in my private chamber and making demands on how I grieve over my dead wife is where it ends. You do not know how I feel, so you cannot possibly understand. In fact, you have never had a wife." David pointed at him. "Judging by the way you treat women after you decide you are finished courting, I doubt you have ever cared for anyone the way I cared for Emma, much less loved them. You, dear brother, are not qualified to judge me, so I would appreciate it if you would stay out of my affairs. Now hand it over." David extended his palm and crooked his fingers.

"Gladly," Conrad held the garment out, but when David reached for it, he snatched it back. "But first, tell me, did Charlotte give this to you like she did the miniature portrait?" He pointed at the image on the table.

"Yes, and she has done no wrong, so leave her alone."

"It is for me to decide." Conrad threw the gown at David.

"You are not her father." David shook out the material where it had been wadded up in a ball. His mouth twisted in dissatisfaction. "I heard what Charlotte said to you earlier. If you still have any interest in her like you once did, this is not the way to win her heart." David shrugged and tilted his head. "Looks like you might have some competition for the first time in your life—real competition."

"I do not know what I want when it comes to Charlotte. She confuses me." Conrad let the truthful words tumble from his jumbled thoughts.

"Do not take too long. Time is short, and you may not have as much of it as you think." David ran a hand through his hair. "Look at what happened to Emma and me."

"I appreciate the advice." Conrad pointed to the gown. "But what was the purpose in giving you Emma's clothing? You cannot wear it." Conrad scratched his temple in confusion and paced around the narrow bed. "It is almost as if she is determined to rip open your grief each time you make a bit of progress."

"You make too much of her intentions, Conrad," David said, sitting back on the bed. It creaked under his weight. "When she gave it to me, she asked me to save it for Ashlynn. She thought Ashlynn might one day want to own a gown worn by her mother—a mother she will never have the chance of knowing."

"It sounds like a noble cause, but I know Charlotte." Conrad shook his head in denial. He would not believe her intentions were innocent. "I believe she is afraid you will forget her sister. It is Charlotte's morbid way of keeping the memory of her twin alive." He took angry strides toward the door. "Good night, David."

Conrad reached Charlotte's door, but it was closed. If he knocked, it would give her time to think of a reason to reject him. He listened, but all he heard was silence. Gripping the knob, Conrad swung the door open. It let out a low moan, but not loud enough to arouse her. She lay in her bed with her blond hair fanned out on her pillow, facing the window. Enough silvery light from the moon cast a faint glow on her. She looked so peaceful his anger evaporated like water turning to steam.

Unable to stop himself, he ventured close enough to lean over her. If she woke right now, she would probably scream with fright or box his ears. "You look like an angel," he whispered. Thoughts of her aiding his brother's grief crossed his mind, but this time he couldn't muster any anger. She probably thought she was helping David cope. "A meddling angel." Conrad lowered himself and pressed his lips against her smooth cheek.

Charlotte stood on a wooden pedestal while the seamstress, Miss Henrietta Falkirk, measured the hem of her dress from the floor up. She tried to keep still as Henrietta inserted the pins in a horizontal row. The last thing she wanted was to be poked.

When Pamela, the shop owner, introduced Henrietta as her sister, Charlotte was struck by how much she reminded Charlotte of her sister, Melanie, at home. The only resemblance she and Pamela shared were blue eyes. Like Melanie she was tall, but thinner and younger, around twenty-five.

"This blue topaz is a beautiful color on you," Henrietta said. "Is it your favorite color?"

"I declare, it should be," Pamela said with a sigh as she leaned against the door frame and folded her arms. While no other customers were in the shop, Pamela stole a moment to sneak into the back room to take a peek at her sister's handiwork. "You look as if you should be going to a ball, not a simple dinner party."

Pleased, Charlotte looked down and rubbed her palms against the smooth silk fabric of blue topaz. The front bodice folded in feather-like layers into a V shape, while the shoulders tapered in pleats to a short-sleeved design. The collar and shoulder caps were accented with piped pieces in a flower petal pattern.

"There, this should do until I can finish the hem this afternoon while you shop." Henrietta pointed to the corner. "Go see it in the looking glass and let me know if you are satisfied."

"I am afraid I will have to depend upon your good opinion." Charlotte shook her head. It was tempting to take a peek, but she couldn't bear seeing herself. Even after four months, it was Emma she saw, not herself, and the pain felt as fresh as the day she had died. She held her arms up with a shy smile and slowly turned. "Will it do?"

"Absolutely!" Pamela said. "I wish my husband was home from the war and we could attend events like this together."

"Will you be going as well?" Charlotte asked, excited she would know someone else there.

"No, I will stay home with my two boys and daughter." She gestured to her sister. "But Henrietta will be there. She is five years my junior and still unmarried. I hope one of these sailors will be inclined to ask for her hand."

"Pamela!" Henrietta blushed, glancing at the floor. "You should not say such things. You know Charles and I have been courting. I shall not look at another man while he is out fighting this war." Her voice dropped to a whisper as she leaned closer to her sister. "It would not be decent. What kind of person would I be? Besides, I love him."

"Nonsense, he has not asked for your hand and made no commitment other than coming to call on you a few times. There is no understanding between you." Pamela straightened to her full height and squared her shoulders. Her lips thinned, and the air around them chilled. "You do not understand the ways of these men and the games they play. I will not allow you to be hurt." The bell on the front door rang. "Please, excuse me."

A moment of awkward silence passed between Charlotte and Henrietta. She sighed and offered Charlotte a slight smile. "Please do not think ill toward my sister. Before marrying her husband, Ben, she fell in love with a gentleman who properly courted her for six months. He asked her to marry him and the banns were read in church. Once they announced their engagement, his visits became less often. Two months later, we discovered he had a mistress and had gotten her with child. My sister was devastated. By the time I was old enough to come out, she became fiercely protective. She means well."

"But she is married now?" Charlotte asked.

"Indeed, to Captain Ben Grady of the USS *Lawrence*. He writes to her as often as possible, but I can tell she gets moody if too many days pass and she has not heard from him. My Charles is under his command as Lieutenant Charles Bradford. He writes to me as often as Ben writes to Pamela and with as much dedication in length and content. We do have an understanding. He did not want to marry me and leave me a widow. When the war is over, he intends to formally ask for my hand in marriage. I have no reason to doubt him. He is not the same man as Pamela's former beau. Do you not agree?"

She motioned for Charlotte to step down and held out her hand to help her.

"I am not qualified to give advice in matters of the heart. I remain unmarried as well and, unlike you, have never even had an understanding like you and Charles." An image of Conrad came to mind, and her heart squeezed in regret. She blinked and swallowed hard, trying to push her past away and out of her mind. "But I can say I do not feel like one man should pay for the sins of another."

"I agree." Henrietta walked behind her. "Now allow me to help you with these buttons so we can get you out of this gown, and I can complete the hem before you go home."

As soon as Charlotte spoke the words, their meaning sank deep into her heart. Conrad was married to his career. It was the love of his life. She had witnessed plenty of other military men who fought in this war, made a career out of the military, but continued to have wives and children. If Conrad refused to have her, there was no reason why she had to suffer being alone for the rest of her life. Men were as different from one another as women were from one another. Was David, Conrad's own brother, not proof of it? At one time, she thought she would never marry if she could not have Conrad, but age and wisdom and a new loneliness from her twin's death had changed her mind—and she was glad of it.

She needed something to look forward to—a purpose in life beyond raising her sister's children. For one day they would grow up and go their own way in the world, and once again she would be left alone. Charlotte smiled, but not if she had a husband for companionship and precious children of her own. She would go to the dinner party Mrs. Evans was kind enough to throw for them and make the best of it—and any other invitations she would be blessed to receive in the near future.

Conrad lathered his face and picked up his razor and paused, staring at the empty space on the wall above his washbasin where a looking glass used to be. He discarded the razor on the table and looked around his chamber to see if the oval mirror had been moved to another wall. With a frustrated sigh, he wiped his sticky hands on a towel and went in search of a looking glass so he could shave.

None of the upstairs chambers had a looking glass. Returning to his chamber, Conrad picked up the razor and resumed shaving. He preferred to see what he was doing, but there were times when he had done without one before, and today would be no different.

When he completed his task, he wiped his hands and face with his towel and went over to open the window to throw out the foamy water. He set the bowl back on the table and looked up at the empty wall. Who would take such a thing from his chamber?

While Mildred and Charlotte had taken the children out on a morning walk, and David went to pick up their newly hired servants, Conrad had the entire house to himself. As he walked down the hallway on the first floor, Conrad paused to study a landscape painting where he thought a mirror had once hung in a gilded frame. Where did it go and where did this painting come from? Something wasn't right. He could not find any other mirrors anywhere in the house.

If the house once had mirrors, then they would have to be somewhere. He had an idea where they would be. Conrad stomped up the stairs, marched to the end of the hall, and pulled down the door to the attic. He grabbed a lantern and lit it before climbing the ladder. With the slanted beams, Conrad had to duck as he crouched and maneuvered around old toys and trunks full of treasured items, and then he saw a stack of frames leaning up against a beam. As he browsed through the paintings, he discovered the missing mirrors. He grabbed the one belonging in his chamber and left the attic, satisfied he had discovered what happened. Now he needed to know who did it and why.

Conrad sat on the front porch with the mirror lying facedown across his lap as Charlotte and Mildred returned from their outing. Davie saw him first as he raced down the drive toward Conrad. His brown eyes were bright with excitement and his grin beaming between two rosy cheeks.

"Uncle Conrad, we saw two baby deer!" Davie reached Conrad at least twelve paces before the others.

"Slow down, Davie." Conrad reached out a hand to catch him before he fell over the steps. "Did you see their mother as well?"

"No." He shook his head.

"I bet she was somewhere nearby. I am surprised you did not see her."

"What if their mama is dead like mine? Who will take care of them?" He tilted his head up at Conrad, his voice full of sincerity.

"Davie, wild animals are different from humans. They have natural instincts to help them to survive." Conrad gripped his thin shoulder. "Trust me, those baby deer will be fine."

"What are you doing out here?" Charlotte asked, a little breathless from their exertion, and shifted Ashlynn to face Conrad.

The baby could hold her head up well now, and her grayish-blue eyes took in all the sights around her. Ashlynn stared down at Conrad and grinned, a dimple forming on one side of her mouth—just like her Aunt Charlotte. Heaven help them if they were to have two Charlottes in the house, a grown

Charlotte and a little Charlotte. He couldn't resist smiling back at his niece and reached out to touch his fingertip on her nose. She giggled and scrunched up her legs and spread her arms wide. This delightful creature had his heart hypnotized.

"Conrad, what do you have in your lap?" Charlotte asked.

"Something I intend to discuss with you." He flipped up the mirror and held it out to her, but she backed away and refused to look at it, glancing down at the ground and around them. "I would like to know why I had to shave without my mirror this morning and why I had to go digging for it in the attic."

"Charlotte, I will take Ashlynn and Davie inside." Mildred moved next to her and held out her hands.

Without a word, Charlotte relinquished the baby to her. She bent and kissed Davie on the top of his head. "Davie, go inside and wash your hands. Mildred will give you a treat. I made some cookies yesterday."

"Yeah!" He ran up the two steps and to the front door. Mildred followed close behind and had to help him with the doorknob.

Once they were out of hearing, Conrad stood and met her gaze, slipping the mirror under his arm. "Charlotte, I care not how you decorate the house, but taking things out of my chamber without asking me is rude. Why would you do such a thing? In fact, why would you go to all the trouble of removing every single looking glass in the entire house and retiring them to the attic? Did it not occur to you the rest of us might like to have them?"

"I am sorry, Conrad, truly I am, but when I go into your chamber to dust and gather your clothes for washing, I cannot stand to see it."

"Why?" He bent forward and leaned the mirror against the porch pillar. Conrad straightened and crossed his arms, determined to get to the bottom of her strange behavior. "And be honest."

"I did not think you might need it for shaving." She shrugged and lifted her head so he could see her eyes beneath the white bonnet she wore. "I could shave you the next time you need it, if the task is too difficult without a mirror."

"It will not be necessary. I intend to hang the mirror back on the wall in my chamber where it belongs." He stepped closer, and she fidgeted with her hands in front of her but didn't back away. "I noticed you replaced the mirror in the hall with a landscape painting. I have never known you to dislike a looking glass. Why is it necessary to remove all of them out of sight? Charlotte, I intend to have an answer."

"I do not have to tell you a thing."

"Should I ask Mildred?" He lifted a brow as he leaned closer. "I am sure this has caused her a bit of inconvenience as well. I have never known a woman to have an aversion to a mirror." He sighed and shook his head, shifting his weight to his other foot. "But, of course, you are no ordinary woman. You never were."

"Go ahead. Insult me. I do not have to tell you." She brushed her hair to the side.

"Why?" He grabbed her wrist. "I will ask Mildred, but I would rather hear it from you. I am concerned about you, Charlotte."

She tried to pull away, but he tightened his grip.

"All right! I despise looking in the mirror at myself because I do not see me. I see Emma. Before she died, I rarely looked into a mirror, except for when I was getting ready for the day or to go somewhere." Tears filled her eyes, but she tried to blink them back as her nose turned red and her voice choked. "Every other moment of my life was spent looking at her while we talked, played, ate meals together, and lived every moment of our lives together. I always felt like a reflection of her, and I know she felt the same way because she told me so." Her voice cracked as the tears slipped over her eyelashes and fell down her face. Charlotte's shoulders shook as grief overcame her and she broke into sobs. "It is so painful when I look at a mirror. And it hurts even more," she sniffled, her voice fading to a whisper, "because I thought time and distance would dull the sting, but it has not."

Conrad pulled her to him and wrapped his arms around her. He wished he could ease her pain, but he couldn't. All he could do was stand here and comfort her and listen if she wanted to keep talking. For too long she had tried to deny her grief, throwing herself into caring for Emma's children and even worrying about David. Conrad had hoped a change in scenery and time away from the rest of her grieving family would help her recover faster, but it had not. What could he do to ease the pain?

She looked up with red and watery eyes. Desire ripped through him. He didn't see Emma, only Charlotte—a strong, caring woman who filled him with longing. She had the courage and passion to stand up against him even when his own soldiers would not. His gaze dropped to her mouth, her parted lips inviting him. Conrad lowered himself, brushing his lips against hers, tasting the salty tears, and enjoying the warmth of her. Charlotte's lips molded against his in a perfect fit.

At first, she didn't resist, but after a few moments, her eyes widened, her mouth twisted, and she pulled back. Conrad tried to pull her close again, reluctant to let her go and end the tantalizing moment. Charlotte jerked away, but he didn't let her. She squirmed and fought him until she managed to free an arm. She swung back and slammed her palm against the side of his face.

"How dare you take advantage of me in a weak moment!"

16

A flood of confusing emotions enveloped Charlotte all at once as she backed away from Conrad. A red handprint slowly emerged on his face. She shook her hand, still feeling the sting digging at the inside of her palm and fingers. If her hand hurt this bad, she imagined his face stung even more. Remorse and satisfaction passed through her in shimmering waves as her thoughts flickered back and forth.

His hazel eyes stared at her until he blinked several times as if trying to understand what had just happened. He stood with his hands by his side and remained calm. Moisture gathered in his eyes, but she couldn't tell if it was due to tears or the residue of the slap she had given him across the face.

"If you expect me to apologize, I will not," he said.

"I have learned to expect naught from you, since you only do what pleases you with no regard to anyone else around you." She rubbed the soreness as the sting dulled to a throbbing ache. "You demanded to know why I removed the mirrors, and I merely tried to give you an honest answer. The fact I am still grieving for my sister is not a new revelation to you. I am disappointed you have so little self-control you would try to take advantage of me in a weak moment. You are many things,

Conrad, but I have always felt like I could trust you as a gentleman, but after today I am not so sure."

"Charlotte, I am sorry for the bad timing, but I am not sorry for wanting to kiss you—to comfort you. These past few months have reawakened the feelings I have always had for you. I thought I had made the right decision in choosing my career six years ago, but now I am having regrets and hoping we could have a second chance. I see how strong you are and how so many other couples have made it. I was wrong, and I want to make amends."

"You made the right decision, Conrad. You would never be happy with anything else other than sailing the high seas and seeking adventure." She took another step back, unable to handle being so near him. "Do not allow your sympathy for my grief to cloud your judgment. So much has happened since then, and as you once pointed out, neither of us are the same people we once were. We cannot go back."

"I do not want to go back." He took a step closer, but she held up her hand, and he paused, as he continued, "I want to move forward from here—in who we are today."

"We are. You will be going to your next ship as the new captain, and I will remain here to help raise the children like I promised my sister I would do." Her gaze dropped to the mirror. "I understand why you want to rehang the mirror in your chamber. Just know I will not be coming in to dust the chamber or gather your clothes for a washing while you remain here."

"Forget the mirror." His tone tightened as it had in the past when he was uncomfortable. He scratched his temple and licked his bottom lip. "I am more concerned about you."

"No need. I shall be fine for now as long as I do not have to look at any mirrors." Her handprint on his face nagged at her conscience. "I am sorry for hitting you."

"I doubt anything else would have gotten my attention." He grinned, now touching the side of his face. "You have always had the ability to lure me into your clutches."

"But I was never strong enough to keep you. I see that now." She swallowed, determined to confess the truth that he pretended to ignore. "In fact, I believe it is good you will be leaving after tomorrow. You will see, once you are back on the ship, you will be where you belong and you will not feel the same. You always were one for getting caught up in the moment."

"Charlotte, you speak nonsense and you know it." He grabbed her shoulders and shook her. "I love you."

"No!" She pushed away from him, shaking her head and wagging a finger at him. "You do not. You are experiencing inflated feelings, and it will pass. If I gave in, you would come to regret it, and I would be the one to pay—rejected again."

As a carriage came up the drive, she turned to shield her eyes from the sun so she could better see it. She walked toward the road. "We have company."

"It is David. He went to pick up our new servants," Conrad said behind her. "I made arrangements for Mrs. Cooper to watch the children so Mildred could attend the dinner party with us."

"That was very thoughtful of you."

The carriage rolled to a stop in front of them. The horses breathed heavily from their journey. David jumped out with a grin as he reached to assist Mrs. Cooper. Her progress was slow for a woman of her age and plump size.

"This conversation is not over, Charlotte," Conrad said.

"I beg to differ." She glanced over her shoulder to see him frowning. "As of now, it is."

Once her feet hit the ground, Mrs. Cooper hurried toward Charlotte, while David continued to hold the carriage door open for Mr. Porter.

"My dear, I am so glad to finally be here. I hear you have a festive evening planned at Mrs. Evans's. If you do not mind, I should like to know all about the menu when you return."

"Of course." Charlotte nodded, taking her round hands in her own. "Are you certain you do not mind watching the children?"

"Not at all." She waved a hand in the air. A faint scent of cinnamon floated in the air behind her. "I can do much more than just cook, you know. It will do me some good to be around spirited children again."

"Well, Ashlynn is still a baby, only four months old, but Davie is five. He will be the spirited one."

"Even better." She patted Charlotte's arm.

"Mr. Porter, it is good to see you again." Charlotte gave a brief curtsy to the elderly man who walked up to them. He dipped his gray head into a slight bow. He was quite tall and still stout. He reminded her of some of the loggers she had known back home in North Carolina.

"Allow me to show you both to your chambers, so you can get settled in," Charlotte said.

"I hope neither of you have any need for a looking glass in your chambers." Conrad said, dropping into a bow in greeting.

Mrs. Cooper laughed. "Dear me, no, I believe I am long past the looking-glass years."

Charlotte glared at Conrad as she turned to lead them into the house.

He gave her a sarcastic grin and mouthed the words, "Not over."

When Charlotte had descended the stairs in the evening, Conrad's throat burned at the sight of her. She wore a new gown he assumed she had purchased in town. It fit her to perfection in a blue topaz silk accentuating her green eyes, almost making them look a different hue. Her golden hair was swept in waves over the crown of her head and fell into wisps around her face like a bright halo.

Charlotte possessed a sweet spirit, a vulnerable grief that called to him. When she smiled, she was all innocence and charm, but Conrad knew her and could feel how deep her pain flowed beneath all the beauty. David stepped forward to take her hand and winked at her. She blushed, waving his attention away.

"You are beautiful, Charlotte." He blinked back tears. "I am sorry, I know you are tired of always being compared to her." He shook his head. "But tonight, looking at you now, I am reminded all over of how beautiful my wife was and you still are."

"I know, David." She touched his cheek. "Why do you think I have removed all the mirrors in the house? I cannot bear to look at myself. I can only imagine how hard it must be for you, and I am sorry."

Conrad cleared his throat and pushed himself forward. "Well, I am not reminded of anyone but you, Charlotte." He held out his hand to her. "You look lovely."

"Thank you." Her clipped tone was not lost on him as she straightened her shoulders, lifted her chin, and strode forward, ignoring his offered hand.

David gave him a questioning look, and Conrad shrugged. In spite of what Charlotte said, he was not yet willing to admit defeat.

Mildred and David kept up a steady stream of chatter on the way to Mrs. Evans's house. Charlotte sat beside Mildred across from Conrad. She looked out the window and avoided his gaze. They arrived outside a tall brick home where Mr. Porter parked the carriage behind others on a circular dirt drive. David opened the door and burst from the carriage, shaking it on the wheels. Another carriage pulled up behind them.

This time when Conrad offered Charlotte his arm to escort her up the brick walkway, she slipped her hand around his elbow but didn't bother to spare him a glance. He accepted the honor, knowing it at least meant she had no intention of embarrassing him in public. Their private exchange and argument would remain just so—private. It was another reason he loved her. Charlotte possessed honest integrity, and all these years he had taken it for granted. How many times could she have spread rumors about him or shared their confidences—especially after he left for the sea.

Two lit lanterns hung on the front porch as they climbed the five steps to the entrance. A servant was at the door greeting guests and waving them inside to the foyer where candles glowed with more light. Charlotte took off her hat and cloak. Conrad took them from her and gave them to a servant. Conversations buzzed around them as they walked across the polished wood floor where guests were directed into the parlor.

A petite woman played an elegant melody on the pianoforte, giving the atmosphere a gentle ambience. Charlotte learned her name was Miss Adelle Fleming.

Commodore Evans and his wife excused themselves from talking to two gentlemen and came over to greet them with welcoming smiles. "I am so glad to see you all have arrived." Mrs. Evans said. "Miss Morgan and Mrs. Wolfe, you both look simply divine. Gentlemen, now you are in the company of ladies, so you are not allowed to discuss the war and politics. Tonight is about meeting people and forming new acquaintances." She glanced at her husband before allowing her gaze to travel from Conrad to David.

"Well, I can assure you I have no intention of discussing such boring topics," David said, leaning forward and lowering his voice as if they shared a secret.

"Indeed." Commodore Evans laughed. "Allow me to get the two of you a drink before dinner is announced. Nothing like a few sips of wine to take the edge off the burden of meeting new people." He turned and disappeared. A couple approached.

"Charlotte, I would like to introduce you to Lieutenant Charles Bradford." A man wearing a naval uniform stood behind a young woman with auburn hair. Conrad learned Henrietta was the seamstress who had made Charlotte's gown. After Charlotte introduced him and Mildred, he discovered Lieutenant Bradford served aboard the USS *Lawrence*.

Commodore Evans returned with two glasses of white wine and two new friends on his heels. He handed a glass each to Conrad and David. Turning to motion to the young men in uniform, he said, "Allow me to introduce two men who will be sailing by your side on the USS *Larkspur*. This is Lieutenant Jack Larson, your second-in-command." He motioned to a gentleman with the same hair color as Charlotte. It was pulled back by a blue ribbon at his neck. His stark blue eyes matched his dark blue uniform. "And this is Sergeant Kevin Gallagher, also an officer aboard the USS *Larkspur*." He gestured to the tall man on his other side with short, curly brown hair and dark eyes.

Once all the introductions were made, Jack struck up a conversation with Charlotte regarding the winter weather on the lake. While Conrad tried to concentrate on Commodore Evans's description of his ship, Pastor Luke Shaw arrived. Conrad was introduced to two more young ladies before dinner was announced. He looked around for Charlotte, hoping he could escort her but saw Pastor Shaw had claimed the honor for himself. Disappointment filled him as he was given the task of escorting Miss Fleming as she no longer played the pianoforte. David escorted Mildred.

As they walked down the hall, Conrad tried to maneuver near Charlotte and the pastor. This was not how he had intended to spend his last night home.

Since their encounter earlier, Charlotte found it difficult to ignore Conrad. She was painfully aware of everything concerning him, where he stood in the room, who he talked to, and when he moved. When they were all seated in the dining room, she was relieved to have him out of sight at the other end of the table beside Commodore Evans. She sat with Mrs. Evans on her left, Mildred on her right, and the pastor across from her. David sat across from Mildred beside the pastor.

Flower arrangements and candelabras decorated the long table, lighting the dining room with dancing flames. A servant came by and filled her glass with red wine and moved to Mildred. This was the first dinner party she had ever attended like this, and the excitement kept building inside her as the evening wore on.

The first course of potato soup was placed before them. Charlotte waited until Pastor Shaw said grace and Mrs. Evans dipped her spoon before taking the first bite. The soup was warm and spiced with flavored pepper and butter. She sipped three spoonfuls before reaching for her wine to wash it down.

"Charlotte, how did you and Pastor Shaw meet?" Mrs. Evans asked.

"It was at Grady's General Store. I was shopping for some material for new gowns for Mildred and I, and Pastor Shaw happened to come in while I was there." She glanced across the table and met his hazel eyes. While he had the same color as

Conrad's eyes, a tranquil peace lived in the pastor but seemed to be lacking in Conrad. She couldn't explain it, but she sensed a secure wisdom in the pastor she wished Conrad would develop.

"Who could have known a bag of brown sugar would bring me such good fortune?" He grinned at Charlotte. "I have promised the Deaton brothers I would stop by often and check on Charlotte and the children while they are away."

"This sounds promising." Mrs. Evans said. "Would you be willing to bring me on a couple of your visits? Commodore Evans is often off fighting the war and with our children all grown, I grow quite bored and lonely."

"I would consider it an honor. Mine is one of the few professions to exempt me from the war without being considered a coward by my peers. Other men are expected to leave their farms, their merchant businesses, and their trade to enlist. It leaves few able-bodied men at home to protect the homesteads, small towns, and communities. I am afraid we are at risk at times. The English could come ashore at any time and do as they please."

"Charlotte, you are from Wilmington. Have the English come ashore there and terrorized civilians?" Mrs. Evans turned to her, a distressed look upon her face as she wrinkled her gray brows. "I must confess we do not always hear the news from down there as we ought."

"They have come ashore on occasion, but our biggest threat is them capturing innocent fisherman, especially boys, and impressing them into service against their will. With the English blockade up and down the coast, our merchant ships are having trouble getting in or out and our fisherman cannot sail out to sea with the freedom they once had. They must stay within the confines of the sound." She sipped her wine and glanced at Pastor Shaw. "As to your profession, I have heard there are chaplains in the service. Was it something you considered?"

"Indeed, it was." He set his empty bowl aside, waiting for the next course. "In fact, I was on my way to serve as chaplain on the lakes last year, when I discovered the town of Cleaveland. The town has grown because men have brought their families to live nearby, but once they leave to serve on board a ship, there isn't much protection for those left behind. I realized I could be of better service here."

"Do you regret your decision?" Charlotte asked, wondering if he had a pinch of the same wanderlust flowing through Conrad's veins.

"Not at all." He shook his head and picked up his glass. "Sometimes we make plans in life, but God has a better plan in mind for us. We must remain open-minded and flexible so when our plans change, we do not fight God's course of action for us."

Charlotte leaned to the side as her empty soup bowl was taken away. It must have been God's plan for Emma to die. If not, they would have been able to save her life as they had saved other lives. Was it His will she end up here on Lake Erie? If Emma had not perished, she would have never considered coming here. If such was the case, what was God's next plan for her life? Did it make sense to even plan anything or should she just let things take their natural course?

"Wise words, young man," Mrs. Evans said. "I never realized you intended to be a chaplain in the U.S. Navy. Does my husband know?"

"He does, and he respects my decision to stay here." Pastor Shaw leaned back in his chair as a hot plate of roast beef, gravy, and vegetables was set before him. "In fact, I sense it pleases him, since you are here, Mrs. Evans."

"He has always had my welfare in mind and takes such great care of me." She smiled as her gaze slid down the table at her husband. Her eyes sparkled when his gaze caught hers and he gave her a brief nod.

"Your husband acknowledges you among his comrades in spite of all the distracting conversations around him," Charlotte observed, wishing she could have such a meaningful relationship one day. The idea of being loved and cherished filled her with a longing she couldn't explain.

"My dear, when you have been married as long as we have, sometimes words are not needed—only a simple look." She turned and patted the top of Charlotte's hand. "The look Commodore Evans just gave me says he is pleased with the party. I keep the flower arrangements on the table small for the very purpose of being able to see him at the other end. I can judge by his expressions when he is ready to retire to the parlor, if he is bored and I need to intervene and suggest a lively game, or if he is not feeling well and I need to end the evening sooner than planned."

"I never realized a military marriage could be so blessed and close." The words were out before she could stop them. Afraid of how her words could be misinterpreted, Charlotte cleared her throat and searched for a better way to state her thoughts. "What I mean is, since a husband in the military is often gone, I assumed such a marriage might lack a certain familiarity other marriages may not since the couples are always together, but I am glad to know I was wrong."

"Here is a piece of advice I can give and you may apply to many areas of your life. Respect and value the time God has given you. Once spent, you cannot get it back. Make the most of it and spend it in a way to make you and those you love most happy. One hour can be as valuable as twelve hours, if you do not take it for granted."

While Charlotte tried to absorb her friend's words, Pastor Shaw watched her closely and leaned forward. "I am curious, what had you contemplating a military marriage so deeply?"

"I once courted a man who intended to make the navy his lifelong career. He adores the adventures on the sea, and he couldn't seem to fit me into the concept of his military career. In his mind, he had to make a choice, and I lost." Charlotte stabbed her fork into her meat and sawed it with her knife. She had always known Conrad could have made a marriage with her work—if he had been willing to try. It only proved he didn't love her enough—or maybe not at all. How could he be so cruel as to kiss her again and awaken old feelings she had tried to destroy through the passing of time?

"I am sorry, my dear, but a man who loves you the way God intended will be able to make it work. The commodore and I are proof of it." Mrs. Evans covered her hand and offered a sympathetic expression. "Perhaps God has another plan for you after all—just like Pastor Shaw said earlier."

"Indeed," Pastor Shaw nodded, leaning forward. "Whoever the gentleman might be," he lifted a hand, "and I do not want to know, it is his loss. A military career, no matter how enjoyable, cannot take the place of a loving wife and family. He may not realize it, but after a while, his career could become a different kind of prison to him—one lonely and cold."

17

Conrad tried to enjoy the animated conversation around him, but all he could concentrate on was Charlotte at the other end of the table. She spent most of the meal conversing with the pastor and Mrs. Evans. On occasion, she conversed with David and Mildred, but most of her attention seemed to be fixated on the pastor across from her. To Conrad's annoyance, the man never once took his eyes off Charlotte. Why could he not be old and married?

If Pastor Shaw was in the market for a wife, Charlotte could be vulnerable to his attentions. She still grieved for her sister, was far from home and family, and had already confessed her loneliness. What if she mistook her tender feelings for something else, thinking the pastor was the answer to the void and pain in her life? After tomorrow, he and David would not be around to guide her in such matters.

Stark fear shot up Conrad's spine, burning his neck and the base of his skull as a headache spread all over his head. He had promised her father to protect her, but how could he do so, if he was stationed on a ship out in the middle of a lake? Why did he bring her here?

The first time he had left Charlotte in Wilmington and boarded a ship, it had been hard to leave her, but he had no fear of doing so. He had been arrogant enough to believe she was so in love with him she would not marry in his absence. Conrad was right. She had not married, but when he returned for David and Emma's wedding, Charlotte had refused to court him again, saying she would never marry. Conrad had been content with her decision; at least she would still be free if he decided to give up his military career.

This time things were different. For the first time in his life, he didn't miss the sea, nor was he eager to board another ship. His duty to the military seemed more like a burden than an honored blessing. The thought of leaving tomorrow made his chest feel heavy and his breathing harder than usual. He had no idea how to make this feeling go away. It was as if a dozen bricks were lying across his chest.

"Are you nervous about meeting your crew tomorrow?" Commodore Evans asked as he cut another bite of meat, his gaze directed at Conrad.

"No, not at all," Conrad said, picking up his glass and taking a long sip. The red wine was good, but he could use something a little stronger right now. Charlotte and Mrs. Evans laughed at something Pastor Shaw said. His skin crawled in irritation as he forced himself to meet his superior's gaze. "What time should David and I arrive at your house?"

"Six o'clock in the morning. I shall have two of my groomsmen take your horses home. You and your brother will accompany me in my carriage to the lake, which will be about a thirty-minute ride. We will take the rowboat to the USS *Larkspur* where we shall board, and I will announce you as the new captain to your crew. Lieutenant Larson and Sergeant Gallagher will meet us at the shore before boarding."

"Sounds like an excellent plan. I am honored by your hospitality, sir." Conrad nodded toward Mrs. Evans. "And for the warm welcome you and your wife have given to our family."

"We believe in taking care of our own. My wife will be inviting Miss Morgan to many outings, and the church will rally around her as well as your niece and nephew in complete support."

"I wish you well, Captain Deaton," Miss Fleming said, sitting across from him. "My brother will be serving under your command on the USS *Larkspur*. I wondered . . . would you mind giving him a letter for me? His name is Peter."

"It would be an honor," Conrad said. "I may have to return the favor if he gets leave to come ashore and I do not."

"Of course. We all have to rely on each other to keep in touch with our families. War brings much sacrifice and forces us to be creative when necessary." She reached into her reticule and pulled out a sealed letter, pushing it across the table.

"I agree." Conrad picked up the letter and slipped it into the inside pocket of his uniform jacket for safekeeping. He patted the spot and smiled at her. "I will keep it safe until I personally deliver it to your brother."

"Thank you." Relief filled her face as she went back to eating.

"You have reminded me of another promise I made to a worried father back in Bridgeport." Conrad took another sip from his glass. "Do any of you know a younger sailor by the name of Avery Vernon?"

"I do not personally know all the men serving on our fleet," Commodore Evans said, lifting a finger with a winning grin, "but I do have a roster for each vessel. I daresay, we can find him. What kind of promise have you made on this lad's behalf?"

"Apparently, he does not write letters home, and his parents only want to know he is alive and well."

"The name does sound familiar, but I cannot recall where I have heard it before." Miss Fleming touched her chin in thoughtful concentration.

"We shall find him," Commodore Evans promised with a definitive nod. "Now, I am afraid I must break my wife's rule and talk about a few military matters before your arrival upon the USS *Larkspur* tomorrow morning." Commodore Evans leaned back in his chair and finished the rest of his wine. "Commodore Oliver Perry is in charge of all maneuvers on Lake Erie. Most recently, he was brought to Lake Erie and given command of the operation here by President Madison himself. It is my understanding Commodore Perry requested this move, and since it has been granted, he has made some significant changes I consider to be good ones."

"Such as?" Conrad asked before taking another bite of roast.

"He decided we needed more American ships on the lake, and since it is so costly and difficult to build them on the coast and move them to the lakes, he secured funding from Washington to start building ships right here in the wilderness. You may have heard me mention it before." He lifted a gray eyebrow.

"Indeed." Conrad nodded, pushing his empty plate aside. "And I think it is a brilliant idea. It makes sense."

"All the credit goes to Commodore Perry. He is only twenty-eight and is already making a significant mark on his military career and has the president's attention. In fact, some are already referring to him as Admiral Perry. I do not doubt he will soon have the honorable distinction officially." He lifted a finger in warning. "I just want you to be aware of what kind of man whose command you will be under. When the British abandoned Fort Erie back in May, Perry went after the American vessels, had them towed up the Niagara in only six days, and sailed them along the shore to Presque Isle. Nothing is impossible to him."

"Impressive." Conrad sat back and linked his fingers over his flat belly and tilted his head. "Am I correct in assuming the Americans maintain control of Presque Isle and the Niagara Peninsula?"

"And all of Lake Ontario, but since the Niagara Peninsula is between Lake Ontario and Lake Erie, we feel the northern part of Lake Erie is more secure, which is another reason why we are building ships in the town of Erie on the north shore. We still do not have control over Lake Erie and feel the southern shore is more at risk to the British. This includes Cleaveland."

"I see." He now had more reason to be concerned for Charlotte and the children. "I am eager to change that."

"I believe the opportunity for that will be sooner than you realize. Right now Commodore Perry has set anchor at the island of Put-in-Bay, and we have a successful blockade against Barclay. We believe his supplies are running low. Soon, he will have to make the decision to fight or surrender."

"Do we know how much longer he can hold out?" Conrad asked.

"It is uncertain, but Perry has had him blocked for several weeks. And when the USS *Larkspur* sets sail, we will be ready. My man, you could be at battle within a fortnight."

"Allow us to retire to the parlor," Mrs. Evans announced across the table. "Miss Fleming, would you honor us with more music from the pianoforte?"

"I would be delighted," Adelle said, nodding with an appreciative smile.

Charlotte breathed a sigh of relief. She could play some, but she never quite picked up the talent the way Emma had on the pianoforte or Melanie on the violin. Charlotte accepted her lack of musical talent a long time ago and chose to concentrate her efforts on horse riding, but her father refused to allow her to compete. It simply wasn't done. Her mother understood her plight since she had the same dilemma as a young girl. It was why she taught Charlotte archery. Charlotte became quite proficient in archery and shooting guns, although her mother was much better.

Once again, Pastor Shaw escorted her to the parlor. A servant had arranged chairs in three rows facing the pianoforte. Mildred sat on her right, and the pastor seated himself on her left. She wondered what good deed she had committed to deserve the favor of his company, but it didn't matter, because she enjoyed his attention and the conversation they shared. For a long time, Charlotte had craved the loyal company of a man she could trust. Perhaps the good Lord had finally sent her one.

Miss Fleming took her seat at the pianoforte and flipped through the sheets of music. To her surprise, Conrad stood beside her with the intention of turning the pages of her sheet music. Charlotte tilted her head, trying to remember if she had ever heard him play an instrument or talk about music. She could recall no such occasion. If he could not read music, then how would he know when to turn the page?

He bent toward Miss Fleming's ear and whispered. She smiled and nodded in response. Charlotte's stomach tightened and her mouth went dry. How could he be so close to someone else after declaring his love her just this morning? The man was as fickle as a snake. She had been right to reject him. He would only hurt her as he did once before. Charlotte clenched her teeth, determined to pray for Miss Fleming. She seemed so young and innocent. Charlotte hated the thought of her pining away for Conrad, only to have her heart shattered at his lack of sincerity.

Miss Fleming set her fingers on the keys and gave a dramatic pause. A moment later a soft melody drifted into the air, relaxing everyone as they were mentally taken to some other place and time. Charlotte closed her eyes, imagining home when Emma was alive and the two of them ran and played on the beach, laughing and splashing each other. Silent tears crawled down her face, as she realized this time she hadn't needed a mirror to bring back the memories or the pain. She was hundreds of miles away from home, and still, anything could spark her grief. When would it end?

Mildred reached over and slipped her hand in Charlotte's hand. At least one person understood her grief without judging her and trying to fix her. She still grieved for her husband, and at night, Charlotte could hear her sobs when she passed by Mildred's chamber. Charlotte never disturbed her. Mildred needed those times of solace just as Charlotte often needed them. During the day, she managed to keep her mind on other things, but at night in the privacy of her chamber, sometimes she still wept for her sister.

Pastor Shaw pressed a handkerchief in her hand and leaned toward her. "He was not a twin, but I lost my brother last year. He was killed in the war."

Charlotte turned to look up at him through her teary-eyed gaze. No condemnation existed in his eyes, or a lack of patience, only understanding and a connection she had not realized they shared. She hoped he could see the gratitude in her eyes as she unfolded the handkerchief and mopped at her eyes, wishing she had been able to hold back the tears. She hated how tired and heavy her eyes felt after weeping.

"The music reminded me of my sister," Charlotte whispered. "She often played Beethoven's 'Moonlight Sonata.'" It was one of her favorite pieces."

David got up and stepped out of the parlor.

"I should go to him."

Pastor Shaw grabbed Charlotte's hand and shook his head. "Allow him some time alone to recover. Men react differently than women." He gave her hand a gentle squeeze. "Trust me."

"I do." Charlotte nodded, surprised by how much she did trust him. She turned her attention to the front and saw Conrad watching her, a perplexed and wounded expression in his hazel eyes. He must have seen his brother leave the room, and now, he had noticed her tears. Was Conrad testing them to see how much they had overcome Emma's passing? Could he actually be so cruel?

The next selection was much more cheerful, and Charlotte's eyes dried. David returned with a glass of wine. She wanted to disapprove, but how could she? He had done so much better of late. He had not had a drink any of them knew about in a long while. After a few more selections, Mrs. Evans stood. "How about we dance now? I will play while Commodore Evans turns my music sheet. This way Miss Fleming will have a turn about the room."

Everyone stood, and the men moved the chairs to the walls. Mrs. Evans took her place on the bench in front of the pianoforte with her husband at her side. "Let us begin with the 'Thornton Waltz,'" Mrs. Evans said. "Pick your partners. Places everyone."

"May I have this dance?" Pastor Shaw leaned forward and held out his hand.

"I was not aware clergymen were allowed to dance," Charlotte said, unsure if she had the energy to keep up with the steps.

"The Bible says King David danced in the street, so I see no reason why I cannot." He grinned and winked at her.

"You are full of surprises." She placed her hand in his. "So, in this case, yes."

The ride home was silent. Each of them was tired and trying to process the evening. When Mrs. Evans had suggested dancing, Conrad hoped he would be able to convince Charlotte to dance at least once with him, but she refused. She danced with the pastor several times and even granted dances to Lieutenant Larson, Sergeant Gallagher, and David.

Charlotte closed her eyes as she leaned back against the seat and slumped over to the side against the wall. Conrad longed to poke her and see if she only pretended to be asleep to avoid him. He wanted to talk to her before he left, to come to some kind of understanding. If anything, he wanted her forgiveness for being such an idiot six years ago, not only then, but now. He had wasted the last few months denying his feelings for her. Instead of comforting Charlotte through her grief, he had tried to push her beyond it, so he wouldn't have to endure seeing her pain. He had done the same thing to David, and they both resented him for it.

"It was kind of you to turn the pages for Miss Fleming," Mildred said.

"Indeed, since when could you read music?" Charlotte's dry tone carried across the wheels turning and churning over the dirt and gravel road. Conrad straightened in his seat, glad to know she was still awake.

"In spite of what you think, you do not know everything about me, Charlotte. One of my navy friends liked music. Whenever we put into port somewhere, he would find a pianoforte, and I would end up turning the music sheets for him. He taught me a few of the symbols. I am not coordinated enough to play, but I can follow along with some of the notes."

"Of all the songs you could have helped her choose, why the 'Moonlight Sonata'?" Charlotte asked, still keeping her eyes closed. "I think David found it a little hard to take as well."

"Indeed," he nodded. "There are some songs I do not ever wish to hear again."

"I thought the title of it sounded romantic." Conrad shrugged as guilt poured through him again. "I saw how it upset both of you, and I am sorry. Believe me, it was not intentional. The last thing I wanted to see was Pastor Shaw falling all over you in an attempt to console you." Her eyes flew open, bathed in the silvery moonlight from the window. "I see I finally got your attention."

"Only because it is a lie," she snapped. "I suppose I shall never understand you, Conrad." She folded her arms and shifted to a more comfortable position where she leaned back against the cushioned seat. "You spend all your time trying to make everyone as miserable as you, and when they do not comply with your wishes, you try to treat everyone like part of your crew, barking orders, and demanding we do things your way. You thought we could make little soldiers of the children, so we could keep to your travel schedule on the way here. I have no doubt you somehow managed to manipulate Miss Fleming into playing Emma's favorite song. Did you do it so you could prove David's continuous grief and chastise me once again for bringing Emma's things to keep her memory alive?"

"Nonsense." Conrad rolled his eyes as another headache began to pound in his temples. He touched the side of his head. "I cannot believe you could think I would be so heartless. I will probably regret admitting this, but I had you in mind, Charlotte. The title sounded romantic, and I mistakenly thought you would like it. Forgive me for being wrong. As I always seem to be whenever it comes to you."

"Charlotte, I must admit your accusation is a bit far-fetched even for Conrad." David sighed. "Was Charlotte responsible for the handprint on your face earlier today? I thought she might be, after you refused to talk about it when I returned home." David cleared his throat. "What did you do this time?"

Conrad groaned and slouched in his seat. He had no desire to divulge more of his transgressions. If Charlotte wanted to tell on him, it would be her choice.

Awkward silence followed. He waited, but Charlotte said nothing—to his relief.

"I see. Neither of you wants to elaborate," David said. "Somehow, I am not surprised."

A few moments later, the carriage rolled to a stop in front of their house. In such a short time, he had come to think of this place as his home, and at the center of it was Charlotte. Would she court Pastor Shaw in his absence? As her pastor, he would be seeing her on a regular basis, and he would have plenty of time to work on her emotions and gain her trust. Guilt ripped at Conrad as he realized how much time he could have had with Charlotte. He had no one to blame but himself. He had been a fool, and now, he would have to suffer the consequences.

He and David followed the women out of the carriage. Conrad glanced up at Mr. Porter. "Thank you for your service tonight."

"You are welcome, Captain."

As they walked into the foyer, Mrs. Cooper came down the stairs with a satisfied grin. "Davie and the baby are both asleep. He has a lot of energy—that one."

"Yes, he does," David said, sounding like a proud father. "Now, if you all will excuse me, I am going to bed. Conrad and I have an early start tomorrow." He headed toward the stairs.

"What time will you be leaving?" Mildred asked, watching his dark head retreat. He paused and turned to look at her. "We have to be at Commodore Evans's house at six, so we will be leaving around five-thirty."

"So early? I had hoped to see the two of you off." She glanced from David and turned around to Conrad. "If I do not wake up in time, I will be praying you both return safely. We both will, right, Charlotte?"

"Of course," Charlotte looked up at David, and then gave a hesitant glance at Conrad. If his heart could have pumped outside of his chest, Conrad was certain it would have at this moment. "No matter how much you anger and annoy me, Conrad, I have never wished you any harm. I will be praying for both of you."

Charlotte stayed at the foot of the stairs conversing with Mrs. Cooper about the children after Mildred and David went upstairs to their chambers. Conrad lingered at the rail, hoping to speak to her alone. Before he left, he wanted one thing—her forgiveness.

Mr. Porter came in, and Charlotte spoke to him a few moments as he bolted the door. Both servants retired to their chambers. Conrad managed to hide in the shadows as Charlotte blew out the candles downstairs. She carried a lit lantern as she climbed the stairs. Once she reached the landing, she paused, seeing him waiting for her.

"What do you want, Conrad? I am tired, and I do not wish to repeat what happened earlier today." She sounded as weary as she claimed.

"I wanted to say I am sorry and to ask for your forgiveness." He walked toward her, gripping the rail in an effort to keep from grabbing her and pulling her close to him again.

"For what?" She brushed a lock of hair from her forehead. "For kissing me earlier today or for something else?"

"I am sorry for upsetting you earlier today, but I want your forgiveness for leaving six years ago. I was a kid and so narrow-minded. I did not see all the ways a marriage could have worked with my career, but seeing the Evanses and others now in the middle of a war, I realize how wrong I was. I still love you, Charlotte. Whatever you think of me, I never stopped loving you."

She didn't respond, only stood in silence until his nerves ate at him. He forced himself to stand still and breathe in and out slowly. It wouldn't be fair to rush her or make her feel like he was forcing her.

"Conrad, I forgive you for what happened earlier today and for leaving so many years ago, but I also thank you. By doing what you did, you kept me from making a mistake I would spend the rest of my life regretting. Pastor Shaw is helping me to see sometimes our plans do not work out the way we want, because God has something better planned for us. I am hoping it is why I am here. Perhaps the kind of life meant for me would not have been possible at home, and the people I am meant to meet are here."

This was not what he wanted to hear, but she had granted him the forgiveness he wanted. What else could he ask for? "Could I at least have a hug?"

"Yes." She walked into his outstretched arms and embraced him like she would a brother. The realization made his eyes sting with tears. He was thankful it was too dark for her to see them. She still held the lantern, and it bumped against his side.

He smothered his face in her hair and inhaled the scent of juniper. "I love you."

She didn't respond. Instead, her breath hitched in her throat and she started to tremble. Charlotte pulled away and rushed from him to her chamber where she slammed the door. Sobs echoed on the other side.

A deep ache pounded inside him. It was obvious she still had feelings for him, but it was no longer enough. Charlotte had lost her trust in him. The realization shook him to the core.

18

Charlotte woke to sounds of people moving about other parts of the house. Low voices rumbled in the distance, and she recognized Conrad's voice talking to David and Mildred. The smell of bacon, eggs, toast, and honey drifted beneath her door. Charlotte closed her eyes and squeezed out hot tears as she realized Mildred had gotten up and made them a warm breakfast—something she should have done. Instead, she allowed her conflicting emotions to keep her from doing what was right. She should have been as considerate as Mildred and gotten up to send them off with well-wishes and a hot meal in their stomach.

She spent most of the night awake, thinking about what Conrad had said. He didn't understand real love. If he truly loved her, he would not have been able to walk away from them having a life together. How could she be sure he wouldn't do the same thing again? He only knew the moment, and right now she existed in his moment. As soon as he boarded his ship, he would forget about her just as he did before. She had finally gotten over all the pain and rejection. Did she really want to give him the opportunity to destroy her again? This time it would be much worse. She didn't have Emma to help her get over him.

If Conrad loved her, he had plenty of time to express it—to show it. Why did he wait until the night before boarding his ship to tell her how he felt? There was plenty of time to discuss their relationship while sailing up the east coast to Bridgeport and crossing the wilderness in a covered wagon. Anger washed through her as another realization pounded her heart like crashing waves on the shore. Perhaps Conrad waited so he could once again be seen as the dashing hero in her eyes with little risk of having to prove himself since he would be leaving the next morning. He said he had changed, but apparently he had not. She would be a fool to trust him.

Due to the struggle she still had with her feelings and how the man could keep her up most of the night, she could not go downstairs, say good-bye, and watch them depart. Right now she felt too weak, and part of her wanted to believe Conrad loved her and had changed enough to make a commitment. If she ventured downstairs, she feared her emotions would cave under the stress of seeing him one last time before sailing into battle. No, staying here in the cocoon of her chamber would spare her from further heartache and lies. This way Conrad would escape on his ship with his beloved sailors and she would soon be a memory. She had no doubt his feelings would evaporate with the next captivating adventure to come along.

Charlotte ignored her rumbling stomach and flung the covers back. She bathed in the wash basin, brushed her hair, and dressed for the day. Putting on a pair of slippers to ensure her feet would remain quiet when she walked, Charlotte went to her chamber door. She tiptoed to the rail at the staircase landing and crouched on the floor, looking through the white bars. David and Conrad walked to the foyer and grabbed their hats.

Both men carried a bag of belongings over their shoulders as they reached for their military hats.

"Please be careful and make sure you both come back." Mildred hugged them.

"We will. I tried to explain everything to Davie, but I do not know if he clearly understands," David said, rubbing his eyes. "Will you try to talk to him again? Make sure he understands I love him and have not abandoned him. I will be back."

Charlotte's throat constricted as she thought about the possibility of Davie thinking his father had abandoned him. Avoiding Conrad was one thing, but neglecting David was another. She had promised Emma to take care of David as well. Charlotte pushed herself up and gripped the rail.

"I will, David. I promise." Mildred walked with them to the front door.

"Mildred, will you promise to write me and let me know how Charlotte is doing? She may refuse to write me since we had a disagreement, but I still care. I want to know she is all right. Will you do that for me?" Conrad asked.

Charlotte closed her eyes as hot tears slipped beneath her lids and rolled down her face. How could he act like a man in love one minute and completely turn on her the next? Turmoil and confusion swirled inside her as she listened to Mildred's response.

"I promise to write and let you know how she is doing. Whatever happened between you, I am sure she will soon overcome it. Charlotte is reasonable, and I trust her to do what is right. I have never known her to stay angry for too long."

Charlotte wiped the tears from her face. She had no idea how blessed she would be when her father hired Mildred. The woman was a rare gift. She would have to find a way to convince her to stay even after Ashlynn is weaned. The front door opened and footsteps carried outside. Charlotte ran to the hallway window, but she couldn't see them for the porch roof. Disappointment filled her as she pressed her hand against the glass, hoping for one last glance. Should she risk going down to see them or stick with her earlier decision?

The black carriage waited in front of the porch. Harnessed horses pranced with agitation, but Mr. Porter contained them. Charlotte glimpsed Conrad and David throwing their bags on top and securing them. Conrad opened the door to the carriage and turned one last time to wave at Mildred on the porch. He looked up as if committing the house to memory. Charlotte waved, but he didn't respond, so she assumed he didn't see her. A moment later, he ducked inside the carriage, and David followed. Mr. Porter flicked the reins over the horses, and they lurched into motion.

As they drove away, Charlotte watched the dust from the road form a cloud around them. She leaned forward and pressed her hand against the hard glass. An ache throbbed in the back of her throat. What if she never saw them again? The carriage now looked like a tiny speck in the distance. Her heart thumped with loneliness, as she leaned her forehead against the cold pane.

"Captain Conrad Deaton, I love you, too." The whispered words faded into an eerie silence she feared would haunt her in the days to come.

As Conrad came aboard the USS *Larkspur* to meet his new crew, the men were lined up at attention in three rows across the main deck. Commodore Evans spoke to them first, telling them about Conrad's experience. After he finished speaking, he stepped back and motioned to Conrad to take his turn.

Stepping forward, Conrad linked his hands behind his back and took a deep breath. "I have reviewed Captain Stallings's notes and learned you all are a capable and excellent crew. I am honored to be your captain. I have no intention of changing the way this ship is run unless I discover something is not working as well as it could be. You will find I am a fair, but firm captain. I will ask naught of you I will not do myself. Over the next fortnight, we anticipate a battle with Barclay and his ships. We will face the enemy. I will not be sending you into battle. I will be leading you into battle. We Americans will take over Lake Erie as we have done on Lake Ontario. Many of you have wives and children you would like to return home to, and I want to remind you the sooner we claim victory, the sooner we can return home victorious." Conrad paused and raised his fist. "Are you with me?"

"Yes!" they responded in unison.

"With the exception of the ship's officers, you are all dismissed!" Conrad motioned for them to go.

The crew dispersed, each one heading to his station. The officers lined up before him. Conrad shook each man's hand as they introduced themselves, their rank, and their position on the ship. Once they finished, Conrad dismissed them as well. Only Commodore Evans, Lieutenant Larson, and Sergeant Gallagher remained.

"Gentlemen, show your new captain to his quarters and we will discuss Commander Perry's latest orders. A letter arrived last evening during our dinner party. Since it was not urgent, my staff waited until afterward to give it to me."

"This way," Lieutenant Larson said, leading them across the main deck toward the back of the ship.

"Captain Deaton," Commodore Evans addressed him from behind. "The USS *Larkspur* is one of the few frigates on the lake. The rest are sloops and small vessels designed for lightweight maneuverability. Keep in mind while Commander Barclay has fewer ships than we do at the moment, the British have started building ships on the lake as we have. They are building them in Amherstburg and Kingston, Ontario. Barclay has been hiding out in Amherstburg, but when he emerges to face us, we believe he will be equipped with a new ship."

Conrad took in this bit of news as they walked into his quarters, a large cabin with side windows displaying an excellent view around them. A corner desk stood on one side. A table with maps and charts centered the room, A small bar and a wire bottle holder contained five bottles of wine. A number of wooden chairs were along the wall on another side.

"Your sleeping quarters are back there, sir." Lieutenant Larson pointed to a door in the corner. "Your trunks are in your private quarters."

"Thank you." Conrad gave him a nod of approval. "This is nice. I like the view and the spaciousness."

"I believe a man in charge of a ship needs space to think, plan, plot, and pace—especially when at war." Commodore Evans stepped toward the table and pointed. "Gentlemen, allow me to draw your attention to the maps." He pulled one map out and indicated a body of water. "This is Lake Erie. We are here at the Cleaveland shore. Commander Perry has ordered the USS *Larkspur* to sail southwest and join him off the island of Put-in-Bay, right here."

"How long will it take us to sail there?" Conrad asked.

"A couple of days." Commodore Evans shrugged. "As long as the weather holds out. Perry has been anchored in the area. I doubt he has any intention of going anywhere unless Barclay makes a move. He wants you there to strengthen the blockade he already has in place. Since you are new to navigating the lake, Perry would like for you to hold back once Barclay emerges from cover at Amherstburg. The USS *Niagara* and the

USS *Lawrence* will sail into full battle. Your ship and crew will be held for reserve if anything goes wrong, and we both know anything can happen in these kind of maneuvers."

"Am I allowed to use my discretion as to the nature of anything going wrong or must I wait for specific orders?" Conrad asked.

"Use your judgment, but be warned," Commodore Evans wagged a finger, "whatever you do, make sure you have good reason and it can be backed up if questioned. Perry likes taking courageous risks, and so, he expects it of his officers. Just make certain you succeed at whatever you decide to do. He also hates failure."

"Understood." Conrad nodded.

"It is my understanding Perry is sending these same instructions to his second-in-command, Jesse Elliot, on the USS *Niagara*. Do you have any other questions or concerns?"

"If I need to get a message to you, will you remain here in Cleaveland for now?" Conrad asked.

"Yes, I have been managing the fleets until Perry's arrival. Now I am taking a break in my old age from ship duty. However, I will be available as needed for consultation. It appears my experience is still needed even if my physical service is not." Commodore Evans patted his chest and rubbed a hand over his slight, round belly. "He might be young, but as I mentioned before, he is a capable officer, and I trust in his judgment as does President Madison. He will win this lake from the British, and he will lead the rest of us to victory. Mark my words."

"Yes, sir." Conrad nodded, eager to meet the man who had won over the admiration of so many commanding officers. If Commodore Perry was only twenty-eight, they were the same age. Perry had managed to achieve what Conrad had always dreamed for his own career.

"Do you have any other questions or concerns before I take my leave?" Commodore Evans asked.

"No, sir, not at this time." Conrad shook his head, ready to take over command of the USS *Larkspur.*

The house seemed different after Conrad and David left. Charlotte and Mildred had two new servants they needed to get to know better. She and Mildred settled into an alternating routine with the children and household chores. It helped they now had a cook and could spend time tending to other matters. Mrs. Cooper asked Charlotte if she could plant a vegetable and herbal garden nearby. As it turned out, she knew quite a bit about herbal remedies and felt it would be best since they had two children in the house who could get into mischief and come down with common illnesses and colds.

"Mrs. Cooper, I believe a garden would be an excellent idea, but since we are renting the property, I believe it would be best if we were to call on Mrs. Evans and ask." Charlotte sat at the desk in the study.

"I understand, miss," Mrs. Cooper bobbed her head until her round cap looked as if it might fall. She wore an apron over a plain gown of blue linen. Her round cheeks were a rosy glow from the heat in the kitchen. The aroma of baking bread lingered throughout the first floor.

"Mildred has agreed to accompany me into town. We will be taking the children, but I wondered if you would give me a list of things we would plant in the garden?"

"Absolutely, but would you write them down for me? I am not good at spelling." Mrs. Cooper wiped her hands on her apron.

"Of course." Charlotte took out one of the pieces of paper she usually wrote her letters on from the desk drawer. She opened a bottle of ink and dipped her quill. "Let us start with the vegetable garden." Charlotte wrote it as a title and underlined it.

"Beans, broccoli, cabbage, lettuce, carrots, cucumbers." Mrs. Cooper counted them off on her chubby fingers faster than Charlotte could write them.

"Wait." Charlotte dipped her quill again and continued writing as fast as she could.

"Corn, onions, peppers."

"Corn?" Charlotte paused to look at her. "How many rows?"

"Just one." Mrs. Cooper held up a finger and continued. "Spinach, squash, and tomatoes."

"Are we asking for one row of each?" Charlotte asked, wondering if they would be here long enough for this much work.

"Yes." Mrs. Cooper bobbed her head. "We will need these things this time next year. Right now I am having to depend on the market each week for everything. I would rather depend on the market for our meats and special items. This will get expensive."

"I see. Do you have enough money in the budget to manage for now?"

"Yes. Captain Deaton provided enough for two months. He thought he would be back before then." She tilted her head. "Are you ready for the herbal garden now?"

"Give me just a minute." Charlotte dipped her quill, made a second heading on the right side of the page, and underlined it as she had the first column. "I am ready."

"Basil, chamomile, parsley, sage, and thyme."

"Is this all?" Charlotte asked.

"No, I thought I would give you time to catch up." Mrs. Cooper started over on her fingers again. "Saint-John's-wort, feverfew, aloe vera, and garlic."

Charlotte finished writing the list and waved it in the air to dry. "This should be good for now. Thank you, Mrs. Cooper."

"You are welcome, miss." She dipped her head in a curtsy and continued to linger. "Um, may I ask if you plan to return in time for dinner?"

"Indeed, we shall," Charlotte said, nodding.

Satisfied, Mrs. Cooper took herself back to the kitchen and left Charlotte to find Mildred and the children. It took some time getting everyone ready, but a half an hour later, Mr. Porter brought the carriage around as asked. Mildred carried Ashlynn, while Charlotte held Davie's hand and assisted him inside.

They arrived at noon. Before Charlotte could stop him, Davie opened the door and bounced outside ahead of them. Charlotte grabbed her reticule and gloves to hurry after him. "Davie, wait!"

He ran up the brick walkway and banged on the door since he wasn't able to reach the door knocker. By the time Charlotte climbed the porch steps, she felt winded and out of breath when the butler answered the door. The elderly man stared at her expectantly.

"I am Mr. Deaton, here to see Mrs. Evans!" Davie announced.

Startled, the butler glanced down at Davie and blinked, widening his eyes. A slow grin spread over his expression.

"Please tell them Miss Morgan and Mrs. Wolfe are here to see them, and we brought the children with us as Mrs. Evans requested." Charlotte gripped Davie's tiny shoulders in front of her to hold him still.

"Did I not do it right?" he asked, twisting his head to look up at her.

As soon as the butler departed, Charlotte dropped down to eye level with Davie. He turned to face her, and she gripped his arms. "Do not ever run off like that again." She adopted a stern voice. "You announced yourself perfectly, but we do not run from the carriage or up the walkway to bang on front doors, especially outrunning the adults who are with you. Remember your manners while we are here visiting."

"Am I in trouble?" His bottom lip pouted.

"It depends on how well you behave for the rest of our visit." Charlotte straightened as Mildred arrived with Ashlynn and the butler returned to let them in. Since the weather was mildly cool for early September, none of them had hats or scarves. They paused in the foyer, awaiting further instructions from the butler.

"Commodore and Mrs. Evans are enjoying the day out in the garden on the patio. I shall lead you to them." They followed him down the hall, through the dining room, and out a side door Charlotte had not noticed on the night of the dinner party. The shadows must have hidden it. She held tight to Davie's hand as they stepped down a couple of steps and followed a brick walkway to where their hosts sat at a round table.

"And who might you be?" Commodore Evans stood and leaned over Davie, offering a handshake.

"I am Davie Deaton." Davie slipped his tiny hand into the commodore's large one. "Aunt Charlotte said I have to behave so I will not get into trouble."

"Is it possible?" The commodore lifted a thick, gray eyebrow.

"I do not know." Davie bit his bottom lip with a look of indecision. "I get into trouble a lot."

Commodore Evans and his wife both laughed. She stepped forward and held out her hands. "Please, may I hold the baby?"

Mildred took Ashlynn to her, while her husband pointed at two empty chairs. "Please, have a seat."

"Mrs. Evans, you have a beautiful fall garden," Charlotte said, scanning the view of the goldenrods and perennials until her gaze caught another type of flower she didn't recognize.

"I am sorry, but what is the name of the bright red and pink flowers?"

"Red spider lilies. Are they not beautiful?" Mrs. Evans set Ashlynn on her lap to face her as she made faces and sounds. Ashlynn giggled and laughed, reaching for Mrs. Evans's cheek. "We are so delighted you came today."

"Thank you," Charlotte said.

"Here, I picked a pretty flower for you." Davie ran over and handed Mrs. Evans a spider lily."

"Davie, no!" Charlotte plopped the heel of her hand to her forehead, mortified with embarrassment. "You cannot pick these flowers. They belong to Mrs. Evans's garden."

"But I picked it for her!" He pointed at Mrs. Evans, who covered her mouth in silent laughter.

"I appreciate your thoughtfulness, Davie." Mrs. Evans leaned toward him. "Will you do a favor for me?"

He nodded with wide brown eyes, eager to please her.

"Will you put it on the table in the middle, so Ashlynn cannot reach it? She might try to eat it, and it could be poisonous to her."

"Like my snake bite?" Tears filled Davie's eyes. "I do not want my baby sister to die."

"Davie, come here, sweetie." Charlotte leaned to the side and held out her arms to him. He ran to her, and she picked him up, setting him on her lap. She brushed his hair from his eyes, the tips curling like his father's. "Flowers are beautiful and fine, but they are only poisonous if we eat them. You and I know we should not eat them, but Ashlynn will not understand, even if we tell her."

"Because she is a baby?"

"Exactly, she needs to be older. Right now anything she gets in her hands, goes straight to her mouth, so we have to be careful not to let her have certain things." Charlotte gave him a big hug before he wiggled off her lap and ran to explore the rest of the garden.

"He was bitten by a rattlesnake on the way here," Mildred said. "We feared he would not make it, but God answered our prayers."

"Oh, dear, how terrible." Mrs. Evans clutched her throat with her free hand and frowned, most likely imagining the ordeal.

"Mrs. Evans, while we are here, I wanted to ask if we could plant a vegetable and herbal garden at Captain Stallings's house." Charlotte pulled out her reticule and unfolded the slip of paper where she had written Mrs. Cooper's list. "This will give you an idea of what we had in mind."

Mrs. Evans handed it across the table to her husband. "I see no reason why they should not. If Captain Stallings returns with his family, it would only serve as a blessing to them. What do you think, dear?"

"I am in complete agreement." He nodded, handing the paper back to Charlotte. "I suppose you would like an update on Captain Deaton and his brother?"

"Of course." Charlotte nodded, leaning forward to give him her full attention.

"Yes, we have been wondering how they are doing." Mildred said.

"Well, I can only give an account of the day I took them to the ship. They both arrived without incident. The next day they set sail for Put-in-Bay Island where several other warships await them. We have created a blockade of the British fleet. We expect a battle to follow any day now."

19

As they sailed into the Put-in-Bay harbor, Conrad was reminded of the Pamlico Sound off the shore of North Carolina back home. Lieutenant Larson gave him pointers on where to avoid shallow waters with the patches of green vegetation waving above the surface. The sight of two other frigates, a few sloops, and gunboats brought the old excitement of sailing back again. Lake Erie was beautiful and huge. With the exception of the salty air, he didn't miss the sea as much as he feared.

He pulled up beside the USS *Lawrence*. It looked like the USS *Niagara* was on the other side. "Give the order to drop anchor," he said.

"Yes, sir." Lieutenant Larson leaned over the railing, cupped his mouth with his hands, and bellowed the order.

As much as Conrad loved being on a ship and sailing through the waters, he missed Charlotte and the children even more. Since he had left a couple of days ago, she had been on his mind at every turn, especially at night when he was alone and resting in his cabin.

His gaze fell on his brother, pulling on the ropes to drop the anchor. The moment the two of them boarded the USS *Larkspur*, David was led away to the sailors' quarters. He slept in a hammock and probably had no moment's peace among his new comrades. Conrad wondered if any of his sailors figured out he and David were brothers. With the same surname and matching features, an astute mind would recognize the resemblance. This ship would be different from the *Victorious*. Neither of them knew the crew, and both still had to prove their right to be here. On the *Victorious*, he had sailed with those men for years, and they knew him well. When David arrived, they didn't question his judgment or worry about unfair treatment—at least he did not know of any.

"Sir, Commander Perry is on deck of the USS *Lawrence* beside us and would like to speak to you." Sergeant Gallagher came up the steps to the quarterdeck.

"Thank you." Conrad turned from the wheel, straightened his hat, and descended to the main deck. He stopped in front of the rails and saluted Commander Perry on the other ship. Perry returned his salute.

"Did Commodore Evans speak with you?" Commander Perry asked.

"He did."

"Excellent." He grinned and turned to one of his officers, gave an order, and pointed toward the USS *Larkspur*. "Prepare for me to board your ship."

"Yes, sir!" Conrad motioned toward it. "Secure our side."

Perry's crew launched a stern walk, a board placed to cross to the ship. The sailor moved forward and tied a rope, securing it to the rails.

"Prepared for boarding, sir," Conrad called.

Commander Perry climbed upon the board and walked over to the USS *Larkspur*. He had dark brown hair combed in waves around his face with long sideburns curling onto his cheeks. His decorated uniform shined like a beacon in the sun. He stepped down on the main deck, a few inches shorter than Conrad.

"Captain Deaton, pleased to meet you, sir." Conrad saluted him and gestured to his second-in-command. "Lieutenant Jack Larson and Sergeant Kevin Gallagher."

Perry gave a brief nod to both of them, acknowledging their salutes, and met Conrad's gaze. "I would like to speak to you alone in the captain's quarters, please."

"Yes, sir." Conrad gestured in the direction of his cabin. Perry strode forward, and Conrad followed, knowing Perry was well aware of the layout of a frigate. Once inside, Conrad was thankful there was enough sunlight filtering through the windows he would not have to light any lanterns. He motioned to the bar. "Would you like a drink, sir?"

"I will take simple wine since it is still early." Perry chose a wooden chair and sat, crossing his booted ankle over his knee. "I understand most of your experience is on the sea."

"It is."

"How do you like Lake Erie? Do you find the differences a stark contrast?"

"I miss the salty air and the large swells. I found them comforting at night when I needed sleep." Conrad poured two glasses half-full and brought Perry's to him. He accepted it and took a long swallow, while Conrad dragged a chair closer and faced him. Conrad sat and leaned back, attempting to appear as relaxed as possible in spite of the circumstances.

"At least you are honest," Perry said. "There was no hesitation in your answers, and I find I agree since most of my career has been at sea as well." He took another sip. "Do I have your word what I am about to say will remain in your confidence?"

"Yes, sir." Conrad nodded, taking a long sip from his glass in anticipation.

"As you may have heard, Captain Jesse Elliot served under Commodore Isaac Chauncey on Lake Ontario. At the time, he was captain of the USS *Madison*. In February of this year, I was promoted to Master Commander over Elliot, but he did not take the news well. I have been hearing reports he feels like he was overlooked for the position. He claims he has more experience than I do. My initial reaction was to ignore these reports, but in recent months I have observed a certain disrespect, and it is becoming quite alarming and disturbing since he is my second-in-command. Elliot is entitled to his feelings and beliefs, but I must be able to trust him in the midst of battle. I am concerned this is no longer the case, but I have no choice since I have no proof—only a gut instinct—which rarely fails me."

"Sir, with all due respect, I do not understand how this concerns me." Discomfort gnawed at Conrad's conscience.

"If we go into battle as I suspect, in the next few days, I would like you to hold back and keep your ship out of gunfire range. Keep watch, and if anything untoward happens, follow your instinct. Elliot and I will be going full force on a frontline attack against Barclay. Your ship and a few others will stand as a line of defense, if we do not succeed. Regardless of what happens, we must win at any cost, so do what you must."

"You do not think Elliot's resentment runs so deep he would fire upon your ship—one of our own American ships?" Conrad gave him a skeptical look.

Perry paused, actually considering the question, but shook his head. "No, but I do have doubts if I needed his personal assistance, he might look the other way. Our ships are not built to handle heavy gunfire at close range, and Barclay's cannons are much more powerful than ours and can shoot at a longer range. In order for ours to make an impact, we must sail at close range. Elliot and I will be in great peril, which is why we need another line of defense, and it is you."

"I understand, and you can count on me, sir." Conrad nodded.

"Good, I was hoping to hear you say so, but I thought it only fair for you to know what you will be sailing into. Our lives and those of our crew are at stake when next we meet the British." He finished his glass and stood. "I anticipate this will be the largest engagement to take place on Lake Erie. Whoever wins this battle will win control over the entire lake, and it must be us."

Before Charlotte and Mildred departed from the Evans home, she was given a sealed letter from her mother. The courier brought it the day before, and Mrs. Evans promised she would deliver it. Charlotte kept turning it over and over, fingering the dried ink on the outside as they rode in the carriage. Eagerness almost stole her breath away as lingering thoughts of her mother kept burning in her heart and mind, making her miss her family even more. She prayed all was well with everyone.

"They are so nice," Mildred said, bouncing Ashlynn on her lap. "And so good with Davie."

"Like perfect grandparents," Charlotte said. "At times they remind me of my parents. One day I would like to give my parents grandchildren."

"They already have grandchildren, do they not?" Mildred gave her a confused look.

"Yes, but I want to see them love my children. I miss them, Mildred, and here I am making a whole new life here."

"It does not have to be forever." Mildred leaned forward and covered her hand. "You are making a life here in Cleaveland for now, until it is time for you to move on to another place or for you to go back home." She patted Charlotte's hand. "Believe me, I never would have thought I could end up here, loving a family I never even knew this time last year."

"It goes back to what Pastor Shaw was saying the other night at the dinner party," Charlotte said as Mildred sat back and rocked Ashlynn. She tilted her head in question. "I cannot remember his exact words, but something on the order of—we make plans in life, but God has a better plan in mind for us. We must remain open-minded and flexible so when our plans change, we do not fight God's course of action for us."

"What he said is so profound and wise." She smiled with a pensive expression. "It makes me want to write it down in my journal so I could look at it on those days when I am questioning my life, because there are times when I do. It is so hard for me to understand how it could be God's plan for me to lose my husband and my tiny son. As much as I love these children and your family, I still want my own family back. I cannot imagine a better plan." Tears welled in her eyes, and she kissed the top of Ashlynn's head.

Charlotte gulped and looked away. Mildred's pain felt like her own. She had two natural-born sisters, but over the last few months, Mildred had become like a sister to her. A few moments later, the carriage rolled to a stop in front of their house. Charlotte rubbed the sealed letter in her hand one more time. "Will you be all right with the children, while I go upstairs and read my letters?"

"Of course, take your time." She gathered Ashlynn close, while Charlotte grabbed Davie's hand and opened the door to help him out. She waited until Mildred stepped out with the baby and helped them inside.

Charlotte hurried upstairs and closed the door to her chamber and sat on her bed. She broke the seal and unfolded the letter. Another letter fell out. She set it aside and read the first one from her mother.

My dear Charlotte,

I was so relieved to receive your letter once you reached Cleaveland. The house sounds beautiful. I hope you have hired some servants to help you once David and Conrad leave. How is David? I've been praying for him—for you both.

Is Davie fully recovered from the snakebite? Does he have a scar or hurt from it? How is Ashlynn? Is she crawling? Eating table food? I wish I would have thought to have a painting done of them before they left, but everything happened so fast. Please, do not let them forget about us. Tell them how much we love them.

Scott and Duncan have begun to remodel the house David and Emma lived in. They have painted the outside a beautiful green, your favorite color, with white trimming. All the rooms on the inside are being painted and receiving new wallpaper. With the exception of family heirlooms, they are even replacing the furniture. I think they believe you will want it one day when you come home again. Every decision they make, they consult Melanie and I on what you would like.

Charlotte stopped as tears filled her eyes and she could no longer see the words. She lifted the hem of her dress and mopped at her eyes before continuing.

Melanie has announced she is pregnant again. She is not yet showing, but I suspect it will be any day now. She and Rob are so excited.

As for your father, we felt your anger from your last letter, and it has hurt him deeply. He only asked Conrad to look after you because you had just lost the most important person in your life and David was in no condition to make promises. We realize your history with Conrad has been a shaky one, but he has kept his word to your father and written us faithfully. We are glad we asked Conrad to keep us informed. He has written us at times when you have not. We love you, Charlotte, but please, do not shut us out in the midst of your grief. Life is short, and we need to make the most of it, even if we can only do so through letters. Write your father and let him know you forgive him.

I love you, sweet girl.

Mama

Charlotte took a moment to wipe her eyes again and digest the news of Melanie's pregnancy. She will soon have another niece or nephew. Will she ever have a chance to meet the child? She would have to write Melanie and congratulate her, but first she needed to read the other letter. Charlotte picked it up and recognized her grandmother's scrawled handwriting. She broke the seal and unfolded it.

My Dear Charlotte Girl,

I felt led to write you after I learned of your anger against your father and Conrad. I realize you feel betrayed and are still hurt by Conrad's rejection so long ago, but you have to let it go. Forgive Conrad—and your father.

I know you remember the story of Malcolm and I, how he stole me from my family in Scotland as revenge against my father and sailed me across the ocean to the colonies. If I could forgive him, you can forgive Conrad. Has he hurt you again? Is it why you are so angry? Write to me and let me know what is REALLY going on. I may be old, but because I am old, I might have some perspectives you may not have considered. I miss those days when we used to sit on the edge of my bed and talk about everything in your life. You always listened to me and took my advice. Please hear me now. Forgive Conrad. He was young and foolish six years ago. Allow him the chance to grow up. He deserves at least that much.

My hand is starting to shake with my arthritis, so I will end this letter. I love you, Charlotte Girl!

Grandma Lauren

Conrad stretched and yawned as he walked outside his cabin to take in the morning. Clouds were in the sky, but not so low it was foggy. A sailor brought him a steaming cup of coffee.

"Thank you." Conrad sipped the warm liquid. It wasn't Charlotte's coffee, but it would do. During their four months of traveling together, either her cooking had gotten better, or he had gotten used to it.

"You are welcome, sir." The sailor walked away, and Conrad walked out onto the main deck.

"Pull anchor! The British are on the move!" Someone shouted from Perry's frigate beside them. The sailors on the USS *Lawrence* flew into motion.

The men on deck of the USS *Larkspur* all turned to Conrad for direction.

"We will wait! Give them time to get into position." Conrad pointed to one of his sailors. "I need my officers awake and alert. Go find Lieutenant Larson and Sergeant Gallagher."

"Yes, sir!"

"I need my spyglass." He climbed up the stairs to the quarterdeck and stood in front of the wheel where his men expected to see him. He sipped his coffee while he waited. Someone brought him his spyglass. The USS *Lawrence* pulled out ahead of them. Conrad motioned to Captain Elliot on the USS *Niagara*. He motioned back and ordered his anchor up and his sails down.

Lieutenant Larson joined him. Conrad handed him his coffee so he could adjust the spyglass to see better. The British were indeed on the move, and the morning wind was in their favor. The USS *Lawrence* did not have as much speed, but it didn't matter with the British fleet heading straight for them.

Conrad reached for his coffee again as he handed the spyglass to Larson. "The British are heading this way, but we have been ordered to hold back as the final line of defense. Perry and Elliot are going straight at them on the offensive."

"How long do we hold back and do nothing?" Larson asked, handing back the spyglass. His tone sounded frustrated and disappointed.

"I have my orders directly from Perry himself. I intend to follow them," Conrad said. "The rest is up to my discretion and it all depends on what happens."

A few schooners and gunboats sailed beside the USS *Lawrence*, as the USS *Niagara* pulled out behind them. Conrad sensed his men getting frustrated at being left behind. He took another sip of his black coffee. Once the USS *Niagara* moved away, Conrad took a deep breath. "Hoist the American flag to the top and pull anchor!"

He turned to Larson and Gallagher. "Order the gunners to their cannons and the ammunition to be loaded at each station. No one fires until I command it. Since Perry has ordered us to hold back as the final line of defense, we must stay out of firing range for as long as possible. Are we clear?"

"Yes, sir!" both men answered.

"Wait another twenty minutes until we are moving and drop the sails," Conrad said.

Gallagher went to the gun deck to deliver the orders, while Larson strode to the main deck to carry out the rest of the orders.

Conrad stood at the wheel and finished sipping his coffee, hoping he appeared calm and unworried to his crew. They needed a leader, not a fearful fool barking out crazy orders at them. "Lord, give me wisdom and courage to do what I need to do."

After the USS *Niagara* sailed ahead, Conrad ordered the USS *Larkspur* to follow. For the next couple of hours, they sailed around the island to meet the British fleet. By noon, the wind shifted in Perry's favor and he picked up speed.

"The USS *Lawrence* is sailing right in the middle of the entire British fleet." Larson shook his head. "They are too vulnerable; the British ships will destroy them. I believe in bravery, but this is . . . crazy!"

"He is not supposed to be alone." Conrad lifted his spyglass again. "The USS *Niagara* is supposed to be beside the USS *Lawrence* on the offensive and it includes the sloops and schooners holding back with the USS *Niagara*. What is Elliot doing? He looks to be at least a mile away . . . maybe more."

"Move forward," Conrad ordered.

"I thought we were ordered to hold back?" Larson asked.

"We were, but he also told me to use my discretion if things did not go according to plan. He had a feeling Elliot would do something like this and he was right." Conrad slammed his fist against the rail. I will not willingly sit by and do naught while a whole crew of men are slaughtered because other ships refused to do what they are supposed to do.

"Full sail ahead!" Conrad called.

The booming sound of a cannon echoed in the distance. Conrad lifted his spyglass. "A British ship fired at the USS *Lawrence*, but it fell short." He shook his head. "I fear we will not make it in time to help."

"Well, we shall do what we can. We have two long-shot cannons and the rest are short-shot carronades. Should I have Gallagher order the long-shot cannons to fire as soon as we are in range?"

"Yes, and make sure we target whichever ship is firing the most against the USS *Lawrence*."

Larson disappeared below. Conrad judged the distance and the wind and realized they were going in at the wrong angle. "Slight right to starboard!"

To Conrad's disappointment, the USS *Niagara* stayed where she was, but the other schooners and sloops followed Conrad forward to aide their fellow American ship. By now, several cannons had fired and the USS *Lawrence* had already suffered several hits. The other British ships had moved in on the USS *Lawrence* and now had excellent range; two in particular were pounding the USS *Lawrence*.

The schooners and sloops began returning fire against the British, but they didn't have as many guns nor the depth and power needed. The first shot from the USS *Larkspur* rocked the entire ship. It was one of the long cannons. Larson had gotten word to Gallagher. A second shot fired. Conrad gripped the rail along the quarterdeck as Larson returned, climbing the steps.

"Good job, Larson!" Conrad lifted his spyglass to check the status of the USS *Lawrence*. Another round hit them, and the deck splintered into a million pieces as men and body parts flew in every direction. Closing his eyes, Conrad hung his head, sorry they had not made it in time to save them.

The USS *Larkspur* closed the distance, filling in a huge gap as a round of carronades pounded one of the British ships. If they were now in firing range, it meant they would soon receive their fair share of return fire. The USS *Larkspur* shot two more long-range cannons.

A moment later, a cannonball ripped through the center of the ship. The blast flipped Conrad on his backside. His bruised tailbone burned, but he could move so it wasn't broken. Larson lay on his side and crawled back to his feet. Smoke came up from the center of the deck. Conrad worried one of their guns had been taken out.

"I need to know the extent of the damage to the ship and weapons," Conrad said.

Larson nodded and staggered down the steps. Conrad pushed himself to the quarterdeck rail where he could support himself and leaned over to assess the deck. The sails were still in operation. "Keep going! Do not give up."

They battled for another hour, taking hit after hit. Still, they continued to fire as long as they had abled-bodied men, cannons, and ammunition. The USS *Lawrence* had stopped firing, and the British ships eased up on her but seemed to be turning their attention upon the USS *Larkspur*. A round of cannon shattered the USS *Larkspur* in every direction. The blast threw Conrad across the deck. Pain sliced through his skull as his vision wavered into a hazy blur.

20

Pastor Shaw sat across from Mildred and Charlotte in the parlor. Mrs. Cooper brought in a tray of hot tea and sugar cookies. Mr. Porter stoked the small fire in the hearth. The early morning hours were now chilly, and by mid-morning, Charlotte thought she would keep the fire going one more hour for their guest.

"I want one!" Davie bounced up from the floor where he had been playing with his toy soldiers.

Charlotte pressed her finger to her lips and turned to Mrs. Cooper. "Thank you."

She nodded and left the room.

"Now can I have one?" Davie asked, tilting his head.

"You may." Charlotte smiled. "Pastor Shaw will you take one or two lumps of sugar?"

"Two, please." He accepted the small plate with two cookies. Charlotte stirred his tea and handed it to him. "My, Ashlynn has grown in the few weeks since your arrival. Am I right in assuming she may soon be crawling?"

"I suppose. I believe my sister Melanie's baby began crawling at five months. Ashlynn is the same age now. When we lay her out on a blanket, she manages to wiggle her way off of it, so she is definitely getting more mobile." Charlotte looked at Mildred. "Would you like for me to spread out her blanket now, so you can drink your tea?"

"An excellent idea," Mildred nodded. She unwrapped the blanket from around the baby and held it out. Charlotte spread it out on the floor, but far enough away from Davie's play area. Mildred went over and laid Ashlynn on her tummy while Charlotte prepared Mildred's tea.

"What news do you bring us from town, pastor?" Charlotte asked, handing Mildred her tea and turning to prepare her own.

"There are rumors a battle has begun near Put-in-Bay, but I have no idea how true it might be. People like to speculate and talk." He relaxed back in his chair and crossed his ankles. "If a battle is happening, we will no doubt know for sure in a few days."

"What about the wounded? How will they be cared for?" Charlotte asked, scooting to the edge of her seat as fearful thoughts for Conrad and David swirled in her mind and heart. "Unless I am mistaken, there is not a hospital around for miles."

"I imagine something would be set up nearby. They could open a building, set up tents, or a church could open its doors. People all around will need to volunteer their time and service. We could send a few volunteers from our congregation." He shook his head. "But there is no need to panic. Most of the time these ships only engage in small skirmishes, and the wounded are few compared to the larger battles."

"What has happened on the Great Lakes so far?" Mildred asked.

"Most of the action has taken place on Lake Ontario. Little has occurred on Lake Erie so far," he said.

"If you send volunteers from our church congregation, I would like to be among them," Charlotte said, linking her fingers in her lap in an effort to hide their trembling. "After all, Conrad or David could be among them. It is the least I can do."

"I will keep it in mind." He sipped his tea and bit into a cookie. "Mmm, this is very good."

"Thank you," Charlotte said. "We are blessed to have Mrs. Cooper with us. She has quite a talent for baking and cooking. We may need to go on longer walks to keep our waistlines from increasing."

"Let us talk of something more pleasant," Pastor Shaw said. "I have heard a large ball will be taking place in October."

"Indeed?" Charlotte sat back, the idea more appealing than it would have been years ago back in Wilmington. So many changes were taking place in her, she could hardly understand it all. The idea of dancing and lively music lifted her spirits. Could she be depressed? She hoped not. "Who will be hosting it?"

"I am uncertain as to who, but it will be in the town of Erie. It is about a hundred miles from here and would be a three-day journey." He lifted an eyebrow and shrugged. "It might be nice to get away for a while and attend something to bring you some joy, however temporary. I am offering my services to escort you, if the two of you decide to go."

"I could not leave the children for that long." Charlotte shook her head, already deciding it would be impractical for her. "And I would not want to haul them so far and inconvenience their schedules so I can attend a ball. It almost seems . . . selfish."

"Of course, I understand." Pastor Shaw nodded, a look of disappointment lingering in his expression as he glanced at the floor. "But I thought I would mention it, just in case it was something to appeal to you."

"It might if it was being held closer to home. I thank you for keeping us informed," Charlotte said.

"Yes, indeed." Mildred sipped her tea with a slight smile.

"Well, I had better be going. I need to prepare for Sunday's sermon. Before I go, I would like to bring in some wood for you and a bucket of water from the well." He stood. "Is there anything else I can do?"

"It is not necessary, but we thank you for your thoughtfulness." Charlotte set her cup on the table and rose to her feet.

"What about your letters, Charlotte?" Mildred asked. "Could he not take them to the courier for you?"

"Indeed! Thank you for reminding me." She glanced up at Pastor Shaw. "Would you mind?"

"Not at all." He grinned and set his black hat upon his head. "While I am collecting the wood, why not get your letters?"

"I will be right back." Charlotte left the parlor and hurried up the stairs to her writing desk in her chamber. The sound of the front door opening and closing indicated that the pastor had gone outside. Thankful she had already sealed each letter. Charlotte grabbed the stack and went back downstairs where she waited for Pastor Shaw to return. He carried an armload of firewood and set it on the grate in the corner. He dusted off his hands. Charlotte walked toward him. "I appreciate your delivering these to the courier for me." She held them out, and his hand grazed hers as he accepted them. "In fact, I have told my family back in North Carolina about you and how you have welcomed us here in the community."

"You warm my heart, Miss Morgan." He tucked them in his jacket pocket and patted them for safekeeping. "I look forward to my next visit in a couple of days."

Conrad slammed against the side of the wall as another blast splintered across the deck, shattering the wood into tiny pieces. His right shoulder burned like fire and more lightning crackled through his skull. Everything went dark, but the explosions continued to strike around him. The screams and cries of his men in anguish ripped through his soul as he staggered to his knees and blinked to wipe away the darkness. Light and fuzzy shapes in dark shadows filled his mind. He blinked again and wiped sweat from his brow, trying to focus. Blood soaked his arm and where he had rolled up his right sleeve on his forearm. Was he bleeding?

"Captain, are you all right? You have a nasty gash on the side of your forehead." Lieutenant Larson crawled to him, gripping his arm.

A gut-wrenching groan rippled through Conrad and erupted into a roar as the burning in his shoulder shot through his arm and neck like a torpedo. "I think my shoulder is dislocated."

"Sorry, Captain." Larson jerked his hand away from his arm and scooted up onto his knees, wincing. "I can help you put it back in place. Feels like all my joints and bones are still intact. Just a bit of bruising is all."

"What about the ship physician?" Conrad asked, preferring someone with more experience. The throbbing in his shoulder grew intense with each breath he took.

"Sir, if he is still alive, I doubt he will be available for a while." Larson leaned back so Conrad could get a better view of the state of his ship. A two-foot-wide gap split the top deck in half. The sails were ripped with holes, and pieces of canvas flapped in the wind. The watchtower was gone from the mainmast and half of the foremast lay across the jib sails. The smell of burning smoke accosted his senses as it clung in patches like thick fog. A mixture of blood and water soaked the deck where some of his crew had fallen to their deaths like discarded clumps of debris.

His stomach revolted, and Conrad fought the rising nausea as the fate of his comrades clung to his conscience like a fly caught in a web. He swallowed the rising bile and, with a forced effort, swayed to his feet. Conrad gripped the side of the rail with his good hand and clenched his eyes from the painful tremors shaking his body.

"Have you done this before?" Conrad glanced at his shoulder for emphasis.

"No, but I have seen it done. I know what to do." Larson wiped his sweating brow and left a smudge of soot on his face. "Once I heard a doctor tell a patient most shoulder dislocations are only partially out of the socket."

"If this is a partial dislocation, I would hate to feel a complete one."

"We need to brace you against something." Larson dropped his hands on his hips and surveyed what was left of the ship. "We shall use the mizzenmast. It is still stable and upright. Can you make it?"

"Of course." The moment the words were out, Conrad wondered if he had just told a lie. His vision faded to black as Larson gripped him by his good arm and made an attempt to help him.

"I am afraid you are losing a lot of blood, Captain," Larson said, glancing at the wound on his head. "I suspect you have a concussion."

The ship shook beneath them, and Conrad realized his gunners were still firing at the enemy. If they could still fight back, they were not yet finished. Encouraged, he tried to muster more energy as they made their way around dead bodies, scattered wood, broken barrels, and flapping sails. Once they made it to the mizzenmast, Conrad leaned his good shoulder against it and looked into Larson's blue eyes. "Be swift."

Larson lifted his arm at the right angle. Conrad clenched his teeth and closed his eyes. It would be better if he didn't know when the jab would come. He didn't want to wince or move the wrong way and cause Larson to miss, prompting more damage. Larson gripped his elbow and shoved his arm into his shoulder. His bones snapped and intense pain sliced through his arm, into his chest, and throughout his entire body. Conrad shouted in pain, as the veins in his head pulsated with quick gasps of air. Dropping to his knees, Conrad let his wounded arm hang at his side, afraid to move it again and reawaken the pain as a throbbing ache began to set.

Grabbing a portion of discarded sails, Larson came toward him. "Captain, we have to wrap it. Your arm will be swollen until it heals. You should not move it." Larson bent toward him. "Can you lay it across your chest? I need to make this secure and as comfortable as possible."

The USS *Larkspur* rocked and shimmered as it took another hit below them. Conrad fell on his backside, while Larson lost his balance and caught himself to the side with his palm against the deck.

"We had better hurry before another blast comes at us," Larson said, scrambling to his knees.

"Indeed." Conrad nodded, using his good arm for balance as he climbed to his knees and stood to his feet. Like before, Conrad braced himself against the base of the mizzenmast. "Let us get this done." He groaned, forcing his injured arm across his chest.

Working fast, Larson wrapped the sail around him, looped it up over his good shoulder and tied it tight. More blood dripped down Conrad's face and into his eye. He blinked and wiped it away. Sergeant Gallagher walked toward them looking as dirty and rumpled as they.

"Sir, we are down to four guns Almost all our gunners are dead. The lower levels are already taking on water. I do not know how much time we have before we sink," Gallagher said.

"Sergeant, we shall make the most of what we have left. Double-load those four guns, and bombard those blasted British." Conrad didn't know where his sudden strength came from. Perhaps it was from pure anger or disgust, but either way, his officers blinked in surprise and hesitated. "Go, I do not intend to allow the USS *Larkspur* to go down without fighting."

"Yes, sir." Sergeant Gallagher saluted him and turned to make his way down to the lower deck.

Conrad turned to Lieutenant Larson. "I appreciate what you have done for me. Now we must concentrate on saving what lives we can. Gather able men and prepare the rowboats to save the living. We need to be ready when the USS *Larkspur* succumbs. Row them to the other American ships."

"What about you, sir?" Larson asked.

"Go without me if you must." Conrad pointed toward the front of the ship where he knew David had been stationed earlier. "I am going up to the foremast to see who may have survived."

He didn't wait for Larson to respond as he climbed over the fallen mainmast and jumped over the two-foot hole in the deck. Conrad was prepared for the action to jar his arm and shoulder, but what he wasn't prepared for was the dizzy spell that came over him. He paused to gain his bearings, hoping he wouldn't pass out. After a few moments, he kept going.

A pair of feet peeked beneath one of the sails. Conrad hurried over and pulled it aside, careful not to jar his injured arm. He didn't recognize the unconscious sailor. Bending to his knees, Conrad felt for a pulse in his neck. There wasn't one.

He repeated the same process with three more soldiers. Only one could be roused. Conrad sent him in Larson's direction. He continued searching for survivors and found David lying on his side. His heart quickened, no longer thinking like a captain, but a brother.

Conrad rolled him over and breathed a sigh of relief when he discovered David still breathed. He slapped his cheek and winced from the pain in his shoulder. "David, wake up." Frustrated he didn't move, Conrad grabbed his chin and shook him. "You have to wake up. David, you have kids who need you."

This time, David blinked, his face contorting as he became conscious of pain. "Hurts."

"Where?" Conrad asked, searching his body for wounds. He didn't see any other injuries.

"Head." David lifted a hand to the back of his head.

Conrad reached around and found a growing lump. "You probably have a concussion. I am sorry to do this, but you have to stand. I cannot move you by myself. I have a dislocated shoulder."

"Leave me alone."

"I cannot. David, the ship is sinking. We have to get in the rowboat." He waited a moment for his words to penetrate. "Now come on." Conrad offered his good arm. David accepted, and together they made their way over to Lieutenant Larson. Two men lowered the rowboat, while Larson ordered instructions.

"Are there any others?" Larson asked.

"David is the last." Conrad shook his head. He pointed to the rail. "Hold on here," Conrad pressed David's hand around the rail, "while I go to the deck below and search for more survivors."

His brother didn't answer as Conrad walked away toward the steps. Another cannonball hit the top deck. Wood flew in every direction as the USS *Larkspur* bounced and rocked in the water. Losing his grip, David fell into the water.

"David!" Conrad ran to where he had been standing and leaned over the side. The water swayed and moved, but David was gone.

Charlotte contemplated her thoughts in silence as they rode the carriage toward Commodore and Mrs. Evans's home where they had been invited to spend Friday afternoon. Her thoughts drifted toward last Sunday's church service at Mercy Community Church. Pastor Shaw had preached on the book of Ecclesiastes. He said there was a time for each thing and it has its own season. Two passages stood out most to Charlotte, one was *a time to live and a time to die*, which brought images of Emma to mind. Sadness filled her. The other passage was *a time for peace and a time for war.* A new fear rose inside her—a fear of losing those she loved who were still alive. An image of Conrad and David came to mind, and her heart lurched with anxiety.

Her stomach rumbled in hunger, and she wondered what they would serve. Davie sat beside Charlotte and kept swinging his legs over the seat, kicking the bottom.

"Davie, please stop," Charlotte said, exchanging a weary glance with Mildred. She smiled as she continued to breast-feed the baby, while they still had privacy. Mildred had become adept at throwing a blanket over herself and Ashlynn, so Davie wouldn't see.

"When will we be there?" Davie whined, turning to the window.

"Soon, I promise, but you must behave or you will not be allowed to go outside and play in this beautiful weather."

Charlotte leaned toward him, knowing how hard it was for him to sit still. Regardless, she had a responsibility to try and encourage him to behave properly. "If you keep up your good behavior, I might allow the commodore to take you fishing. How does it sound?"

"When?" He whirled, twisting on the seat with his eyes growing wide with excitement. "Today?"

"First, you will have to eat the meal Mrs. Evans has prepared for all of us, but then you may go with the commodore if the weather holds out."

"Thank you, Aunt Charlotte!" To her surprise, Davie swung his tiny arms around her and squeezed. She wasn't sure if his hug was from gratitude or genuine love or a combination of both, but she was grateful. Charlotte wrapped her arms around him. These moments weren't often for a lad his age who was always busy running and playing. A pool of warm love settled in her heart.

"Charlotte, will you burp Ashlynn while I right myself?" Mildred asked, holding the baby out to her.

"Of course." Charlotte sat Ashlynn on her lap and patted her back.

"When will she be able to eat like the rest of us?" Davie asked.

"Very soon, we will be able to mash some of the softer foods and give it to her," Charlotte said as a loud burp came from Ashlynn's throat. "We have to be careful until she has teeth to chew."

A moment later, the carriage rolled to a stop. Commodore Evans and his wife were waiting to greet them, along with Pastor Shaw. Even though she wasn't expecting to see him, Charlotte's heart beat faster, and she realized she was glad to see him. He stood tall beside the commodore with his broad shoulders and black hat. He wore dark boots and the same black jacket he had worn at Mercy Community Church.

Commodore Evans stepped forward and opened the carriage door. Davie bounced out first, while Charlotte maneuvered the baby and accepted the commodore's assistance. Mrs. Evans came forward to greet her while her husband turned to assist Mildred.

"Since it is such a pleasant day, I have arranged for us to have our meal outside in the garden. Would this be agreeable to you?" Mrs. Evans took Charlotte's hands in her own and gave her a hopeful smile. "Afterwards, I believe the men intend to go fishing, and they hoped to take little Davie with them."

"Indeed," Charlotte nodded toward Davie. "I have promised Davie he may go as long as he behaves." He bounced on his heels with a huge grin but managed to remain silent as he rubbed his palms together in anticipation.

Mrs. Evans led them to the left side of the house where the gardens began at a brick archway and continued around to the back of the large two-story house where they had sat once before. They passed a small lily pond Charlotte had never seen and came to a rectangular table, set with plates, glasses, and silverware. A white canopy tent was erected over the table. With the colorful display of flowers surrounding it, the setting looked beautiful.

Once they were all seated, a servant brought a tray of tea. A moment later, she set a basket of fresh-baked bread before them. The main course consisted of pheasant, corn on the cob, squash, and spinach leaves. A disgusted expression crossed Davie's face as his mouth twisted into a frown, but he caught Charlotte looking at him and managed to hold his tongue. Pastor Shaw said grace, and they all dug into their plates.

The pheasant was tender and layered with spices. Charlotte laughed as Davie bathed his corn with butter and made a mess getting it on his cheeks. Mildred had to scoot back from the table as Ashlynn's little fingers grabbed at everything, and she would cry each time Mildred took it away from her.

"Pastor, what will next Sunday's sermon be about?" Commodore Evans asked.

"Overcoming grief." Pastor Shaw pushed his empty plate aside and wiped his mouth with his napkin before sitting back in his chair and relaxing. "In light of the anticipated battle taking place on the lake, I am concerned we may have some grieving widows and children to console."

"Well, let us not dwell on such things now," Mrs. Evans said. "In fact, here comes the pumpkin pie for dessert."

"Yay!" Davie waved his arms at the servant carrying the round dish. Charlotte lifted an eyebrow at Mrs. Evans, who nodded and motioned her to serve Davie first.

"The food has been excellent as always, Mrs. Evans," Charlotte said.

The older lady beamed with pride. "I am pleased to have the company."

After consuming the pie, Mrs. Evans glanced from Charlotte to Pastor Shaw and tilted her head with a gleaming smile. "I believe Mildred and I shall take the children to the well to wash their faces and hands. In the meantime, the servants will need to clear the table. Pastor, will you not take Charlotte on a stroll around the gardens?"

"What an excellent idea," he said, standing. Pastor came around the table and offered his arm. Unwilling to disappoint her host, Charlotte smiled, recognizing Mrs. Evans's obvious attempt at matchmaking. She accepted her escort's arm and allowed him to lead her toward the lily pond.

"I must admit I am glad to have a few moments alone with you," he said.

"Why?" she asked, hoping he would take things slow and not force her to reject his attentions. She liked him, but she needed time to discern how much she liked him. Charlotte sensed they could be compatible, but was it enough?

"Well, I have been wanting to get to know you better." He paused and took a deep breath as if trying to decide how to phrase his next words. "I realize I have not known you long and you are still in partial mourning for your sister, but I hope you will allow me to spend more time in your company, for it is the only way we can get to know each other better."

"It sounds reasonable." Charlotte nodded in agreement. "What exactly do you have in mind?"

"A formal courtship and, if you agree to this courtship, you may call me Luke." He patted her hand on his arm. "I long to hear at least one person call me by my given name. I would be most obliged if it was you."

Her heart fluttered with flattery. Did this mean she liked him in the same way? Indecision wrestled inside her as she thought back to moments with Conrad—and how she had longed for him to kiss her. Passionate heat always flowed through her veins when Conrad was around. Was it lust or something more?

"I must confess it is a little intimidating to court a man of God." They paused in front of the lily pond where she looked up into his hazel eyes. "I fear you will be quick to see all my faults and will soon grow displeased with me."

"Nonsense, we are all flawed." He took her hands in his. "And I fear I will disappoint you in not living up to the standards you expect of a godly man. I, too, am human."

"Will you give me some time to think about it?" she asked. "I will consider it."

"This is exactly what I had hoped for." He nodded and set her hand on his arm again. "Now allow us to return to the others before we go missing for too long."

When they returned, Commodore Evans paced in front of the tent with a slip of paper in his hands and rubbed his temple in distress.

"What is it?" Pastor Shaw asked.

"I just received a message. Our American fleet met the British fleet on Lake Erie this morning. A battle has begun. We do not yet know the details or the outcome. All I know is it occurred right off the shore of Put-in-Bay."

"Were Conrad and David involved?" Charlotte asked, glancing to the side as Mildred and Mrs. Evans returned from the well with the children.

"I am most certain they were," Commodore Evans nodded.

21

Another explosion shook the ship, and both Conrad and Larson were thrown overboard. The shock of the cold water jolted Conrad as held his breath and kicked to the surface using only one arm. Pain spiked through his skull, and he wondered if he would make it before passing out. A moment later he broke through the surface and gasped for air. The USS *Larkspur* burned, lighting up the sky and filling it with dark black smoke. The rest of the ammunition would soon cause more explosions. He had to get away.

Conrad paddled with one hand and kicked as hard as he could until he reached a chunk of floating wood. He hung on with his good arm and took a moment to catch his breath. Cannon fire continued to rage over his head as he tried to regain his thoughts and his bearings. He wished he knew the outline of the lake better.

Another man lay across a wooden plank bobbing in the water. He didn't move. Was he alive? Conrad blinked, kicking toward him. It looked like David. Taking a deep breath, Conrad paddled harder, but he felt like he wasn't making any progress. "David!" The man didn't move. Inch by inch he grew closer until he was certain it was David lying there unconscious. At least, he hoped his brother was unconscious. The other alternative was unthinkable.

He finally reached David and let go of the piece of wood and grabbed onto the board where David lay. It tilted, and Conrad feared dumping him into the water. He moved to the other side to give it balance. Conrad hung on with his good arm. "David? Can you hear me?"

No response. Fear spiked through his heart as anxiety took his breath. Conrad swallowed, trying to concentrate on what he should do and not panic. He called for help, but his voice was drowned out by more explosions and gunfire. It would do no good to stay here floating in the midst of so much danger. He turned the board around and kicked toward one of the American ships. Perhaps if they could get close enough, someone on board would hear him and bring them aboard.

"Lord, help me get away from the USS *Larkspur* before she explodes again." How many times had he wondered if God was listening to him in the past? Before when he questioned God, nothing in his life had been out of balance. He only questioned because he wasn't getting the response he wanted, but now he was in turmoil and his life hung in the balance—his and David's. If ever there was a reason to believe in divine intervention, he had to believe in it now or give up. At a time when no one else could hear him, Conrad was convinced God was the only one who could.

He kicked until his legs and lungs burned and grew heavy from exhaustion. Soon his muscles would be so numb he might not be able to move them. A huge explosion rocked the water into swells. Conrad could feel the heat even from this distance as the USS *Lawrence* succumbed to flames. Certain the USS *Larkspur* would not be far behind, Conrad kept going, but a wave stalled him. He almost lost his grip on the wooden board.

Splinters were already digging into his palm. Another wave came at them, and Conrad prayed David wouldn't slip.

The other swells following were smaller and calmer. Out of the burning smoke came a rowboat with only a few souls on board. Conrad called to them, but they were too far away to hear him. Coming from the USS *Lawrence*, they were survivors from the crew. Leading them in front was Commander Perry, standing tall and carrying a banner he couldn't see from such a distance. The scene encouraged Conrad, and he kicked harder, determined not to be left behind.

Perry rowed toward the USS *Niagara*, where it still lagged behind by at least a half mile. The ship appeared to be unscathed and not engaged in battle. Conrad imagined what kind of battle might follow between Perry and Elliot once he reached the USS *Niagara*. Cannon and shrapnel continued to reign around Perry as the British tried to finish him off. Every shot missed him, and the smaller American ships fell back without Perry's leadership. Conrad sighed. Was this the end? Had the British won?

He glanced over at his brother and realized he needed to get him to a boat or to shore so he could take care of him. Even the rowboat moved away faster than Conrad could kick. At this rate, he had no hope of catching them. He wished the wind would turn in his favor and blow them to shore. At least he could see land, which had to be a good sign. Exhausted, Conrad lowered his head on his elbow and rested his legs. The numbness set in and claimed his entire body.

Images of Charlotte came to mind, and he knew he had to keep going. He couldn't leave her alone with the responsibility of the children, and they needed their father. Glancing over at David, he made the decision to keep trying. Conrad took a deep breath and forced his legs to move. After a while, the rowboat disappeared from his vision. He hoped they made it to the *Niagara* without any further injuries.

Another explosion erupted behind him. Conrad turned to look over his shoulder and saw the rest of the USS *Larkspur* reduced to flames. Disappointment filled him as he mourned for his crew and prayed no other souls were caught aboard. The British slowed their fire, probably assuming they had won. The knowledge left a bitter taste in his dry throat. At this point, there was nothing he could do but survive.

A few moments later, a movement caught his attention. The USS *Niagara* was turning, and a new flag was being hoisted. In fascination, Conrad watched the USS *Niagara* sail right back into the British fray. The USS *Niagara* waited until she was close enough and set off a charge of fire, never letting up. Wide awake now, Conrad knew in his heart Perry had made it aboard the USS *Niagara* and relieved Elliot of his duties.

By the way Perry fired at the British, Conrad could tell he had his gunmen double-loading the cannons. All eight of the remaining American ships sailed toward the British and let loose more fire. The British were bombarded until two British ships collided into each other. It was a sight Conrad would never forget.

Sweat continued to drip down his face. At first, he thought it was where water had splashed up on him from the swells and waves due to all the action from the ships, but then he looked at his hand and saw blood. The gash in his head hadn't stopped bleeding. If he didn't hurry and make it to shore, he could soon be as unconscious as his brother.

For two days, Charlotte waited to hear news about the battle on Lake Erie. As the hours passed by with no word, her fears grew stronger. At first, she and Mildred had discussed their concerns but then lapsed into a quiet sadness, seeming to make the house heavy with despair. What would she do if the children lost their father? If she lost Conrad?

She wanted to stay positive and have a strong faith, but hadn't Emma's death proven that prayers weren't always answered and that bad things did happen to fine and righteous people? She didn't know anyone better than Emma, except Davie and Ashlynn. They were two innocent children who had already lost one parent and didn't deserve to lose another. It wasn't fair.

Tears stung her eyes as she pricked her finger with a needle. She needed to repair a button on Davie's shirt, but right now her nerves trembled throughout her body. Whatever made her think she could sew at a time like this? With a sigh, she set her sewing aside and walked to the window. A carriage came up the drive. It looked like Commodore Evans.

"Someone is coming," Charlotte said, her heart pounding.

Mildred paused from reading her book.

"It looks like Commodore Evans." Charlotte pressed her nose to the window and squinted. "I believe he is alone. Why would Mrs. Evans not come with him?" Her breath hitched in her throat as fear clawed around her neck, increasing her anxiety. "Something is wrong. He is bringing bad news or he would have brought his wife with him."

"Charlotte, you are jumping to conclusions. You do not know for sure. Perhaps he was out and about and decided to stop by and check on us." Mildred set Ashlynn on a blanket on the floor since she could now sit up by herself. Davie sat beside her playing with his toy soldiers. Mildred walked over to Charlotte and wrapped an arm around her shoulders. "Whatever it is, I will be here with you. Your family has become my family as well."

Blinking back tears, Charlotte nodded, unable to speak. Instead, she patted Mildred's hand on her shoulder. They needed each other.

She stepped out onto the porch as the carriage rolled to a stop. The door opened, and Commodore Evans stepped out. He looked tired, and the lines around his eyes formed deeper circles than she remembered. He grinned, but unlike in the past, his smile didn't reach his eyes as he walked toward them. Was it her imagination or did he lean on his cane more than usual?

"I realize you were not expecting me, but I have news I need to give you," he said, climbing the two steps to their porch.

"Commodore Evans, you are always welcome no matter if we are expecting you or not." Charlotte hoped her voice sounded as sincere as she needed it to be. She held out a hand and motioned him through the door where she had left it open. "You may proceed to the parlor where Mildred is waiting with the children. We only have two servants, and I sent Mr. Porter on an errand in town."

"Very well." He nodded as he moved passed her. "I know my way."

He went on and greeted Mildred as Charlotte closed the front door and prepared herself to hear what he had to say. She wanted to beg him to skip the formalities and just tell her the news, but she knew it would be impossible. When she walked into the parlor, Commodore Evans had already sat in a wing-back chair by the window facing Mildred on the settee. Charlotte chose to lower herself onto the settee beside Mildred.

"Would you like some tea?" Charlotte asked. "I am sure our cook already has some prepared."

"No, thank you." He shook his head and set his cane against the side of his chair. "As you probably suspect, I have some difficult news I must share with you, and I am trying to figure out the best way to state it."

"Just say it," Charlotte's patience ran out as she scooted to the edge of her seat. "Are they dead?"

His gaze fell on the children, specifically Davie, but the child paid them no heed as he played. She realized he wanted to be careful as to what he said.

"Davie, would you go ask our cook to bring us some tea and cookies?" Charlotte asked.

"Cookies!" Davie bolted to his feet and ran from the parlor.

"As you know, a battle took place on Lake Erie early Friday morning and carried out for most of the day," Commodore Evans said. "The conflict took place near Put-in-Bay. While the Americans suffered great losses, the campaign was an overall success. A little after four, Commander Perry sent the message, 'We have met the enemy and they are ours.'"

"But what about Conrad and David?" Charlotte wanted to get to the point of his visit.

"The USS *Larkspur* went down and so did most of her crew. Captain Conrad Deaton and Private David Deaton are both among the missing. I am so sorry."

Both? Charlotte tried to ignore the pain erupting in her head. "Is there any chance they might have survived?" she asked.

"Very little." He shook his head. "I do not want to give you false hope."

Mildred burst into tears.

"Is no one looking for them?" Charlotte refused to believe the worst so quickly. "Both of them are excellent swimmers, and they might have made it to shore."

"Miss Morgan, I promise, we are doing everything in our power to ensure all survivors are accounted for." He held up a finger in warning. "Based on what we know, the chance of Conrad and David's survival is remote. You need to prepare yourselves."

The finality of his words sank into her mind until she wanted to deny it. Sharp pain sliced through her chest as it ignited into a burning desire to believe they were alive. She could not give up. It was too soon. Charlotte lifted her gaze. "I understand your cautious warning, but I believe there is still hope and both Conrad and David will be found. When everything seems impossible, it is when we need a miracle the most."

Conrad managed to reach shallow waters where he could touch the bottom. Using his legs as momentum, he dragged the floating board with one hand, hoping to save his brother. Not once had David responded to his calls or shown any signs of life. Such lack of activity wasn't so unusual from a man who had been unconscious for as long as David. Still unable to use his injured arm, he took much longer than usual to drag the board onto land. Breathing heavy, Conrad fell to his knees in the sand.

The lake wasn't surrounded by tall sand dunes like the sea, but there was more sand than he had anticipated. He took a deep breath, attempting to recover his strength and gather more willpower. After a few moments, the effort paid off and his breathing eased. Conrad crawled over to his brother and shook his arm. He lay stiff and lifeless. An unsettled feeling kicked Conrad in the gut. Surely, David only felt this way because he had been in the water for so long. The small swells and waves from the battle kept washing over him.

Feeling for a pulse on David's wrist, more alarm coiled inside Conrad when he found none. He shook his brother's shoulder and winced at the blast of pain shooting through his injured shoulder. No response. Conrad shook him harder.

"Come on, David, you have to wake up!" When he still didn't respond, Conrad braced himself and rolled his brother over. A pool of blood leaked around a large piece of metal shrapnel buried deep into his chest. The life had already drained from him and the water must have kept washing away his blood. While trying to swim and hang onto the board with one hand, he had not been able to check David's pulse until now.

He let go of David's body and slammed a fist into the sand beside him. It flew up like powdered dust as he attempted to deal with his shocked disbelief. This whole time he had been fighting to save his brother's life, while he had already died. What were his last words to David? He couldn't even remember. Ever since the day they had boarded the USS *Larkspur*, he had been so busy getting to know his officers and crew, helping them prepare for battle, he and David hadn't spent any time together. How could he have let his younger brother die? He was supposed to look out for him—and the whole crew.

Sinking in the sand, Conrad shivered from the cool breeze blowing against the wet clothes now pressing against his body. Grief settled over him like a monsoon of despair, exploding through his nerves and shocking his system into a state of despondency. How could he go back home and face Davie knowing he not only lost his mother, but now his father as well? And Ashlynn, she would never know David or Emma. The only consolation he could fathom from this terrible ordeal was that his brother had been reunited with his beloved Emma. Had it been David's wish all along?

He should have been more patient with David as he had grieved over his wife. Closing his eyes, Conrad thought of all the times he should have had more compassion. Instead, he had tried to push David and Charlotte beyond their grief, so it would be easier for him to bear their pain. Guilt plunged through him, raking his soul in anguish as he rocked back and forth like a child, grateful for the solitude he had not granted his loved ones when Emma had died.

An image of Charlotte's tear-stained green eyes came to mind, all the days she wore black as it ate at him, and the pain—how could he have been so selfish? The idea of saying good-bye to a brother who had always been there through every part of his life—through all his mistakes and achievements and loved him unconditionally in spite of himself—how could he say good-bye? He could only imagine how much harder it must have been for Charlotte to lose Emma. Thoughts of her tumbling in the ocean waves in a sea of black flooded him. He wanted Charlotte. He needed her.

Conrad blinked to focus as he leaned over David one last time and touched his brother's cold arm. "I am going to miss you more than you will ever know. I only wish I could have had the wisdom to tell you how much you mean to me before it became too late." Tears choked his words and strangled his throat. Conrad swallowed, determined to carry on. "I shall be back for you. We will give you a proper burial. I promise."

Struggling to his feet, Conrad swayed as a wave of dizziness came over him. He tried to keep his balance as he looked around. All he saw was a barren wilderness of trees and wildlife, no houses or people. Taking a ragged breath, he pushed himself to walk in a random direction, hoping he wouldn't have to go too far before he found help. His throat was dry, but at least it seemed his head had stopped bleeding. If only the headache beating at his temples would subside.

Conrad walked for what seemed like hours through bushes, weeds, and woods. He fought constant waves of nausea and with each tide prayed the sick feeling would go away. Several times his vision faded, and he feared passing out in the middle of nowhere. He mumbled desperate pleas for help until he rambled just to hear himself talk. Hearing his voice gave him comfort he was still alive and moving.

Dusk began to claim what was left of the daylight. He tried to increase his pace, but he stumbled and tripped over tree roots. Groaning from the fierce pain in his shoulder and the new bruise on his hip, Conrad forced himself up and eventually found a path he could follow. It had to lead to somewhere—to someone. He crossed a harvested field and saw a dim light in the distance. As he pressed forward, the image of a small house came into focus. Conrad climbed the few steps to the front porch and hugged the pillar, resting for a moment. A dog barked from inside, and someone came to the door. Conrad couldn't see the person as his vision faded once again.

"Help me." He felt himself sliding to his knees.

22

As soon as the carriage rolled to a stop, Charlotte shoved the door open and bounded outside. She rushed up the walkway to Commodore Evans's house. He would not have sent a carriage for her if he didn't have news regarding Conrad and David. The fact he told the driver to suggest Mildred should stay home with the children made her anxiety even worse. She banged the brass knocker against the wooden door.

The butler answered and directed her to the parlor where Mrs. Evans waited on a settee and Commodore Evans paced around the room with his hands locked behind him. Both looked up as Charlotte entered. Her heart pounded so hard, it felt like it would come up her throat.

"Thank you for coming so quickly. Please sit down." Mrs. Evans patted the seat next to her. "I am afraid my husband has some distressing news."

"Indeed." He nodded, resuming his pacing. "After the battle on the lake, two ships were turned into a makeshift hospital to care for the wounded. Neither Conrad or David were among them, so when they did not turn up, we thought they might have gone down with the ship."

"You mean you found them?" Charlotte scooted to the edge of her seat with hope.

"David was wounded and lay on a wooden board. Conrad swam and pushed him to shore, but David did not make it."

Eerie chills crawled all over Charlotte's body as she digested the news. Thoughts of how she would tell Davie pierced her heart. Now he and Ashlynn were completely dependent upon her and Conrad. She jerked her head up, as fear coiled in her stomach ready to spring. "What about Conrad?"

"Conrad is alive but barely. He has a concussion and lost a lot of blood. His right shoulder was out of socket and is badly bruised. He also has two broken ribs. The doctor bound his ribs and cleaned the cuts all over his body. With a little rest and care, he should be back to himself in a few weeks."

Relief poured through her as silent tears blinded her vision. She looked down and tried to wipe her eyes, but the burning tears continued to flow. "Bittersweet news," she whispered.

"I am sorry." Mrs. Evans leaned over and covered her hand. "Captain Deaton has been asking for you. We put him in our guest chamber upstairs. The doctor is with him now." She turned to her husband. "My dear, would you take Miss Morgan upstairs to see Captain Deaton?"

"Of course." He walked over and offered his arm.

Charlotte sniffed and wiped her eyes as she lifted her chin, determined to be strong when she saw him. She could only imagine the horrors and suffering he must have endured. Was he with David at the end? Would it change him?

"I would offer you a handkerchief, but I believe I have already given them all to my wife." Commodore Evans gave her an endearing smile and winked, no doubt, hoping to cheer her. She placed her hand on his arm and allowed him to escort her up the staircase. Once they reached the landing, they walked down the hall and passed several doors. He paused by the fourth door on the right and knocked.

"Come in," came a muffled reply.

Commodore Evans turned the knob, and it clicked. The hinges squeaked as he eased it open. "Miss Morgan is here."

"Good, bring her in. I doubt Captain Deaton will get any rest until he sees her." The doctor set a bottle of medicine on the table beside Conrad's bed. He closed his black bag and stepped back. "He has been asking for you since I arrived. You might want to get in as much conversation as you can because I gave him some laudanum, and he will soon be fast asleep."

A bandage was on the side of Conrad's temple and across part of his forehead, and another one was wrapped around his shoulder and around his chest. He had cuts and bruises on his arms and hands, but when his hazel eyes met hers, she burst into tears of relief. She came closer to his bedside and gripped the hand he offered her. A mixture of relief and profound sadness filled his eyes as he looked up at her. She sensed a connecting bond between them that had not been there before.

"He should not move or sit up. His broken ribs will need a few weeks of healing. I bound them as tight as I could." The doctor shook his head as he walked behind her toward the door. "I have no idea how he managed to swim in his condition."

"Miss Morgan, please sit down." Commodore Evans slid a chair over for her. "I will be right outside in the hall talking to Dr. Blevins." He followed the doctor out of the chamber but left the door open.

"I was afraid you would not come," Conrad said, tightening his grip on her hand.

"And why would I not?" She pressed her other hand around his knuckles. "We are family, and I care deeply about you." Her voice dropped into a whisper as her chin trembled. "I always have, and it will never change no matter how angry you make me."

"Charlotte, you may not believe me, but I love you. Six years ago, I was so young and foolish. I thought adventure would give me a fulfilling life, but it never completed me the way I had hoped. I did not realize what was missing in my life until I came back and the emptiness subsided. Being around you—spending time with you—completed me. When I left you here with the kids, the emptiness came back again. I know we belong together."

Her heart beat as hope soared inside her. Could she trust him? She wanted to risk believing him, but thoughts from the past continued to sail through her mind. There was no doubt she still loved Conrad. She had to force herself not to think about him. Whenever she considered Pastor Shaw's request to court her, it was hard not to compare him to Conrad, which she knew was unfair.

When she heard Conrad and David were missing, she had worried about David like a brother and had mourned for the children, but the idea of losing Conrad ran much deeper. It felt as if her entire future was at stake. The connection was similar to how deeply she felt the loss of her twin. It was like losing part of herself. For the first time, she understood what Emma had felt for David. Charlotte had always thought she loved Conrad, but now her feelings for him had deepened to a level she had not known was possible.

"Charlotte, say something before this medicine knocks me out." Conrad's speech slurred as he dropped his head on his pillow in a groggy state. "I need to hear your voice."

"I love you, Conrad. I have always loved you, but I am afraid you will change your mind again and choose the sea." She squeezed his hand and brought it to her lips to kiss the top of his knuckles. The small layers of hair on his hand tickled her nose.

"No chance . . . of it happening. I could not wait to get off the ship and come back to you." His eyes rolled shut, and he said no more. Charlotte pressed her hand against his cheek and let the silent tears of relief fall as she listened to his steady heartbeat.

Conrad woke from a number of nightmares and each one showed David dying from the blast on the ship. He jerked awake, sweating and panting as if someone chased him. His shoulder and ribs throbbed. He winced aloud as he tried to move to a more comfortable position.

"What is wrong?" Charlotte's worried voice carried to him from across the chamber. Her skirts swished along with the sound of her footsteps as she came near. A warm hand laid over his arm. "You slept most of the morning away and it is now mid-afternoon. Are you hungry?"

"Thirsty."

He blinked to clear his vision as she poured a cup of water from a pitcher on the nightstand. She pressed the rim to his lips and tilted it enough for him to sip. It was cool and felt like a healing balm on his dry throat. He sipped as much as he could until his neck hurt and his ribs intensified in pain.

"Where is my brother?" he asked.

"What do you mean?" Fear laced her voice as if she questioned his sanity.

"I mean, where did they put his body?" He sighed in sadness, wishing he did not have to ask these questions. "I am not crazy. I realize he is dead, but I want to know what arrangements have been made. He was my brother. If I could not save him, the least I could do is make the arrangements for his burial."

"Conrad, you cannot blame yourself. You nearly died trying to save him." She sat in her chair and took his hand in hers. It felt smooth and soft, but strong. He needed the strength and clarity of mind she offered him. "If it had not been for you, we would not have his body so we could give him a proper burial."

"Where is he?"

"At the morgue being prepared. Commodore Evans provided a proper uniform for him. Everyone has been so comforting and helpful." Her voice faded into silence. He sensed the pain and burden of the responsibility she felt. "Pastor Shaw has agreed to officiate the service, and they will bury him in the church cemetery."

"I need to write our parents." He dreaded telling them the news. His mother would be devastated. David was the baby of the family, and they had always expected Conrad to take care of him. He wondered if they would inadvertently blame him. He remembered the time when they were seven and nine, when David was bitten on the hand by a dog. His mother had chastised Conrad for allowing him near the dog.

"I have already taken care of the matter," Charlotte said, leaning over to kiss his cheek. He wanted to feel her lips and reached over to pull her closer, but she leaned back before he could manage it. Frustrated he didn't even have the strength to give her a proper thank-you kiss, Conrad closed his eyes with a sigh. "Do not get angry, but I told them what happened to you as well and you are in recovery."

"How could I be angry?" he asked. "I am thankful you thought of it. When is the burial?"

"This afternoon. We cannot wait through the night. His body is already decomposing." She brushed his hair off his forehead. "I am so sorry. I know what it is like to lose a sibling. It will take time and the pain is hard enough, so do not compound it by blaming yourself."

"It seems as if you have thought of everything," he said.

"Not everything. I have not been able to bring myself to go home and tell Davie. I wrote Mildred, but I told her I wanted to tell Davie myself. I want to be there to comfort him when he learns the truth. He is still so young, but he now comprehends his mother will not be coming back. I have no idea how he will react to the news of his father's death."

"We will both do it. Ask Commodore Evans to bring him here. I can still talk and make decisions." He reached for her hand and linked his fingers with hers. "Which brings me to another decision, and I want no argument from you."

"What?" She arched a beautiful blond eyebrow in suspicion.

"I intend to be at my brother's burial." Her eyes widened, and he could see the look of shock and denial on her face. "Do not deny me, Charlotte. You of all people should know what this will mean to me. I will have enough resistance from Dr. Blevins and everyone else. I need you to be on my side in this." He gave her a pleading look. "Please."

She hesitated and straightened her shoulders like a peacock, ready to go into battle.

"Charlotte, I need this closure. Allow me the opportunity to say good-bye to David on my own terms. Think back to how you felt about Emma and put yourself in my shoes."

Her defenses crumbled and she relaxed. "All right, but you have to allow Commodore Evans to assist you and be willing to sit in a chair by his graveside."

"It sounds like a reasonable compromise." He nodded. "I believe this marriage will work out after all."

"Marriage?" She lifted wide green eyes as her mouth dropped open in disbelief. "Captain Conrad Deaton, is this your idea of a proposal?"

"Forgive me if I do not bend down on one knee or produce an engagement ring." He grinned. The idea of marrying her was the only thing to make him smile at the moment. He needed something positive to look forward to as he recovered from his wounds and grieved over his brother's death. He needed her by his side, and a proper engagement would keep the gossips from tarnishing her reputation. "Charlotte Morgan, I love you, and I want to spend the rest of my life with you. Will you consider marrying me in a few months when you are out of mourning?"

"Of course I will. I have been waiting six long years for you to ask me." She smiled as she leaned forward and pressed her soft lips against his. The kiss was gentle and too brief, only a glimpse of the promise to come. "In the meantime, you must rest and I will go tell the others you intend to go this afternoon. I shall have someone bring a tray of food. You will need the nourishment for your strength."

"Do not forget about Davie," he said. "Send for Mildred and the children."

"I will." She closed the door behind her, and his heart felt much lighter than it had when he first woke. Charlotte made all the difference in the world, and he looked forward to having her by his side for the rest of his life.

A fortnight later, Charlotte instructed Mr. Porter to set up a table with chairs outside in front of the house by the lake. The mid-morning breeze was cool and refreshing. It reminded her of how soon autumn would be here. Tiny waves lapped against the rocks in a gentle rhythm as pieces of light glistened on the water's surface on the sun's pathway. She enjoyed the serenity and peace here, but the love of home still tugged at her heart.

She gripped Conrad's uninjured arm where they paused on the porch and prepared to step down. While his physical body continued to heal and he improved each day, Charlotte could see and feel his grief for his brother. In spite of his physical and emotional pain, Conrad had held Charlotte's hand while she broke the news to Davie. Together, they comforted him and answered questions as Davie tried to process another death in his young life. As promised, Conrad attended David's burial, but the effort cost him the rest of his strength, and he slept the rest of the evening and most of the next day.

"It is so good to be outside again." Conrad covered Charlotte's hand on his arm. "You have taken such excellent care of me, and I am determined to stop being an invalid."

"Nonsense. If anything, it has been a challenge to keep you lying still as the doctor ordered." She took a deep breath, allowing the cool air to fill her lungs as she strolled through the yard beside him. A few leaves were now tinted yellow and orange, while others remained green. Birds chirped and sang around them, flying from tree to tree.

"Lying around gives one too much time to contemplate the sorrows of my life and all the mistakes I have made. I do not wish to become depressed and agitated. I feel better when I have my mind occupied and something to do." He leaned over and gave her a warm kiss on her cheek. "Thank you for bringing so many books and letting me complain when frustration gets the best of me."

Warmth pooled in the top of her stomach as she imagined her face turning a rosy hue. The announcement of their engagement was met with sincere congratulations from their friends, but Charlotte couldn't help wondering if Pastor Shaw felt uncomfortable around her. She hoped it wouldn't be too awkward at church next Sunday.

They reached the table, and Conrad pulled out a chair, motioning for her to sit down. She gave him a skeptical look as she did so. The last thing she needed was for him to overdo it this first day outside.

"It is time I get back to being chivalrous again." He settled in the seat across from her and grinned. "Besides, we have lots of plans to discuss."

Charlotte searched his face for signs of pain or discomfort. To her relief, she didn't see any. Conrad seemed to be in perfect health and enjoying the outdoors as much as she. Of course, in her case, it pleased her more to be in his company. She would have to be careful she didn't show too much adoration for him or he might grow a swollen head from all the attention.

Mrs. Cooper approached carrying a tray of tea and biscuits. Gray curls covered a portion of her forehead beneath her white cap, but her winning smile reminded Charlotte of how wonderful it was to have her helping them. "Would you like for me to pour some tea for you?"

"You can leave it." Charlotte motioned to the table. "I believe Conrad was about to discuss some important plans with me." She met his gaze and winked.

"Well then, I shall leave the two of you to have your discussion." She turned and walked away.

"I hate to ask this question, but I need to know." Charlotte poured a cup of tea and set it in front of Conrad. "When will they make you go back to war?"

"Not for a while." He sipped his tea while she poured a cup for herself. Conrad swallowed and took a deep breath. "What I want to talk about is our wedding day. What have you always envisioned?"

The question took her off guard and filled her with sadness. He blinked in concern as her smile faded. An image of her and Emma standing in beautiful wedding gowns in front of the altar at their home church came to mind. Before Emma married David, Charlotte had always envisioned them getting married at the same time. When she and Emma had met Conrad and David, the prospect of her ideal wedding grew even larger in Charlotte's mind until everything fell apart and reality ruined it.

"What I had always envisioned was a childhood fantasy and unrealistic." As she set her cup back on the saucer, it clinked. "I realize it now. At any rate, it is now impossible."

"Why?"

"Because . . . Emma and David are dead."

Conrad's eyes widened in shock. He sat back in his chair as he contemplated her words and nodded slowly. "I see. You wanted to have a double wedding with your twin sister." He pressed his palm to his forehead. "I am so sorry, Charlotte. How many of your dreams did I manage to ruin with my foolishness?"

"It no longer matters. What I wanted back then is no longer what I want now." She leaned forward and stretched her hand across the table.

"Tell me what you envision now, and I will do my best to make it up to you." Conrad sat up and linked his fingers with hers. He gave her a gentle squeeze to emphasize his determination. "Did you and Emma ever discuss it?"

"When we were children, we laughed and dreamed about how our future would be, but when we started courting two brothers it almost seemed imminent." His thumb circled the top of her hand, encouraging her to continue. "Emma's love for David gave her the courage to abandon such childhood fantasies. I always admired her for it, and now, it is my turn. My love for you will give me the courage I need to let go of my past and step into the rest of my life. I am still afraid you will change your mind, but I am determined to trust God will get me through it if you do. I must also trust the Lord we will have a good marriage, if you do not change your mind, because I never want you to regret your decision of wedding me."

"It will never happen, Charlotte." He leaned forward and cradled her hand in both of his. "I am scared to death something will happen to you because I do not deserve you. David's death has brought a reality to me I did not see before—how life can be so fragile. We must make the most of the time we have been given. I never imagined a double wedding like you did, but I always thought David would be there by my side as the best man at my wedding."

"Do you know where I have always felt more at peace than anywhere else?" she asked.

"No, but I want to know." He shook his head. "I feel as if I ought to know."

"Where you found me on the day of Emma's burial. I want to be married on the beach, Conrad. I want my toes to be digging in the warm sand with beautiful seashells around us and the sound of the waves as our music." Excitement built inside her as the new dream formed in her mind and built a foundation in her heart. "When this war is over, I want to go home to the MacGregor Quest, so we can be by the sea again."

"But what about your uncle? Did he not inherit the estate from your grandfather, Malcolm MacGregor?" Conrad raised an eyebrow in confusion.

"He did indeed, but in the hope of enticing me home again, they are fixing up David and Emma's house and saving it for me. If you remember, it is beside the original MacGregor Quest, closer to the sea. It could be ours, Conrad."

"I do not know . . . it would not be on a piece of land we could call our own." He hesitated, looking doubtful.

"Since when do you want land? You are a sailor. You could never be landlocked, and I love you too much to do that to you." She shook her head. "No, we will buy a small parcel of land from my uncle where the old house now stands, but you will sail, and I shall sail with you when I can. You could go into shipbuilding. Would it not suit you better? I already have a brother in the business."

"Why did I ever hesitate to marry you?" he asked, staring into her eyes with so much love she wanted to push the table away and kiss him. "No one could understand me better than you."

"Back then I did not understand you as I do now." She smiled up at him as her heart flooded with warmth and a new peace settled over her—a peace she had not felt since Emma's death. "We were not meant to have a double wedding. Conrad, our time is now. God preserved our relationship and put us back together at a time when we can be more mature and in the right place to raise David and Emma's children as our own." She pushed the chair back and went to stand behind him where, mindful of his recent injury, she leaned down and wrapped her arms around his neck and shoulders. "Our lives have not turned out the way we planned, but we have survived, and we have each other. Right now, I could not ask for more."

Group Discussion Guide

1. Before the book begins, Charlotte lost her identical twin. On a few occasions, Charlotte compares her relationship with her twin to be as deep as a relationship with a spouse. Do you believe twins have a deep bond like this?
2. Charlotte is afraid to trust Conrad because he hurt her six years ago when he chose his navy career over her. How often do we allow the past to make decisions for us in the present?
3. It pained Conrad to see Charlotte and David grieving over Emma, but it took losing his brother to see how he had tried to prevent their grief. What other steps could Conrad have taken to help them overcome their loss without hindering their personal grief process?
4. Conrad believed Charlotte changed after her twin's death and saw a side to her that he had never noticed before. Do you believe those qualities were already present in Charlotte and Conrad merely saw her differently, or did she really change as much as he imagined?
5. When Charlotte arrived in Cleaveland and met all the women with husbands in the military, it made her realize that the life she had wanted with Conrad could have been possible. How often had you been closed-minded about how to make something work in your life like Conrad?
6. On a couple of occasions, Charlotte was reminded of the Ecclesiastes 3 verse where it says there is a time to kill and a time to heal . . . a time for war and a time for peace. What do you think God means by this verse?

7. At what point in the story did Conrad begin to see that his love for Charlotte was stronger than his fear of being landlocked and away from the ocean? When has your love for someone else given you the strength to see beyond a particular fear in your life?
8. When Davie was bitten by the snake, Charlotte began to question her ability to be a mother to Emma's children. When have you questioned your ability and decisions as a parent? If you are not yet a parent, what do you believe would be your greatest challenge as a parent?

Want to learn more about author
Jennifer Hudson Taylor and check out other great
fiction by Abingdon Press?

Sign up for our fiction newsletter at
www.AbingdonFiction.com
to read interviews with your favorite authors, find tips
for starting a reading group, and stay posted on
what's new on the horizon. It's a place to connect
with other fiction readers or post a
comment about this book.

Be sure to visit Jennifer online!

www.Jenniferhudsontaylor.com
http://jenniferswriting.blogspot.com
http://carolinascots-irish.blogspot.com

We hope you enjoyed Jennifer Hudson Taylor's *For Love or Liberty*, the final book in her MacGregor Legacy series. If you haven't read the first two books, *For Love or Loyalty* and *For Love or Country*, we hope you will be inspired to check those out as well. Here's chapter one of *For Love or Loyalty*, which details the thrilling story of how the MacGregors came to be a great American family.

1

A feeling of foreboding crawled over Malcolm MacGregor like a colony of insects picking at his skin. He gripped the reins as he inhaled the crisp March air, but it burned his lungs with the residue of tainted fire. A cloud of dark smoke hovered over the wee village of Inverawe—home. Fear coiled inside Malcolm's gut as he urged his mount forward.

His brother kept pace beside him. At a score and four, Thomas was two years Malcolm's junior. He favored Malcolm with the same stubborn chin and broad shoulders from hard work.

Distant moors lined the overcast sky. Morning fog hovered over the glen, blending with heavy smoke. As they drew near, their eyes stung and the burned smell accosted them until they coughed. Keening scraped his ears like a tormented bagpipe.

They reached the stone huts, packed with dirt and topped by straw roofs. At least the village homes weren't on fire as he originally feared. Piles of furniture and personal items burned in front of each hut. Weeping echoed from every direction.

Malcolm's throat constricted. His chest tightened in a mixture of compassion and fear for his family. He maneuvered his horse between the huts, heading toward the center of the village, seeking the home where he had grown from a lad into a man. Engulfed in flames, it blazed to the sky.

"Mither an' Carleen . . ." The words fell from Malcolm's swollen tongue, stalling in the air as his thoughts shifted to their youngest brother, Graham. At only twenty, the lad would have done anything to protect the women in their absence.

"Malcolm, ye're back!" Heather strode toward him, her eyes red and swollen. Words stalled upon her tongue, increasing his anxiety as he waited for her to collect her emotions and continue.

"What happened?" Malcolm asked, pulling his horse to a stop and dismounting. It was an effort to keep his voice calm, but he tried for Heather's sake, though his insides quaked.

"'Tis the worst." Heather succumbed to tears, shaking with grief.

"What is it, lass?" Malcolm shook her, hoping to force her out of her temporary stupor.

"Where's Mither an' Carleen?" Thomas strode toward them, his voice betraying his fears.

Heather sobbed, falling against Malcolm's chest. On instinct, his arms slipped around her. He looked up as the rest of the villagers approached with sorrowful expressions.

"The Campbells were here." Roy strode foward, his red eyes weary with similar grief—his right eye swollen and his lip cut. Even in his late fifties, Roy was healthy and robust. It would have taken several men to bring him low. "They took Iona an' Carleen."

"Took them?" Thomas gave the elder man a look of disbelief. "Where?"

"How long ago?" Malcolm pressed Heather into the arms of her mother, who came up behind her. He turned back to his horse and prepared to mount.

"Nay! There's too many o' them. Sixty or more." A strong hand grabbed his shoulder. "Listen to me, lad. Ye canna help yer mither an' sister if ye're dead."

"I've time to catch them if I leave now." Malcolm pulled away. More hands grabbed him. He didn't want to fight his own kinsmen, but they wouldn't deter him from his mission. He had to act now before it was too late.

"Let me go!" Thomas yelled, fighting a similar battle.

"I've got 'im, Da." Strong arms belted around Malcolm's neck and jerked him backward, cutting off his air. Malcolm coughed. He swung his elbow into Alan's ribs.

"Argh!" Alan relaxed his hold but didn't let go.

"Listen to reason, lad. The rest o' us are too auld an' wounded to be fightin' ye." A fist from another angle slammed into Malcolm's jaw. "But fight ye we will if it's the only way to save yer life." Roy's voice echoed over the multiple hands and arms keeping him down.

Never had the villagers fought him like this. More dread pooled in the pit of his stomach as he realized there had to be a reason for their adamancy. What had they not yet told him? They were right. How could he and Thomas expect to best sixty or more Campbell men? This feat would require his wits, and he wasn't thinking, only reacting.

"All right." He clenched his teeth, willing his body to relax against their resistance. "Tell me why I shan't go after them. It does not make sense to lose precious time."

Following Malcolm's example, Thomas also surrendered.

"Duncan Campbell came to collect the rents," Roy said. "But he arrived with an army of warriors. He did not come hither on business as he claims. His purpose was to cause trouble, an' he chose yer family to be the example."

"They were not supposed to come for another fortnight." Malcolm jerked away from Alan, who sported a bloody lip, already swelling, and a long sword gash upon his arm. Malcolm frowned. Only the Campbells would have been carrying broadswords. Blood soaked Alan's sleeve, probably more so from his skirmish with Malcolm. Guilt lacerated Malcolm's emotionally scarred heart. How long must they go on living like peasant pawns for the Campbells' entertainment?

"They did all this over unpaid rents?" Malcolm lifted his hands in disbelief. "We took the cattle to market an' we now have the rent. 'Tis all for naught!" His voice cracked as he ran a hand through his hair. A deep ache twisted his gut.

"Listen to Da." Alan wiped the back of his hand across his lip. "We need a plan. The Campbells want us to come after them in a mad rage. They have the king's favor an' all the wealth they need. We canna fall into their trap again."

"We can gather more MacGregors an' break into Kilchurn Manor." Thomas walked over. The others stepped aside to let him through. "We'll get Mither an' Carleen out. We canna abandon them."

" 'Tisn't that simple. I wish it were." Roy rubbed a wrinkled hand over his weathered face with a broken sigh. "Even if we gather more MacGregors from other parts of Argyll, we may not be strong enough to break through Duncan Campbell's forces. He has too many allies. If we succeed an' bring them home, how will we stop the Campbells from coming again?"

Roy and Alan stood still, watching Malcolm and Thomas as though they would tackle them again if need be. More villagers crowded around. All of them looked like a sorry lot, the men having been beaten, the women wearing expressions of grief and sorrow. Soot layered their faces, arms, and clothing.

“ ’Tis possible they have taken them to a debtors’ prison,” Mary MacGregor maneuvered around her husband and son, “since yer mither did not have the rent money.”

“If that is the case,” Malcolm said, “they will have to release Mither an’ Carleen once I pay the rent.”

“Duncan raised the rents again, plus he’s charging interest,” Mary said. “He took our furniture an’ burned what he did not want.” Tears filled her eyes. “William an’ Graham are young an’ foolish to try to fight them. They killed William this day. How many more do ye think we can stand to lose?”

“An’ Graham?” Malcolm staggered at the news. He closed his eyes, rubbing his brows. William and Graham were inseparable. Had Graham suffered the same fate? Heather broke into more weeping, and Malcolm’s chest tightened. The lass had been sweet on their youngest brother as soon as they could walk. Now he understood the extent of her grief. “Where is Graham? Did they take him too?” Malcolm clenched his fists at his sides, attempting to calm the rising tide of anxiety. “Is he alive?”

“Aye, but barely,” Roy said. “I’m sorry, Malcolm. We tried to fight them, but there were too many . . .”

“Take us to ’im,” Thomas said in a gruff voice, moving to stand beside Malcolm.

“Greg and Colin are tending to ’im. The Campbells beat him bad an’ hung ’im on a tree.” Roy’s voice faltered. “To make an example out o’ ’im.”

“By the neck?” Malcolm followed Roy and Alan to their hut. Fear clawed at his heart and gripped his lungs, stealing the breath from him.

“Nay,” Alan said. “With his arms spread out. We think both shoulders are dislocated.”

They stopped before entering Roy's hut. "They left us only one bed so that is where we put 'im." Roy held up a palm and shook his head. "Prepare yerself, lads."

Malcolm bent through the threshold and blinked, allowing his eyes to adjust to the dim candlelight. Their small huts contained no windows for daylight to filter inside. He walked across the dirt floor to the tiny bed. Graham's long legs hung over the side. His height matched Malcolm's at six four. Among the three brothers, Thomas was the shortest, shy of them by a couple of inches.

Colin looked up from where he hunched over stitching a wound in the lad's side. Greg cleaned his bruised face from the other side. Neither of them spoke as they concentrated on their tasks.

Both Malcolm and Thomas dropped to their knees. Thomas groaned and gulped back a threatening cry. Malcolm searched for his voice, but it lodged in his throat as a sickening pain clutched his soul and wouldn't let go. They stayed that way for several moments, trying to make sense of it all.

Colin cleared his throat. "The lad fought bravely, like a Highland warrior if ever I saw one."

Graham disliked fighting. Unlike the rest of them, who thrived on the sword, Graham preferred his wits to outsmart the wretched Campbells. He held out in stubborn pride, believing forgiveness and reason would bridge the great divide between the Campbells and the MacGregors. Today, he discovered the truth, and his faith almost cost him his life.

"Is he . . ." Still unable to say it, Malcolm laid a hand on Graham's chest. A faint heartbeat pulsed beneath his palm. Malcolm closed his eyes in relief.

"He passed out from the pain when I reset his shoulders back into the sockets," Greg said. "As soon as Colin stitches his side, we'll bind his ribs."

"At least he's alive," Thomas said, shaking his head in disbelief. "I always teased him about being the bonny son. Now look at 'im. I fear he will never be the same again."

"Graham was never vain." Malcolm gripped Graham's limp hand. "I worry 'bout the lad's spirit an' his broken ideals. He will blame himself for not saving Mither an' Carleen. No doubt, he will feel naïve he ever thought reconciliation with the Campbells was possible."

"Aye, 'twill take him a while to recover," Thomas said with a sigh. "Did Mither an' Carleen see what happened to 'im?"

"Nay," Colin shook his head. "The Campbells split up. Scott Campbell took them away while his father stayed behind to cause more damage." Colin rubbed his eyebrows and sat back. "That one has the heart of the devil, he does."

"I shall get revenge for our family an' the whole MacGregor Clan. The Campbells have wronged us for two centuries. They have tried to wipe out the MacGregor Clan, an' here we survive against all odds." Malcolm raised a fist and growled. "This time, I care not what it takes." Malcolm turned to Roy. "We shall send a scout to Kilchurn Manor to see if Mither an' Carleen are being held there and also to the nearest debtors' prison. We will move our family to Glenstrae under the protection of the MacGregor Clan Chief." He shoved a hand on his hip and rubbed his eyebrows, fighting the onslaught of a headache and too much regret. "Should have done it a long time ago after Da died."

"Ye were but a wee lad." Roy shook his head. "Do not do this to yerself. 'Tisn't yer fault."

"Aye, I've tarried long enough. I almost lost my family because of it." Malcolm glanced down at Graham, fear spiking inside him. He hoped it wasn't too late.

"Where ye going?"

Lauren Campbell jumped with a start, throwing a hand over her hammering chest. She placed a finger across her lips to shush her sister of ten and two. A quick glance around the busy kitchen assured her no one paid them any attention. Cook put away uneaten food while the rest of the servants cleaned up where the Campbells had broken their morning fast.

"Do I have yer word to say naught?" Lauren peeked at her sister's wide brown eyes, curious as Blair twisted her lips into a mischievous grin.

"If ye take me with ye." Blair nodded, and her sandy brown hair slid over her face. She brushed the long strands out of her eyes with an impatient sigh.

"I canna." Lauren shook her head, biting her lower lip as she placed biscuits in a basket. " 'Tis dangerous where I'm going."

"Where?" Blair sidled up to the counter beside Lauren, excitement building in her tone.

"I'm going to the ancient castle of Kilchurn." Lauren's heart swelled as her sister's eyes widened in admiration.

"All alone? Ye know Da would not approve if he was home." Blair lowered her voice to a whisper. "He will be angry if ye do not take cousin Keith."

"Keith is studying to take orders next week and will give his first sermon," Lauren whispered, touching the tip of her sister's nose and grabbing a block of cheese. "I canna interfere with the Lord's work. Besides, Kilchurn Castle is part of our estate. 'Tisn't as if I'm leaving the grounds."

"But ye're leaving Kilchurn Manor," Blair said.

" 'Tis only a short ride." Lauren covered the basket with a cloth and tucked in the edges. She paused, considering her sister's hopeful expression.

"I want to go, please." Blair linked her fingers as if she was about to pray. She wore the Campbell plaid over a dark blue dress and frowned with a sulky pout as she crossed her thin arms. "Lauren?"

"Run along and get ready. Meet me at the stables," Lauren said. "I shall see that your horse is saddled and ready."

Blair disappeared. Her footsteps pattered down the hall. Lauren chuckled and shook her head, knowing the child ran in haste. She hoped Blair would not tumble into one of the servants. With her basket of goods in tow, Lauren let herself out the side door and made her way to the stables.

It was a crisp morning, bright with sunshine and promise. Lauren loved the ancient relic of Kilchurn Castle now crumbling on the far side of Loch Awe. The short journey would take them less than an hour on horseback. On the days she walked the grounds, Lauren loved imagining what it must have been like centuries ago when the castle passed from the MagGregors to the Campbells through marriage.

Lauren entered the shaded stables. "Aidan?" Lauren called to the stable lad. "Are ye there? Blair and I are going for a ride." No one answered. Strange. Lauren shrugged and stepped back, trampling on a pair of booted feet. A man's hand clamped over her mouth, shoving a piece of cloth inside to silence her scream. Another hand pulled her by the hair and jerked her back against his hard body. Her basket of goods flew over a nearby stall. The horse inside stomped and snorted.

"I took care o' the lad," said a gruff voice at her ear. "Just needed to get 'im out o' the way. 'Tis Duncan Campbell's daughter I want."

Lauren's heart pounded in her ears as she kicked behind her, but he slammed a fist against her temple. Pain sliced through her head. He wrapped an arm around her neck, cutting off her air, and dragged her into a dark corner.

"Lauren?" Blair called. Her footsteps came closer. "Are ye here?"

Closing her eyes, Lauren stopped struggling, praying God would spare her sister. The man breathed heavily at her ear, his grip intense. To Lauren's relief, he appeared to be alone, and he did not go after Blair.

"Aidan?" Her sister sighed with frustration. "Where did everyone go?" She stomped out of the stables and back toward the manor.

As soon as Blair disappeared, the man slipped a knife to Lauren's throat. "Go." The blade nicked her skin as he pushed her forward, leading her out of the stables on the other side. The gag tied in her mouth made her jaw ache and dried her tongue. He dragged her into the woods where a horse waited.

Lauren tripped over a fallen branch, but he caught her and shoved her against a tree. Her bruised hip stung as he pulled her arms behind her and bound her hands. The man slung her over his horse and mounted behind her. Between a dizzy spell and a wave of nausea, she caught a glimpse of his MacGregor plaid.

They rode toward Inverawe where Lauren often visited the poor and brought them food. Iona and Carleen MacGregor always welcomed her and shared their faith. Iona's sons were not quite as friendly, but Graham was open-minded and kind. Lauren supposed because he was the youngest he wasn't as set in his ways as the other two. He was closer to Lauren's age at twenty.

When they arrived at the village, Lauren wasn't prepared for the devastation she witnessed. Ashes simmered in gray piles. Grief-stricken faces glared at her with hatred. Several people spit at her, and one threw a rotten onion in her face. The putrid smell made her stomach roll.

They came to a pile of rubble that should have been Iona and Carleen's hut. Hot smoke still pumped from the smoldering remains. Lauren's chest tightened as tears sprang to her eyes. Her father and brother were supposed to arrive here and collect the rents. Surely, they were not responsible? Her heart ached, fearing it was the truth she wanted to deny.

Her abductor stopped at one of the huts where smoke pumped through the chimney. He grabbed Lauren by the arm and yanked her down. She stumbled to her feet, finding it hard to regain her balance. He pushed her toward the door as others surrounded them.

"Why did ye bring a Campbell 'ere?" a woman asked. "Do ye not think they have caused enough trouble?"

"Aye," a man said. "The whole lot o' them will come looking for 'er."

"Malcolm! Thomas!" Lauren's captor ignored them and banged on the worn wooden door. "Open up. I have Lauren Campbell."

The door swung open and Malcolm's tall form emerged. He crossed his arms with a menacing scowl. "Colin, ye were supposed to find my mither an' sister, not bring back a hostage."

"Iona an' Carleen were not at Kilchurn." Colin's words came out in a rush as he tightened his grip on her. "But she was."

"What are we supposed to do with her?" Malcolm pointed at Lauren, venom coating his tone. "This was not the plan."

"We have no plan since they were not at Kilchurn," Thomas said, coming to stand behind Malcolm. "Mayhap, she can be the plan. Who else is goin' to be as important to Duncan?"

"She canna stay here," another man said. "Her father will destroy the whole village lookin' for her."

"Aye, but she's here now," Mary MacGregor said. "The damage is done. Ye should make the best o' her situation. Could we exchange her for Iona or Carleen?"

Shock vibrated through Lauren. What had her father done? Although the MacGregors had never been cruel to her, most, except Iona and Carleen, were wary and reluctant to befriend her. Now that the villagers had good reason to be seething in anger and resentment, she had no idea how far they would go in using her. She wondered if anyone at home had discovered her disappearance.

"What if he comes back an' burns the rest o' our homes?" a woman asked.

"He owns all these huts. If he burns them all, he canna rent them out." Malcolm scratched his temple and glanced at Lauren. "Remove her gag. She may know something."

"How ye plan to get 'er to talk?" Colin asked, jerking at her bindings. The cloth fell from around her head, and Lauren spit out the other piece.

"Speak up, lass." Malcolm stepped toward her, his height more like a tower than a mere man. "Where did yer da take my mither an' sister? The sooner we find out, the sooner negotiations can begin an' ye can go home."

"All I know is that he intended to collect the rents and go to the harbor."

"The harbor?" Thomas joined his brother, his palm up against the side of his head, pondering the possibilities. "Why would he do that?"

"Only one explanation," an older man said, lifting a finger. All eyes turned to him. "To sell them. What else?"

The women gasped, some wept, while the men groaned and complained in outrage. Colin jerked Lauren by the arm and shoved her to the center. "We have one of their own!" She stumbled and fell to her knees. He pulled her hair. Fire burned her scalp. She prayed her neck wouldn't break from the pressure. Tears stung her eyes. *Lord, I thank You for sparing Blair.*

"What would Duncan do to save this bonny face?" An elderly woman bent to squeeze Lauren's cheeks. The others came at her all at once with raised hands. Lauren closed her eyes, expecting a beating.

"Stop!" Malcolm's firm voice sliced through the mob like a king. With the MacGregors scattered throughout Campbell lands that used to belong to the MacGregors, none of them had a clan chief. The exception was Glenstrae farther north in the heart of the Scottish Highlands. Yet no one laid a hand on her. They obeyed Malcolm out of respect.

"Let us think about our actions an' how the Campbells might retaliate." Malcolm lifted his hands and pointed in the direction of Kilchurn Manor. "As long as the lass lives an' remains unharmed, we have something to bargain. None o' us wanna worry 'bout being murdered in our beds at night or forced to flee to the hills again."

Eyes widened, mouths dropped open, and heads shook back and forth in slow motion. Some of the villagers' skin turned paler. They backed away from her.

"Duncan an' Scott Campbell have a good head start. At this point, we would be guessing which harbor they went to an' taking the lass at her word," Malcolm said.

"Taynuilt Harbor is the closest," Roy said. Lauren had heard one of the others call him by name. He was a middle-aged man who looked at her with so much malice her skin itched and burned. " 'Tis on Loch Etive an' leads out to sea."

"Aye." Malcolm nodded, rubbing the back of his neck. "First, I want to ensure Graham's safety 'til he heals, as well as the villagers'. I shall find her wretched father." His boiling gaze landed on Lauren, and their eyes met. If the good Lord hadn't been holding her together, she might have crumbled in fear, but Lauren not only found the courage she needed but also managed to lift her chin and keep her peace. Later in solitude she would bear her burdensome fear to the Lord.

"Let us bring her inside while we tend to Graham an' make our plans," Malcolm said, turning to the others.

Colin shoved her. Lauren stumbled into Malcolm. He reached out a steady hand and gripped her arm. She assumed the action was only out of instinct, not for her welfare.

"What happened to Graham?" The words tumbled through her lips. Of all the MacGregor men, he had always been kind to her.

Malcolm paused, his lips twisting in anger. "Yer da ordered him beaten. They tied him to a tree, pulled an' tortured him 'til his shoulders snapped out o' the sockets. They murdered his best friend, William."

Lauren cringed as her mouth drained dry and her stomach twirled. The temptation to deny his words frayed at the edge of her mind as she followed him inside.

Malcolm directed her over to a large figure lying motionless on a small bed. A candle burned on a makeshift table beside him. She took small steps, her heart pounding into her throat.

"Graham?" Lauren leaned over him, taking in the sight of his bruised and disfigured face. The memory of his handsome features was like a vision. Graham didn't respond. Deep sorrow filled her soul as she imagined what agony he must be enduring. "My . . . da . . . did this?"

"Aye," Malcolm's tone dripped with bitterness. "I was not here, but they tell me he tried to protect my mither an' sister—yer friends." He emphasized the last words as if she had betrayed them herself.

"They are my friends," she whispered, unable to wipe at her tears with her hands bound behind her. Bile rose to the back of Lauren's throat, threatening to overcome her. Graham's wounds would be branded in her brain forever. What would become of

Iona and Carleen? She slid to her knees as grief wracked her body. Lauren had never been able to deny the emotional tug of compassion. While she wondered what was to become of her, Graham's grave condition weighed on her heart along with the spiritual state of the souls within her father and brother.

Lauren turned and tried to wipe her cheek on her shoulder. Malcolm strode toward her, his mouth set in a grim expression. She resisted the desire to cower and forced her muscles to remain still.

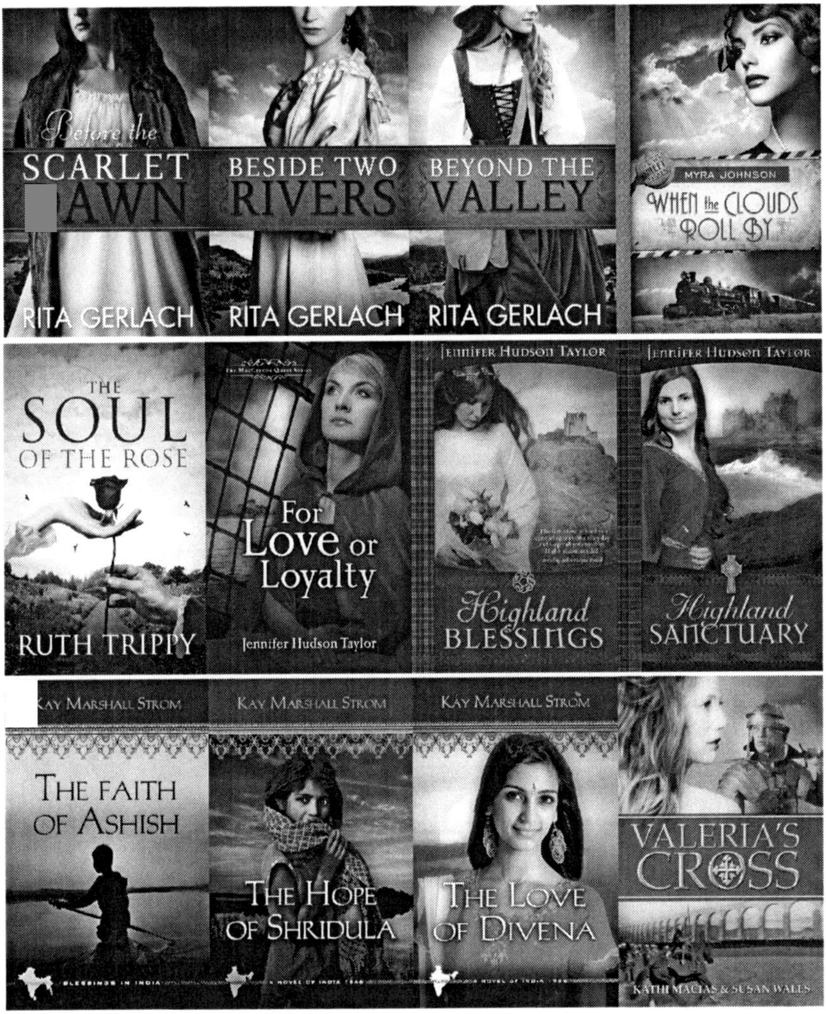

Before the
SCARLET
RITA GERLACH
BESIDE TWO
RIVERS
RITA GERLACH
BEYOND THE
VALLEY
RITA GERLACH
MYRA JOHNSON
WHEN the CLOUDS ROLL BY
THE
SOUL
OF THE ROSE
RUTH TRIPPY
For Love or Loyalty
Jennifer Hudson Taylor
Jennifer Hudson Taylor
Highland
BLESSINGS
Jennifer Hudson Taylor
Highland
SANCTUARY
KAY MARSHALL STROM
THE FAITH
OF ASHISH
KAY MARSHALL STROM
THE HOPE
OF SHRIDULA
KAY MARSHALL STROM
THE LOVE
OF DIVENA
VALERIA'S
CROSS
KATHI MACIAS & SUSAN WALES

CPSIA inform
Printed in the U
BVOW04s023

374385B